CHRISTMAS IS DEAD...AGAIN

EDITED BY
ANTHONY GIANGREGORIO

OTHER LIVING DEAD PRESS BOOKS

TWISTED FISH: AN AQUATIC ANTHOLOGY
THE DEAD OF SPACE BOOK 1 AND 2
PLAYING GOD: A ZOMBIE NOVEL
THE TURNING: A STORY OF THE LIVING DEAD
NIGHT OF THE WOLF: A WEREWOLF ANTHOLOGY
JUST BEFORE NIGHT: A ZOMBIE ANTHOLOGY
THE BOOK OF HORROR* KNIGHT SYNDROME
THE WAR AGAINST THEM: A ZOMBIE NOVEL
CHILDREN OF THE VOID * DARK DREAMS
BLOOD RAGE & DEAD RAGE (BOOK 1& 2 OF THE RAGE VIRUS SERIES)
DEAD MOURNING: A ZOMBIE HORROR STORY
BOOK OF THE DEAD: A ZOMBIE ANTHOLOGY VOLUME 1-5
LOVE IS DEAD: A ZOMBIE ANTHOLOGY
ETERNAL NIGHT: A VAMPIRE ANTHOLOGY
END OF DAYS: AN APOCALYPTIC ANTHOLOGY VOLUME 1-4
DEAD HOUSE: A ZOMBIE GHOST STORY
THE ZOMBIE IN THE BASEMENT (FOR ALL AGES)
THE LAZARUS CULTURE: A ZOMBIE NOVEL
DEAD WORLDS: UNDEAD STORIES VOLUMES 1-7
FAMILY OF THE DEAD, REVOLUTION OF THE DEAD
RANDY AND WALTER: PORTRAIT OF TWO KILLERS
KINGDOM OF THE DEAD * DEAD HISTORY
THE MONSTER UNDER THE BED * DEAD THINGS
DEAD TALES: SHORT STORIES TO DIE FOR
ROAD KILL: A ZOMBIE TALE * DEADFREEZE * DEADFALL
SOUL EATER * THE DARK * RISE OF THE DEAD
DEAD END: A ZOMBIE NOVEL * VISIONS OF THE DEAD
INSIDE THE PERIMETER: SCAVENGERS OF THE DEAD

THE DEADWATER SERIES

DEADWATER * DEADWATER: Expanded Edition
DEADRAIN * DEADCITY * DEADWAVE * DEAD HARVEST
DEAD UNION * DEAD VALLEY * DEAD TOWN * DEAD GRAVE
DEAD SALVATION

COMING SOON

BOOK OF CANNIBALS VOLUME 2   DEAD ARMY (Deadwater series book 10)

CHRISTMAS IS DEAD...AGAIN

For more info on obtaining additional copies of this book, contact:

www.livingdeadpress.com

Illustrations by Gary McCuskey

Table of Contents

SANTA'S L'IL HELPERS
NORTH POLE

SANDY CLAWS' SECRETS

CHARLES VERSFELT

Santa smiled, his beard parting and revealing a vast jolly grin as another child climbed onto his lap. One of the good ones, Santa knew. This was a blond-haired boy with short-cropped hair, and he stared at Santa quizzically through blue eyes enlarged through thick eyeglasses.

Behind Santa's head, a huge bow-covered wreath on the wall seemed to create a red and green halo. To the right of his high-backed chair, a vast Christmas tree stood, decked out with beautiful ornaments, garlands and white lights. To his left, a small table with a tablecloth of fake snow held a stack of wrapped gifts and a small snow globe.

"You're not the *real* Santa," the boy said, sounding like he was speaking through his nose.

"Oh, I'm not, am I?" Santa asked, and then laughed jovially, his nose and cheeks seeming to become, amazingly, even redder, the color of blood.

"'Course not," the boy said. "The *real* Santa's at the North Pole, working with the elves and preparing his reindeer. Tonight is the big night. He doesn't have time to sit in a New Jersey mall."

"Well now, young man, you do have a point," Santa said, placing a gloved finger under his beard to scratch his chin as he patted the boy's back with his other hand. "I'll let you in on a little secret. You would be absolutely correct about that, roughly about 99.994% of the time. Santa's helpers are almost everywhere you go, dressed up as me, inviting children to sit on their laps. Nevertheless, today is different, you see, not only because it's Christmas Eve, but also because, I assure you, I'm the one true, genuine and bona-fide, Santa Claus. Now that that's settled, what would you like for Christmas?"

"Yeah, right," the boy said, his precocious voice dripping with sarcasm. "Okay, how about a 1986 Hess fire truck? My dad's been getting them for me on eBay. I almost got the whole set. That's the only one I'm missing."

"That's a hard one," Santa said. "You sure that's that you want?"

"Yeah," the boy said. "But I want it in blue." He grinned mischievously revealing the gap where his two front baby teeth were missing and his adult teeth hadn't come in yet.

Santa's eyes widened. "Blue, now?" This was a trick, Santa knew. A test. The 1986 Hess fire truck was red. There *was* no blue 1986 Hess fire truck. "If you had one, would you play with it? You're not going to turn around and sell it again on eBay, are you? You're not going to use the money to buy a slingshot or a BB gun to harm innocent animals with? Worse yet, you're not going to leave it in its box and put it on a shelf to collect dust, are you?"

"Naw," the boy said. "I want to play with it."

Santa laughed heartily. "Of course you do," he said, putting a hand on the boy's shoulder. Santa lifted his snow globe, shaking it gently. Snow fell softly on the fake grass inside. Through the tiny arc of glass, Santa saw the boy, excitedly running his blue fire engine along the carpeted floor of his home, making fire engine sounds. He didn't need to see this to know the boy was telling the truth, but it lightened his heart anyway.

Santa turned back to the boy. "Watch this," he said. Suddenly, sparks seemed to float from Santa's fingertips before the boy's eyes like pixie dust, creating a small, rainbow wave of color that looked and smelled like ribbon candy. Then, seeming to appear from the molecules of the air, Santa held a long, thin box neatly wrapped in green and silver paper, topped with a bow. "Here you are, young man," Santa said. "One blue 1986 Hess fire truck. The only one of its kind. Fair warning, though: if you open it now, or even if you peek, you'll find nothing but a box of coal. This is for Christmas morning."

The boy's face filled with joy. He leaned forward, offering Santa a big hug. Shortly, after posing for the obligatory pictures, the boy departed. Santa watched him leave as a woman joined the back of the line with three children in tow. She stood in an animated conversation on her cell phone as her children writhed and fussed on the carpeted floor.

"But I don't *wanna* see Sandy Claws," cried a small little girl in a bright, frilly dress. "I'm scared."

"Stop being such a fricking sissy," her older brother sneered. He was about eleven, with the pudgy cheeks of a bully, his black t-shirt sporting a bloodied skeleton. The middle child, a boy of about seven in a peace sign shirt, knelt and held the girl by her hand.

Santa shook the snow globe again, and watched as the snow inside fell. It swirled peacefully, and then whipped up into a storm inside the glass, the white snow turning into the yellow color of sand. Santa called his assistant over, a green-clad helper with pointed Spock ears.

"Stop the line after that family," Santa told him. "They're the ones."

The helper nodded, stepping behind the family and setting up a tall sign.

Sorry, Santa needs to feed his reindeer.
Will return at 6:00 PM!
Thanks for visiting Santa at
The Bridgewater Commons Mall

The helper stood by the sign, blocking the entrance to the winding path leading to Santa.

As time passed, the remaining line grew shorter. Incredibly to Santa, the woman at the end of the line never hung up her cell phone, and never once looked down at her children. They were finally the last in line, but they didn't approach. Santa waited patiently, watching them.

"I told Melanie, you need to have those papers to our office by Thursday at the very latest," the woman said into her phone with an impassioned smile. "We're going to foreclose on you, you know. I understand your husband had a stroke, but that's really not our problem..."

The girl was crying again, pulling away while her middle brother just held her, a tired expression on his face. "Don't want to see Sandy..."

The older boy was picking the leaves off the display and then ripping them into little shreds, looking bored.

"Ahem," Santa said. The woman kept on talking. Finally, he pointed a white-gloved finger at the phone, sparks flying from his fingertip.

"So Melanie says to me... Ingrid? Hello? Ingrid? Hmph! Must be a bad connection. Damned cell phones." For the first time since joining the line, the woman looked up. Santa stood before his chair, arms folded, tapping his upper arm. "Oh look, we're next in line!" the woman shrieked in genuine surprise. "Okay, kids, get up there and get your pictures."

"Just a moment," Santa said. "You children wait over there. I want a word with your mother." He marched to the woman, stiff as a toy soldier, and took the phone out of her hand.

"What's the idea?"

"You listen to me, young lady, and listen good. These are your children. They need your love. They need your strength, your guidance. But first, they need your attention. They're starving for their mother. You have plenty of time to be predatory in your office. You don't need to bring your business to the mall with you, with your children, on Christmas Eve. Do I make myself clear?"

"Why, I never! I'll have your job!"

A few more sparks flew from Santa's fingers and across the woman's face. "You'll what?" he asked.

"I... uh... Yes, sir. I'm sorry, sir." Her expression carried deep remorse and humiliation.

"Good," Santa said, slamming the phone back into her hand, wishing his powers could have a lasting effect on the woman. Santa Claus could bend reality, but he couldn't change the human soul, though he could sometimes soften the hardened hearts of people. "Now, since you obviously have no interest in doing so, I'm going to go spend some time with your children." He marched over to his seat and invited the children to come to him.

* * *

"Now, one at a time, I'll talk to each of you," Santa said. "I'll start with the youngest. Young lady?"

The girl's tears had dried. She had been watching Santa, and something about his manner, and the way he'd spoken to her mother had comforted the girl. Suddenly, she wasn't afraid of Santa anymore, and rather looked forward to sitting on his lap.

"Sandy Claws?"

"Yes, dear?"

"My name's Christa," she said. "I'm four," She held up four small fingers.

"Are you having a rough time at home?" Santa asked.

The girl nodded, sniffing. "Sometimes. Dale is nice, he helps me out, but Allen's always mean to me."

"What about your mother?" Santa asked.

"Mom is never home. She's always working, or drinking those smelly drinks with all the men she brings home. Then she falls down on the couch with the man and tells us to leave her alone."

"I see," Santa said, a tear rolling down his cheek toward his white whiskers. He knew not to ask about their father. He knew he hadn't been around for a very long time. Santa hugged her, reaching behind her back to lift the snow globe.

"What's that?" the girl asked.

"Snow globe," Santa said. "It sometimes shows me the future. Right now, I'm looking into the past."

Again, the snow turned to sand, a sandstorm whipping inside the globe. There was a beach, wind and waves. From the waves, Santa saw a hand, the hand of the girl. She was screaming. Drowning. With a sad sigh, Santa set down the snow globe.

"You're a good little girl. I'm going to ask you what you want for Christmas, but I'm not going to ask now. A little later. First, I want to talk to your brothers."

He set Christa onto the carpet, and turned toward Dale.

"Hi, Santa," Dale said.

"Why, hello. I understand you're Dale?" Santa said with a gentle, ho-ho-ho laugh. "So how are things? Have you been a good boy this year?"

"You bet," Dale said. "I'm trying to keep my grades up. I got some A's. I got a C in math. I have a hard time studying sometimes, 'cause I have to watch my sister a lot."

"That's not so bad," Santa said. "Not everyone can be perfect all the time."

"I have to study hard," the boy said. "I want to be a botanist some day. Either that or an archeologist, like Indiana Jones."

"I see," Santa said, gazing into the snow globe at the spindrift of sand. He saw a small hand, raised over the sand, and then falling into the cool splash of the blue water. A bright sun beating down over their heads.

"Christa!" the boy's voice called from inside the globe. "Hang tight! I'm coming to get you."

The image faded, and Santa turned toward Dale. "You're a good boy, Dale. One of the best. A very, very good boy."

"Thanks, Santa. I don't think I'm so good though." But before Dale could say another word, Santa set him aside, and turned towards Allen.

"Well, Allen, would you like to come up here?" Santa asked.

"I guess I have to," Allen said. "I really don't want to, on account of, uhm, you kind of stink."

Santa gave him a stern look. "Is that right?"

"Yeah, 'cause there is no real Santa Claus. Santa is for idiots. You're just some stinky, smelly senior citizen old person who farts all the time and is here trying to steal money from people with your stupid fake..."

Santa wasn't listening. He peered into the globe, and watched as the sand whipped around. There were voices crying inside the globe.

"Stop it!" Christa shrieked.

"You're such a baby," Allen said. "Like yesterday, when you stepped on my sand castle. I hate you. You should go swim in the waves."

"She can't swim," Dale said. "You know that. Don't do that to her."

Santa watched as Allen spun the little girl, blood appearing on her legs as they scraped on the boardwalk, splintering. Then he flung her into the ocean.

"No!" Dale screamed while Allen laughed, looking at him. "Not like last time, not again!"

Santa watched as the girl flew out into the ocean where, strangely, the bodies of the dead stood, watching over the children; sneering, blood-covered corpses, just standing in the water, watching, waiting, staring angrily at Allen.

Santa set down the snow globe. "There was another, wasn't there Allen?"

"Another what?" Allen asked. "Are you stupid or something, old man?"

"Another child," Santa said. "Your other sister. Sarina."

"Don't talk to me about her," Allen snapped. "What do you know? What do you know about her, you stupid old man? Don't you talk to me about her!"

"I know," Santa replied. "I know." His face changed, turning pale white, and then blue, like a strange sea creature. His teeth were suddenly sharp, triangular shark's teeth, and his eyes grew cold.

"And another thing," Santa said, his spiked fingers cutting into Allen's arms, sharp as small knives. "Don't address me as 'old man.' My name is... *Sandy... Claws*! And you! You are very, very *naughty*!"

A moment later, Santa's face returned to normal. His eyes settled back to comfortable blue with puffy cloud eyebrows. His cheeks were rose red. Overhead, the gentle melody of *Santa Claus is Comin' to Town* played over the mall speakers. He turned toward the two younger children and then, as if nothing unusual had happened, Santa's smile returned and he asked, "Pictures?"

* * *

The picture taking finished, the mother turned toward Santa. "Thanks for your time," she said. "They're such a handful."

"Yes," Santa said, unsmiling. "They are."

"Well, come on, kids," the woman said.

"Just a moment," Santa said, a spark floating from his fingertip.

"What is it?" the woman asked.

"Your phone," Santa said. As if on queue, the woman's cell phone sounded, a haunting ring tone rendition of *Silent Night*. The woman pressed the button and then listened, her face growing pale.

"What? Is she all right? I'm coming. What do you mean, I can't bring the kids? They don't have day care in a hospital? Well, I certainly can't bring them to John. No, that's right. Yes, he's still in the Bahamas, with that bitch girlfriend of his. Well, I'll think of something."

The mother's eyes were bugged out, crazy. She ran a hand over her forehead, frazzled.

"Mommy, what is it? What's wrong?" Dale asked.

"What do you care, butthead?" Allen snapped, pushing him.

"It's Grandma," Mom said. "She's had an accident."

"Is she all right?" Dale asked.

"She's going to be, but she's in a lot of pain."

"Excuse me," Santa broke in. "I'm sorry to interrupt, but I understand you're in need of a babysitter?"

She breathed hard. "Yes, but..."

"But nothing! I'm just going off duty. The mall Santa... well, that is, I mean, the other mall Santa... he's coming in at six. I have the rest of the evening off. I can take care of your children for you!"

"You're insane," the woman said. "I don't even know you. You could be some pedophile for all I know."

A twinkle formed in Santa's eye, and there was a sparkle in the air. There was a strange scent, like candy canes mixed with rich, green pine trees. "You don't know me?" Santa laughed. "Why, you've known me since you were a little girl! You've always known me!"

The woman looked confused. "Wait. I think I remember."

Santa laughed again. "Of course you remember! There's nobody you trust more than you trust me!"

She nodded, zombie-like. What was that smell? "Of course. How could I have forgotten? There's nobody else I'd trust more than you."

"Mom, what's wrong with you?" Allen asked, suddenly interested in what was going on. "You're not really going to leave us with this freaky old man, are you?"

"Of course I am, Allen," Mom said. "There's no one I trust more than him!"

"Listen to your mother," Santa said to Allen.

"Listen to your mother," Mom said to Allen.

"You've got her hypnotized or something!" Allen threw up his hands. "Mom, you can't! He's some kind of monster!"

Mom grabbed his ear and smacked him hard in the face.

"That'll be enough," Santa warned her.

"That'll be enough," Mom repeated with a nod, looking at Allen. She bent over, kissed Dale on the forehead, and picked up little Christa. "Mommy's going to be back for you a little later. You're going to stay with this nice man for a while."

"Yay!" Christa called. "We get to spend the day with Sandy Claws!"

Christa ran over and grabbed Santa's leg, holding tight as if she never wanted to let go. Santa could see the joy in Christa and Dale's faces, as if the world had suddenly lifted from their shoulders. He could see the fear in Allen's eyes as well. He patted

Christa on the head, and they watched as Mom disappeared up the escalator, making a hasty departure for the parking garage.

"Well, now that it's settled, Christa, I have a surprise for you. You also, Dale." His face darkened when he said, "And I have a different surprise for you, Allen."

"A surprise?" Dale asked excitedly.

"Yes," Santa said. "You may have heard of a Secret Santa. That's when people get together and exchange gifts but no one knows who gifted them. Well, this is better than a Secret Santa. This is Santa's Secrets. Since we're going to spend the rest of the day together, I'm going to let you in on some of Santa's best-kept secrets.

* * *

Santa led the children down the bleak cement steps to the parking garage, the odor of diesel and garbage in the air.

"I'm actually both more and less magic than many people think," Santa explained, walking them through the lot. Allen's eyes darted left and right, apparently looking for an escape route between the cars.

"I don't really go to *every* child's house on Christmas Eve night. Obviously, there's my naughty list, which is much longer than you might think. Then there are the children who are well provided for, whose parents load them up with gifts. Such children need nothing from me. And, of course, it would be an insult to bring gifts to children who would be opposed for religious reasons. I've been doing this for a long time, so I know who is deserving and receptive of gifts."

"You must be very old," Dale said.

"Older than you might think," Santa agreed. "I'm actually…"

Just then, Allen made a break for it, ducking between two cars and running down an aisle. Headlights appeared and a honking horn.

Santa sighed.

Breathing hard, Allen ducked down, pressing himself against a car. He felt a finger on his shoulder.

"Going somewhere?" asked Santa's pointy-eared helper.

Allen screamed, running between the cars. He looked up the aisle. Santa's helper was standing at the end. He turned and Santa's helper was there, too. Were there two of them? More? Or was this man just everywhere, at once?

Turning back, he found Santa's helper standing directly behind him, laughing in evil hysterics. He ran, and the helper was there, too. Allen ran behind an SUV. He came out on the other side, and found himself before a large red car, a beautiful antique sports car, immaculate, with silver side mirrors and large rear fins. The license plate read "REDNOSE1."

"Look," Santa said. "Allen took a shortcut and made it to the car before we did!"

"But I went the other way," Allen said, hyperventilating.

"I'm sure you did," Santa agreed. "Okay, everyone in the car. And buckle up, kids! I don't want any accidents!"

Eagerly, Dale and Christa hopped in.

"You too, Allen," Santa ordered, pointing a finger at him. "You don't want me to use my pixie dust on you, do you?"

Allen grunted, pouting, He climbed in and buckled up without another word.

"Oh, and Allen?"

"What?" Allen said bitterly.

"You'd better not pout!"

The car went into gear, moving at lightening speed down the ramp and out of the mall parking lot. Christa laughed as the car kicked into high speed. Within minutes, they had made their way out to the highway, and then to the long, winding back roads. Allen watched as the speedometer passed ninety, one hundred...

"I had to get out of sight of the curious," Santa said. "Now watch this." He pulled the hood release, and the hood popped open, completely blocking Santa's vision of the road.

"You're going to get us all killed!" Allen screamed. Then, from under the hood where the engine should have been, a reindeer leaped, followed by another.

"Children, I'd like you to meet some friends of mine," Santa said happily. "You probably know their names."

Dale gasped. "It's Dasher and Dancer, Prancer and Vixen!"

"Yes," Santa said. "And there's Comet, Cupid, Donner and Blitzen." The car was suddenly pulled into the air, toward the night's full moon. "Now, kids, we're going home."

"The North Pole?" Allen screamed. "You're crazy! That will take..." They heard a thump as the car landed on a pile of snow near a giant candy cane.

"You were saying?" Santa asked with a ho-ho-ho. Dale looked at Allen, and then back at Santa Claus.

Santa's stomach was shaking, Dale thought, like... well, it really *was* like a bowl full of jelly!

"I've got so much planned for you," Santa said. He looked at Christa and Dale, who peered up in awe at the amazing sight before them. The large castle stood, beckoning them, the music making them want to dance with joy, the smells of candy and apple pie floating in the air. The snow crunched beneath their feet as they stepped forward. "This is going to be the best night of your life," he said to the younger children. Then, with a sly look at Allen, he added, "Tonight, children, you'll get exactly what you deserve."

"Which way do we go in?" Christa asked, running toward the house.

"I'm going to start you children off in Santa's Fun House. I need to go up ahead and make sure everything's prepared."

Santa's helper gestured toward the side entrance to the fun house, which opened into a maze of mirrors. He shoved Allen in first, who slammed against a glass wall, and then bent down to talk to Christa.

"Hold your hands out in front of you," Santa told her. "You won't hit a wall if you do. You can lead Dale through. Hold each other's hands. Don't worry about Allen. He'll find his way."

Christa no longer saw Allen, but she took Dale's hand and, together, they made their way through the maze of mirrors. Bright, beautiful lights surrounded the mirrors, blinking pastel colors. Laughing, they rounded one corner, than another, finding their way out of a dead end hallway where a dancing snowman pointed a finger to the left, where Christmas trees lined the walls, decorated with garland and balls. The path led them to a miniature train with large green seats. They got in, and immediately the train took off, bringing them through a ride that would have made Walt Disney himself envious. They finally ended up in a large room with a burning fireplace. There, Santa sat at a large desk, a paper before him.

"Why hello," he said, laughing in his usual manner and inviting them in. "Cup of cocoa? A cookie?"

"Thanks!" Dale said, taking the cup and passing it to his sister, than taking one for himself. Two comfy chairs were before the desk.

"I promised I'd tell you some of my secrets. Well, here's one. I don't go out often and visit with the children. There are just too many. That's why I have so many helpers around the world, in the malls and shopping centers, standing on street corners." He chuckled. "Most of them don't even believe in me! But they believe in my message, and that's all that's important. But every year, on Christmas Eve, I meet with at least one child from my good list. This is the child who has the most stars, who made the top of my good list. The best of the best, you might say. And this year, that honor goes to you, Dale."

He pointed at Dale, his face brightening in surprise. Then, Dale's countenance fell. "Thank you, sir. But I don't deserve the honor."

"Santa doesn't lie, Dale. I see what you're doing, all the time, and I know you're a good, good boy. I saw you, that day at the beach. I saw the way you saved Christa."

"Yeah, but what about Sarina?" Tears ran down Dale's cheeks. He wiped them away with his sleeve. "What about the day I couldn't save her?"

"Sarina? Who's that?" Christa asked, her forehead furrowing with confusion.

"Oh, God," Dale said. "You don't even remember your sister."

Santa breathed hard. He put a hand on Dale's shoulder. "You couldn't help what happened, Dale. It wasn't your fault. I can see into your heart, and I know this to be true. You're a good boy. The best of the best. And that's why you and your sister Christa are going to have the best Christmas ever. I'm going to give you exactly what you want and deserve for Christmas."

A kindly old woman came in. "Would you children care for some more cookies and some eggnog? I have some prepared."

Dale's stomach was growling.

Christa looked up at Santa and asked, "Is that okay?"

"Sure!" Santa said with a jovial laugh. "Now, you kids take your mind off all your troubles. Just relax and have fun. It's Christmas! I'll catch up with you later. I have some other business."

"Santa?"

"Yes, Dale?"

"Where's Allen? I mean, he's mean to me, but he *is* my brother and all. He'll want some cookies, too."

"Don't you worry about *him*," Santa said. "He'll get what's coming to him."

Dale nodded, following Mrs. Claus into the next room.

* * *

The ride on the red-backed chair of the rickety old train was a horror ride, worse than any haunted house Allen had ever experienced. The train bucked and jolted, hissing and smelling nasty as it turned through the dark dungeons of the castle. He was certain that some of the bodies he had seen on the ride weren't fake at all, but rather, were the real bodies of the dead. The ride came to a screeching halt, dumping him into the office where Santa sat, eyeglasses on, pipe in mouth, reviewing his notes.

"And here's Allen," Santa said solemnly.

"So what are you going to do to me now, *Sandy Claws*? Kill me? Feed me to a lion? Are you going to turn back into a beast like you did at the mall? Be done with it then. I really don't care." He crossed his arms over his chest defiantly.

Santa puffed his pipe. "That's your problem, Allen. You don't care. You never cared." Santa reviewed his notes, a long list before him. "You started early, I can see. You were no older than your sister Christa is now when you poked the eyes out of a little puppy."

"It was getting on my *nerves*!" Allen raged. "It wouldn't stop whining."

"Then at age five, I see you pushed a classmate down the stairs and broke two of his teeth. You were the youngest child ever expelled from that school."

"Yeah, well he was..." Allen started.

"He was what?" Santa broke in. "That child did nothing to you, and you know it. I saw what was in your heart, Allen. You did it because you thought it would be fun to inflict pain."

Allen folded his arms. "What else?"

"At seven, you beat up a four-year-old girl. That child lost a kidney. And later that year you first caused the death of another child, though most everyone thought it was an accident."

"Okay, so what do you have in mind for me? Military school."

Santa's eyes never left the list. "It just goes on and on. Most atrocious, of course, was what you did to your sisters. What you did to Sarina."

Allen looked at him coldly, arms still folded.

Santa dropped the page, staring blankly at the fireplace. "What you did to Christa."

The boy's anger and frustration was so great that he bit his lip so hard he started bleeding.

"I have one question for you, Allen," Santa said, mustering all the calm he was able. "How long did it go on? The...touching."

"Don't talk to me about that!"

"The way you used the tools in the garage to do... unspeakable things to your sisters."

"Don't say that!"

"I love children, Allen. I've devoted my life, thousands of years of life, to caring for the young, for the innocent. It breaks my heart when a child is born... without a conscience, without a soul. It happens, though, every now and then. Which is why once a year, I have to choose a child, a child who is at the top of my naughty list, or the bottom of my naughty list depending on how you look at it, the worst of the worst. The saddest part is that it's not really your fault. Your parents' neglect is what led to this travesty. But it's gone too far, I'm afraid. The things you've done are simply unforgivable."

"What are you going to do to me?"

Santa sighed, pulled a lever to his right, and the floor dropped out from beneath Allen. He began a mad slide, then a plummet, down, down, until he landed hard in hot sand.

* * *

The sun beat down on Allen, burning his skin. He was at the beach, Wildwood Beach, the same beach where he'd killed Sarina, and where he tried to kill Christa. It was incredible that their mother had even brought them back to the beach after the 'accident' that killed the younger child, but she believed Allen's lame story and had brought them back.

In the distance, Allen saw someone standing in the water. He didn't know how he'd gotten back here, far from the boardwalk where the gray-blue water broke in waves on the horizon. But now, seeing someone in the distance, he regained his hope. Perhaps this was a lifeguard, an adult, someone who could call Mom and get him out of this mess.

"Hello?" Allen called out. "I need some help over here."

But as the figure grew closer, he recognized it as a child. His sister, Sarina. Her blue, bloated body rambled forward, rotting flesh clinging to her bones. There were others in the distance, some he recognized as children he had harmed, some he didn't know, but they were all dead, they were all zombies, moving toward him, their heartless, mindless screams drowning out the sound of the gulls in the distance.

Allen turned to run, but the sand below his feet dragged him down, slowing him. As if running in a dream, the boardwalk seemed to grow no closer, and it seemed to slip away with his feet sliding in the sand. The zombies closed in, clutching him to their dead, rancid-smelling bodies.

He looked down, and he saw a sand castle, a sand castle that looked very much like a larger castle he had seen once; a castle bright and large on a snow-filled mountain surrounded by large candy canes. The sand castle was suddenly swallowed by a sinkhole, and from the hole, he emerged, like a sea creature coming from the ocean's depths.

Sandy Claws.

"Very Christmassy, Santa," Allen goaded, as the zombies held him tight, pushing him toward the hole. "Zombies? Seriously?"

Sandy Claws looked at him, his face morphing for a moment to become Santa again. "More Christmassy than you would think," he said. "Do you know the history of Christmas?"

"You mean the stupid story about Jesus and the manger?" Allen asked?

"That came later," said the beast, his face flickering between Santa Claus and Sandy Claws. "But it was a fitting image for the holiday. Jesus of Nazareth was best known as a man who rose from the dead, taking new life into his body. Even before, Jesus is said to have restored life to the corpse of Lazarus. But Jesus wasn't born in December. Even the Christians' writings say he was born when the shepherds were in the fields, which couldn't have been the time of the Pagan Winter Solstice, the true celebration that would later become Christmas. Long before I was Santa Claus, long before I was Father Christmas, people knew me as Woden, the god that watched over the cycle of life, of birth, of death, of rebirth."

"Why are you telling me all this?" Allen blubbered.

"My globe gives me special vision," Santa said. "I can see the past, I can see the future, and I can see pasts and futures that might have been. I brought you here so that my children may feed, and in so feeding, may bring life to the world. If I'd allowed you to continue in life, you would have brought death and destruction to the beloved world. You would have become a terrorist, the likes of which hadn't been seen since Adolph Hitler or Joseph Stalin. But I see a better future, a future that begins when you cease to exist."

Sandy Claws pointed a clawed finger, and the zombie at Allen's right began biting into his flesh, its teeth ripping out his shoulder and part of his neck.

"If it may be of some solace to you, Allen, unlike the stories of Christian legend, the world of Woden has no room for a place of eternal torment. Instead, you will be eaten, and your body, mind and soul will cease to exist, forever and ever, as in the scriptures the man Jesus once read; ashes to ashes, dust to dust.

Allen screamed horrifically as the zombies devoured his flesh. As each zombie ate, Allen remembered another person he had harmed, another wrong he had done, and each time, he writhed in incredible pain. One zombie slammed a fist into his abdomen and began ripping out his intestines, feeding on them as another tore open his ribs. A moment later, he would have screamed again, but he no longer had vocal cords as another zombie ripped out the rest of his neck. His blood poured into the sand, and as the last ebbs of life left his body, he realized his feet were no longer hot, but cold, and as his blood was absorbed by the sand below his feet, instead of becoming red, it became as white as snow. The last voice he heard was not the harsh, raspy voice of the beast Sandy Claws, but the kind, gentle voice of Santa Claus.

"Allen. You never were."

* * *

Christa sipped her eggnog, looking lovingly at her brother, and at the elderly woman who patted her head. In the distance, they thought they heard a scream. Then it was gone, and they turned to see Santa Claus standing behind them.

"Santa!" Christa yelled happily and Dale looked up with a smile.

"I see you children are having a good time," Santa said.

"I'll say," Dale said. "I can't wait to see the rest of your workshop!"

"I wanna go on another ride!" Christa yelled.

"But wait," Santa said. "Are we missing someone?"

"Well, yeah," Dale said.

"A brother, perhaps?" Santa asked.

"Don't be silly!" Christa laughed. "My brother is right here," she said and pointed to Dale. "Where's Sarina?"

Smiling shyly, Dale and Christa's sister Sarina appeared from behind Santa's robe.

"Sarina! Where have you been?" Christa yelled happily.

"I've been with Sandy Claws!" Sarina said, hugging Dale and Christa.

"A new past, and a new future," Santa told Mrs. Claus slyly. And then, putting his hands on the heads of Sarina and Christa, he added. "And innocence restored. What had been, now, never was."

The children had no idea what he meant. Santa had already seen the future. He knew that Christa would grow up to be a great doctor, and would save millions of lives by finding a cure for childhood diabetes. Dale would grow up to become a great political figure who would mediate peace between many warring nations, bringing hope to generations. And Sarina would grow up to become a scientist who would develop a cheap chemical that could be added to soil to grow crops three times as fast and allow starving people in remote regions to feed their hungry.

"There's still one problem," Mrs. Claus said.

"Yes, their mother. She's still neglectful and lost in her own world."

"That's not what I meant," Mrs. Claus said. "I meant you still haven't asked the children what they want for Christmas."

* * *

Each child had a turn on Santa's lap, and each child was granted a wish. The last wish, the wish that came from Dale, was the one that surprised Santa the most.

At Sarina's request, the family would have a dog. She vaguely remembered having a dog when she was younger, but it must have run away. She wasn't sure.

For Christa, the children would all ride with him that night, on the sleigh, delivering toys and gifts. Of course, not to all of the children of the world, but to those who were the most needy and deserving, and whose traditions and beliefs didn't conflict with their receiving gifts.

But Dale's request was different. Santa spoke it over with Mrs. Claus, and together they made their decision. They wouldn't do this deed with magic. Instead, they worked out a deal with the law firm of Marley and Scrooge, and together, Mr. and Mrs. Cringle sued for custody of the three children. The court fight wasn't long, and each parent was granted generous visitation rights.

The three children would now spend the rest of their lives at a home of wonder and merriment, a home of love. The only down-side to everything that happened was that they never really learned all of Santa's Secrets.

There was a strange rule Santa had and the children had to obey. Every year, on Christmas Eve, they weren't permitted to go into Santa's office.

It was four years later that Dale broke the rule, and after Dale vomited at the sight of the zombie eating some boy from Austin, Texas whose name happened to be at the top of Santa's naughty list, Sandy Claws decided with some resignation to tell Dale the rest of his secrets.

NO MORE CHRISTMAS

ANTHONY GIANGREGORIO

Mike Reynolds stared at his two daughters as they played by the fireplace. Watching the two children, and becoming lost in their imagination as they played with their old toys, he found he could pretend the dead never walked and that the world wasn't an apocalyptic cesspool, filled with rotting corpses and the animated dead.

The calendar on the wall, the one with all the blocks crossed out, said that tomorrow was December 24th.

It would be Christmas in two days and Mike had decided that no matter what, it would be a Christmas his two daughters would remember.

He had decided to leave their small cabin in the woods, about twenty miles from the closest city, and go into the nearest town and scavenge what presents he could find for his family.

Over the past year, their morale had waned and he knew this would be just the thing to raise the children's spirits. Of course, his wife, Sharon, didn't want him to go and had vehemently argued for him to stay.

"But don't you see, honey," Mike had told her the previous night. "The girls need something to remind them of what life was like before the dead walked. They need to feel like the world could be the way it was again."

"But it's too dangerous , you know that," she had said as the two whispered by the fresh-cut Christmas tree Mike had brought into the cabin three days earlier. It was decorated with whatever odds and ends they could find in the cabin, as well as small twigs that had been tied together to mimic garland. The top of the tree had a small wooden carving of an angel. It wasn't a very good likeness, but it was the best Mike could do given his skill level.

"What if you get cornered somewhere?" she asked. "What if you're trapped or hurt? We'll never know what happened to you. What kind of Christmas would it be for the girls then, for me? What if their father never came home?"

Mike had waved away her concerns with his hand. "I've made my mind up, Sharon, I'm doing this. Our girls need to have a real Christmas again, even if it's only for one day, they need to be happy."

Tears welled up in Sharon's eyes as she hugged her husband. "You just better come back to us, you hear?" she sniffed. "You better not leave us alone."

He patted her back softly, then rubbed it in small circles and began caressing her neck. After a full minute had elapsed, he disengaged himself from her and held her shoulders with his hands.

"Sharon, you should know by now that nothing would ever keep me away from you and the girls. Why, death itself wouldn't stop me."

She sniffed a little more and regained her composure, feeling slightly embarrassed by her show of emotion. She knew Mike didn't need her crying like a weak woman and have her welfare on his mind. No, if he was really going out into the world, even if it was against her wishes, she would support him with everything she had.

"I still don't like this, but I have to admit, even though I don't want you to go, it would be nice for the girls to have presents to open on Christmas morning. You just better keep your promise and get back here in one piece."

"I'll be fine," he told her with as much confidence as he could muster. "You'll see, I'll be back before you even know I'm gone."

The next morning found Mike leaving his car and walking the last half mile to the town.

It had been a hard morning for him.

After hugging his daughters and telling them goodbye, Sharon had reconsidered and had begged him to stay with them.

But his mind was made up and he had left her in tears, the girls not understanding why Mommy was crying. She had been on her knees, hugging the two girls as he drove away, glancing in the rearview mirror one last time before he turned a bend in the dirt road and the cabin was lost from sight.

The cabin had been his father's, and when the dead began to walk, Mike knew it was the only safe place to be, that being in the middle of nowhere, where the dead couldn't get them.

Still, every now and then a zombie would find the old dirt road leading to the cabin and Mike would have to put the thing down, using the machete to hack it to pieces like it was cordwood. There was an open pit a hundred feet from the cabin where he dumped the bodies and parts. It was already half full, and when it finally was, he would have to fill it in and make another. But he'd worry about that when the time came.

As he walked into town, he glanced one last time at the car, making sure it was well concealed.

It wasn't perfectly hidden, but it should be fine for the half day he figured he'd be gone. Then, with gifts in hand, he would return to his family and they would all celebrate a wonderful Christmas together.

He hoped to find some canned goods as well, maybe even some sweet potatoes and canned ham. That would make Christmas even better.

In his pocket he had a list of some likely presents. For the girls he was looking for dolls—any kind would do— as well as coloring books and crayons. For Sharon, perfume and any makeup he could find, as well as new pants and shirts. Out of the four of them, Sharon had the littlest amount of clothing and had to wear the same things over and over. Mike knew she would be thrilled to get a new outfit for Christmas.

For weapons, he carried his trusty machete for quiet work and had a hunting rifle slung over his shoulder by a strap. The gun was only for emergencies, as its report would alert the dead for miles that he was in the vicinity, and if that happened, it wouldn't be very good for his plan of going into town unobserved.

He walked slowly through the woods, cutting through the forest instead of following the road into town. He hoped by doing this he could sneak in quietly and unnoticed. He knew there had been rioting after the dead began to walk and frankly, he had no idea what to expect in the town.

Whether danger came from the undead or from fellow living survivors, he didn't know and he didn't want to know. If he had his wish, he would get in, search some homes for possible gifts, then get back out without a soul—living or dead—ever seeing him.

At the outskirts of the town, he paused and just stood motionless for five minutes. He strained to hear anything that would mark the presence of danger. When nothing came to pass, he continued on, stepping out of the treeline and onto the road leading into the north side of town.

It was a small town, no more than three thousand people in total, but how many were living there now was anyone's guess.

Mike assumed the entire town was evacuated when Martial Law had gone into effect, but he wouldn't know for sure until he went into some of the homes.

The first house was only a few minutes walk from the treeline and he approached it cautiously.

The front of the home was decorated with Christmas decorations. A plastic snowman was on the yellow, overgrown lawn and a sleigh with a smiling Santa waving—also made of plastic—sat on the roof, the extension cord for the electricity still dangling from where it had popped off its moorings. Large bulbs of red, yellow and blue adorned the window frames, but all were dark as the power had long failed in this part of the state.

As he crossed the street and onto the front lawn, he paused when he saw a lone figure at the end of the street. It was walking slowly and seemed to pause and look at him. But then it continued on, to be lost behind another building. Mike knew then it had to be one of the walking dead, for a living person wouldn't have continued on like that.

Unknown to Mike, the animated corpse had seen him, but from a distance, the zombie had figure Mike was just another animated corpse so had ignored him.

Mike continued on to the stone walkway and up to the porch of the home.

He barely glanced at the dry and brown wreath on the front door, now a year old.

Not knowing what to expect, he reached out and tried the doorknob.

Turning it slowly, he was only mildly surprised when the door clicked open on greased hinges. As he stepped in slowly, the machete in his right hand, he sniffed deeply for signs of the dead. Their odor was unmistakable, like rotting trash left out in the sun for too long.

Though the house smelled of stale air, he didn't detect the ripeness of the walking dead and he entered with a little more confidence. As he stepped inside, closing the door softly, he looked down to see the skeleton of a housecat. The animal must have been left behind at the evacuation and had starved to death when food had run out. Stepping over the small skeleton with bits of dry skin and fur, he headed deeper into the home, his destination the living room.

Just as he expected, the room was decorated with Christmas cheer. A once fresh tree—now brown, the needles on the floor around it like a carpet—was in the far corner and under the tree, also covered with brown needles, were faded presents, each wrapped and waiting for a recipient that would never be.

But before Mike could inspect the presents, a door at the back of the house banged open and three zombies stumbled into the living room, moaning in that dry rasping voice Mike knew so well. As they approached, their stench hit him and he fought the urge to gag as bile crept up into throat.

His first urge was to sling his rifle off his shoulder and shoot them, but he knew it would be a mistake. Even inside the house, the report of the rifle would alert others to his location, especially when the town was as quiet as a grave. Sound carried far and the rifle shot would be like an explosion in the abandoned town.

No, this was a job for the machete, and with it still in his right hand, he raised it over his head and prepared for battle.

The first zombie to come at him was an old man, looking at least eighty, but due to the withered skin and pale complexion of death, it was hard to tell precisely. Not that it mattered. Even the geriatric dead had a new spring to their step upon reanimating. Perhaps it was that the dead felt no pain, so ailments such as arthritis and cataracts didn't bother them any more.

Mike waited for the old man to get within three feet of him and he sliced sideways with the machete. The blade was razor sharp and it took off the old man's head as if it was made of dry paper.

The head tumbled off the body's shoulders to fall before it, and the shuffling feet kicked it aside before the corpse dropped to the floor, a black ooze seeping out of the jagged neck stump.

The other two zombies barely slowed their gait, but now had to step over or around the now headless corpse. Mike used this hesitation to his advantage and swung the machete like an axe, slicing off the next zombie's hands at the wrists. The ghoul floundered as black blood seeped from the wounds, and as it reached for Mike, not understanding why it couldn't grab him, Mike finished it off with a chop to the head, slicing the dry skull in two. Like a cut melon, both sides spilled over to flop onto each shoulder, more black ooze spilling forth.

The last zombie had been a woman, and still was to Mike. Wearing a red Christmas sweater with withered mistletoe pinned to her chest, even in death Mike could see she had been a beautiful woman. Her blonde hair was plastered to her head, the roots pulled out and bloody in many spots. One of her eyes was missing, and Mike imagined the remaining one had once been a deep blue to match her blonde hair.

She opened her mouth and elicited a dry moan, rasping, like the voice of a heavy smoker. It almost seemed to him that she was trying to...talk.

He hesitated giving her the killing blow and it was almost his downfall. As he stared at her, she suddenly lunged for him, stepping onto the corpse of the old man and then seeming to jump into the air. Before Mike realized what was happening, he was being forced back into the withered Christmas tree, the dead woman on top of him.

In a crash of pine needles and dry branches, they tumbled to the floor amidst the faded presents.

Mike lost his machete in the fall and his rifle became trapped underneath him. All the while, the zombie was trying to snap at him, her once pristine teeth now cracked and yellow.

He reached out for something to use as a weapon with his left hand as his right held the zombie at bay. His fingers wrapped around a present and he tore it open, the chore harder for the lack of two hands. As he tore open the box, he grabbed what was within it and brought it up to use as a weapon. But when he saw it was a video game controller, he realized he had come up empty.

With nothing else to use, he slammed it into the dead woman's nose, the hard plastic smashing it flat. Dry air wheezed forth as yellow mucus dripped out of the open cavity. He used the controller again, slamming it into her forehead, and a soft crack came to him. Still, she renewed her attack, teeth clacking on empty air. Desperate and out of options, he jammed the controller into her mouth, breaking teeth off as the hard plastic slid into her gullet.

He jammed it in there so good it was like a large ball gag, and try as she might, she couldn't get it out.

With her teeth no longer a danger, Mike reached up with his left hand and grabbed her head, then shifted his right to the other side, and with a mighty twist, he snapped her neck, the crack of the spine filling the house like a cannon had gone off.

The zombie's arms and legs stopped moving as the connection from brain to body became severed, but still the remaining eye blinked. The brain was still active.

But Mike knew the ghoul was harmless now and he pushed it off him with a groan. He stumbled to his feet and retrieved his machete, then with one last look at the three destroyed zombies, decided he didn't want to stay in the house a moment longer.

After gathering a few presents up in his arms, he left, relishing the fresh air as he stepped outside. He checked the street and it was clear for the moment—nothing in sight—either living or dead. Sitting on the porch, he began opening the presents, hoping to find something he could use.

He ripped into the first one and frowned when he saw what it was.

An electric razor with a charger.

With no power, it was useless. He tossed it aside.

The second one was no better. A handheld video game system. But it needed batteries and he had run out of batteries six months ago. He tossed it onto the overgrown lawn where it disappeared in the weeds.

The third present was actually something he could use. It was a brand new Stanley claw hammer. He slid it through a loop on his pants for safekeeping. It worked well as a weapon and as a tool, and the one he had at the cabin was more than twenty years old with a wooden handle. The Stanley was all solid metal.

There was one last present and he opened it quickly. As the wrapping paper fell to the ground to blow away, he saw there was another, smaller box within the first one. Opening this one, he found a pair of diamond earrings.

Though items such as gold and diamonds were a thing of the past, he still pocketed them. He would give them to Sharon. He knew she would like them, even if it was frivolous.

As he watched the wrapping paper blow across the street and get stuck in some bushes, he sighed heavily.

Well, what did he expect? That he would enter the first house and come out with all he wanted? Of course not.

Standing, he brushed off the stray bits of paper and tape, and headed down the street, to try another house.

Christmas decorations adorned telephone poles, most now weathered and torn. A plastic reindeer lay in the middle of the road where it had blown out of a yard after a storm months ago. The face was pitted and the paint scratched and faded, and dried blood covered the back of it.

Mike walked around it, barely seeing it. All around him was wreckage. Abandoned cars with their doors hanging open—animals such as raccoons and skunks now using the cars as homes—were everywhere, and many homes showed signs of fire damage. Gutters on the houses were overgrown with dirt, and weeds grew out of them as if they were long window boxes, the vines hanging down.

Kudzu had returned in force, filling once manicured lawns to almost waist high, as well as growing between shrubs and bushes once trimmed and now runaway messes.

As Mike turned a corner, he spotted another lone figure standing in the middle of the road, about fifty feet away. The instant he saw the figure, the figure saw him also, and it began shambling toward him.

As it moved closer, Mike saw it was a man in a Santa Claus suit, only this suit was covered in dried blood and pus. When Santa was close enough for Mike to see the man's face, he saw it wasn't a man but yet one more zombie.

The white beard was gone and Santa's lower jaw was missing. The tongue hung down like a short necktie, the black muscle twitching back and forth. A low, gurgle of a moan escaped Santa as he began to hobble faster toward Mike.

Gritting his teeth at this display of holiday death, Mike raised his machete and prepared to put Santa down for good.

Each figure moved toward the other, and when Mike was close enough, he raised the machete high and brought it down, planning on slicing Santa's head in half. But at the last second, by accident or intent, Santa moved to the side and the machete came down on his shoulder. The blade sank six inches into dead flesh and became jammed between bone. When Mike tried to pull the blade free, he found it was stuck.

Santa barely flinched as his body was impaled by steel, and he reached out with unusually large hands and wrapped them around Mike's throat. As Mike tried to escape, he and Santa fell to the road to begin fighting.

Once more, Mike's rifle was jammed under his body and he cursed his luck.

Santa's tongue draped over his face, only an inch from Mike's nose as he struggled to keep the zombie at bay. Meanwhile, the holiday zombie was squeezing the life out of Mike's throat and he was beginning to lose focus as lack of oxygen threatened to cause him to faint.

Once more, he reached down to his side, desperate to find a weapon, and his hand found the Stanley hammer.

Pulling it free of his pants with a ripping of material, he spun it around so the claw was facing Santa. With a meaty thwack, he brought the hammer down, the claw embedding itself two inches into Santa's skull.

The zombie seemed to grunt as the hammer slammed into his head, but then he continued to try and bite Mike, despite the lack of a lower jaw. With a tearing of rotting flesh and bone, Mike pulled the hammer free and brought it down again. This time the claw went in deeper and managed to hit brain matter. Santa jerked like he was being electrocuted, and his white eyes rolled up into the back of his head as he slumped forward, limp, his hands releasing their death grip on Mike's throat.

Mike didn't move at first, just glad to be alive. Then with a heave, he rolled Santa off him. He rolled a few feet away and lay on the road, panting. His face was covered in slobber and he felt like he was going to vomit at any moment. Small pinpricks of light still danced across his vision and his throat felt raw when he tried to swallow.

Sitting up, he waited for the nausea to pass and then went to his feet. He pulled the machete from the corpse, and after wiping the blade on the back of Santa's red suit, he did the same with the claw hammer. Now, with tools clean, he hobbled away, looking for all purposes like a zombie himself.

He walked another half block before he decided he needed to go someplace and rest for a bit. There was a house on his right that had all its doors closed and windows were intact, so with hopes of a sterile environment inside, one devoid of the dead, he limped to the front door.

It was locked but the hammer took care of that, a few whacks to the doorknob breaking it off. Then, with a good kick, the door flew in.

Mike waited for more than two full minutes, to see if anything or anyone would come out of the shadows and attack him, and when nothing did, he headed inside. He planned on finding a couch or a bed and rest for at least an hour, then he would continue his search.

He made sure to close the door and prop a chair under it. There was a one foot in height crystal statue of an angel on a side table, and he placed it on the chair. If something tried to get in, the statue would fall and shatter, alerting him of trouble.

Barely looking at the house itself, he stumbled into the living room. The couch was there, as it was in every home he'd ever been in, and he fell onto it with a weary sigh.

As he closed his eyes, he never even knew when he drifted off into an exhausted, stress-filled sleep.

Mike snapped awake with a jerk and an intake of breath. Then he winced, the breathing painful thanks to the soreness of his throat. Damn Santa zombie had almost killed him.

As he looked around the living room, he was relieved to see it was the same as when he fell asleep. The house smelled stale but not of death, and it was as empty as when he arrived.

His eyes caught a small birdcage in the corner, hanging from a metal post. Standing on weak legs, he shuffled over to it.

In the bottom of the cage was the dried husk of a canary, the date on the newspaper on the floor of the cage only three days before the world fell apart.

He could read the headline when he cocked his head a little.

IS IT A HOAX? DO THE DEAD REALLY WALK? SCIENTIST BAFFLED! In smaller font, ***Christmas shopping at an all time low due to crisis!***

Scratching his head, he felt his bladder alerting him it needed to be emptied. Wandering down the first hallway he spotted, he quickly found the bathroom. He peed in the toilet and even flushed it. But as the water went down, there was none to refill the tank. The water pressure had failed more than six months ago if not more, depending on the area.

He checked the medicine chest and found two bottles of aspirin and an open box of sleeping pills. He put them all in his pocket. A half empty tube of toothpaste sat on the end of the sink and he took that, too. Then he headed back into the living room to inspect the presents. He had already decided after this house he would head back home. He'd already managed to burn through half a day and he knew he wanted to be home before nightfall. Being December, it was dark by four in the afternoon, and he knew he wouldn't want to be out once the sun went down.

Sitting cross-legged by the withered tree, for all purposes looking like a boy on Christmas morning, Mike reached out and picked up a present. Beside him sat his machete, rifle and hammer.

The box was heavy and for a moment it felt like something was alive inside it, but of course that would be ridiculous. The present had sat under the tree for an entire year, nothing could be alive inside.

He quickly tore off the paper, and as he pulled open the flaps of the box, he was horrified to find more than two dozen mice inside. As he stared at the little creatures, they swarmed out of the box and onto his arms, then onto his shirt. Cringing in horror, despite knowing the mice were harmless, he dropped the box and jumped up, brushing the rodents off him. They fell to the floor and scurried under the couch, chairs, and anywhere else they could find. As he regained control of himself, he looked down into the box and saw two things at the same time. The first was the wrapper of a fruit-cake, now empty and chewed up from tiny teeth. The second was the hole on the back of the present, where the mice had burrowed in and fed on the sweet treat and then made the box their nest.

As the tail of the last mouse disappeared under a chair, Mike shook himself and reached for another present. This time he held it steady and gave it a gentle shake. When nothing moved within, he tore it open and peered inside. It was an iPod. Disgusted at finding another worthless present, he tossed it aside and tried another. This time he had some luck. It was a cashmere sweater. He set it aside to bring home to Sharon.

He went through the other presents and ended up with a pile of junk off to his left. A year ago, the items would have been worth a small fortune, but in the world of the walking dead, they were worth less than rocks. At least rocks could be used as throwing weapons in a pinch.

Standing up, he decided to search the rest of the house before leaving. He didn't like the idea of leaving empty handed and of returning to the cabin the same way. The girls were counting on him as he had told them he was going hunting for Christmas presents.

Leaving the living room with his machete in his hand and the rifle and hammer back on his person, he walked past the bathroom to search the rest of the house. The first bedroom he came to belonged to the adults of the home, and when he peered inside, he frowned at the sight before him. A man, woman and a child, all three bodies long desiccated, lay on the bed together. Beside them on a nightstand, was an empty bottle of sleeping pills. Mike stepped into the room and inspected the bodies a little more. As he did, he saw the large piece of meat missing from the child's left leg and the woman's right arm, as well as the back of the woman and child's head was missing, their dried brains splattered on the wall.

When he looked closer, he saw the man had what looked like dried leather in his mouth, and when Mike was right over the bed, he saw that the man's head had a large gunshot hole on the left side of his head as well. It was easy to figure out what must have happened.

The man, the father probably, had become a zombie and had attacked his wife and child. The wife had managed to shoot the man when they were attacked and then knowing she and the child were doomed, had given the child sleeping pills to kill her, then once the child died, she had put a bullet in her head so she wouldn't rise. Then with her family dead, the wife had placed the father on the bed as well and had taken her own life by eating a bullet.

Mike walked around the bed and found the revolver on the floor the woman had used, but it was empty. He searched for ammunition, and when none could be located, he left the gun. Without ammo it was useless other than as a hammer.

He might have pondered the fate of the family a little more, but the sunlight shining through the window was waning and he knew he needed to get a move on. Leaving the family of corpses, he stepped back into the hallway, closing the door as he left.

There were two more doors in the hallway; one was a linen closet and the other was a child's room. It must have been the room of the child in the bed, he amused.

It was a little girl's room and there, on the floor near the small twin bed, were a pair of dust-covered dolls. Mike was elated at the find. He scooped them up, brushed them off, and used a red sheet off the bed as a sack. He then went through the closet in the room and found dresses and other clothing that would fit his daughters perfectly.

By the time he was finished, the sack was fit to bursting and he had to use another shirt to tie it closed. He tossed it over his shoulder and headed out of the room, feeling good for the first time since his trek began. He went by the kitchen to check it and his luck held. He found a few assorted items to take with him, including a dented can of apricots, a can of beans, some stale crackers and half a bag of rice. Then, way in the back of a top shelf, he found a can of beef stew and was so happy he could cry. After the meager rations he and his family were surviving on, the stew would be a Christmas dinner to remember.

At the front door, he made sure he had everything, and with the machete in his right hand, he used his left and opened the door.

The sack was so big he almost didn't fit through the doorway, but he pulled on it and he slid through. He didn't bother closing the door behind him, as it was too difficult to turn around on the small stoop.

As he walked down the steps and onto the overgrown walkway leading to the street, he never saw the zombie that jumped out of the bushes and sank its teeth into his left wrist.

With a yell of shock and pain, he yanked his arm out of its mouth, blood spraying into the air to dance in the fading rays of sunlight.

The zombie lost its balance and fell to the stone path, right at Mike's feet.

He was so angry he dropped the sack of clothing and toys and swung the machete with both hands on the handle. The blade connected with dead tissue and the head of the ghoul went flying through the air, spinning three times before landing in the tall grass. Even as it disappeared, Mike could hear the teeth continually clacking together.

He fell to his knees and dropped the machete, trying to staunch the flow of blood squirting out of his wrist with his free hand. The wound was bad, real bad.

Like slicing your wrist with a razor blade, the zombie's teeth had torn an artery or vein and the blood was shooting between his fingers no matter how hard he squeezed.

Taking off his belt, he used it as a tourniquet, but even as the blood flow slowed, he knew it was irrelevant. He was bitten, and that could only mean one thing.

But it didn't matter, nothing did but returning home to his family, so he could give them their Christmas presents. He used one of the dresses for the girls as a bandage and wrapped it around the wound, but despite the tourniquet, the bandage was soaked with blood in a matter of minutes.

Shoving the machete into his pants, he picked up the sack and began walking back to his hidden car a half mile away.

It was a hard walk, and by the time he reached the outskirts of town, he was sweating profusely, his shirt a sodden mess of soaked material. A trail of blood drops was behind him, and if anyone was following him, Mike wouldn't be hard to find.

The sun was setting as he reached his car and he fell over the hood and sucked in air, struggling to remain conscious. He wasn't thinking straight anymore, and as fever racked his body thanks to the infectious bite, only one thing was on his mind.

Return home...for Christmas.

It took all his remaining effort to get the sack in the car and for him to follow it. With drooping eyelids and shallow breaths, as well as a complexion that made him look as white as a bed sheet, he managed to get the key into the ignition and start the engine.

Using one hand—ignoring the seeping blood as it soaked into the seat—he backed the car out of its hiding spot and began the drive home, his body going numb as the infection filled him from head to toe.

He would make it, he had to, for his wife, for his girls, he had to get home. For if he didn't, they wouldn't have a merry Christmas.

And if it was the last thing he did in this life, he wanted to give them that.

Sharon was filled with worry.

It was dark out and Mike wasn't home yet.

He'd promised he would be home before it was dark.

She jumped nearly to the ceiling when there was a dull thump at the cabin door. The girls looked up from where they were playing by the fireplace and Sharon told them to stay there after saying, "It's Daddy, he's back, and right on time!"

She dashed to the door, filled with relief that her husband had made it back safely, and with luck, he'd done what he hoped and had found presents for the girls.

Oh, what a wonderful Christmas this would be and now she regretted giving Mike a hard time about leaving.

Without a moment's hesitation, she threw open the door and then stopped cold, a scream on the tip of her tongue as her mouth opened into the shape of an 'O'.

Mike stood in the doorway, swaying back and forth, as if he heard music only for him. He held the red sack of toys and clothes like before, but that was where the picture of normalcy ended.

His clothing was stained a bright red, thanks to arterial spray when the tourniquet had come loose. As he bled out in the car and died, his life's blood had painted him red, making his attire look much like a red suit...a Santa Claus suit. His face was ashen gray, his eyes now white, the pupil's devoid of color. His free hand reached out for Sharon, the gaping wound where the zombie had taken a chunk out of him still glistening as it reflected the firelight from within the cabin.

The girls had jumped up and ran to their mother's legs, wanting to see what Daddy had brought them, when Mike let out a loud moan. To Sharon and the girls it was unintelligible, but to Mike's dead mind, it was his last attempt at speech as he tried to say, "Merry Christmas."

Sharon broke from her stupor as she uttered, "Oh God no, not now, not like this."

Just as she finished speaking, and before she could so much as try and close the door, to keep out the abomination that was her husband, Mike dropped the sack of goodies and lunged for her.

His hands found her neck, the one he'd caressed with lips and fingers only a night previous, and now he squeezed as his mouth opened wide to sink his teeth into her tender flesh. As she stumbled back, Mike followed, and his left foot hit the door, kicking it closed.

The girls screamed, not understanding what was happening, and as Sharon fell to the floor, Mike was on top of her. With the makeshift Christmas tree looking on from the corner, he began to feed, the blood soaking up the firelight and twinkling like lights on a real Christmas tree. The two little girls began to cry, calling out for Mommy and begging Daddy to leave her alone.

Sharon heard none of it, suffering horribly as she died, and still Mike fed on her warm flesh.

Minutes passed, only the slurping of Mike feeding filling the cabin, and the girls sobbing relentlessly as they shook in terror.

Suddenly, Mike stopped feeding and looked up, seeing the two young morsels huddling in the corner of the cabin. Leaving his dead wife, he slowly began to shamble toward the girls as Sharon's corpse slowly began to twitch with renewed life, animating once more as movement filled her corpse.

As Mike leered over his two sobbing children, from behind him Sharon came to her knees and began crawling after him, the warm flesh of the two young girls calling out to her.

The girls, petrified to a state of absolute panic, could only sob and beg, pleading for their parents not to hurt them, but to make things right and protect them from the bad things in the world.

With blood dripping from his chin, Mike reached out for the closest girl, his mouth already open wide for the Christmas feast.

The lone cabin sat in the middle of the woods, far from civilization. Only a few crickets marred the silence, as well as a night bird or two calling out.

Suddenly, from the cabin, shrieks of the two children filled the night, causing the night birds to fly away, startled. The crickets stopped and the forest fell completely silent, with the exception of the girls' screams echoing from within the cabin.

But in time, the screams soon faded and all was quiet once more.

THE LAST NOEL

DANE T. HATCHELL

Santa was making good time flying through the night air of yet another Christmas Eve. He thought about times past when the world's population was smaller. It was simpler times, fewer children to care for, but also his methods of delivery were cruder, too.

All in all, he was proud of the improvements he had made over the years. His recombinant DNA treatment on his reindeer made them fly ten times faster than when they were originally created. The increased number of his robots and the added level of their sophistication allowed him to keep the number of elves at a manageable level.

He would have been out of room at the North Pole a long time ago if everything had to be made by the elves alone. Plus, he didn't know how he would go about feeding a larger number than he had now, those little guys sure could eat.

Keeping up with the electronic revolution had been challenging. But his secret method for Christmas present manufacturing had always been able to match the changing times. The teleportation device that would deliver toys from his shop in the North Pole to his flying sled had never failed to keep him supplied with presents.

Santa looked over at Parko, an elf who earned the right to sit by his side this year, delivering the gifts to all the good girls and boys. His little eyes were wide as saucers, absorbing the thrill of every second that only a few had shared. The innocence in the little elf's face warmed Santa's heart. Not that he was hardened to bringing gifts on Christmas Eve year after year, but that the magic he felt inside could be appreciated by someone other than himself. Santa wished more could share the opportunity to take the ride with him and feel the satisfaction of giving unselfishly.

The next stop on his trek was the tiny the town of Central, Kansas. The reindeer actually knew the route better than Santa did. New streets and developments were built all the time. It was the reindeer's duty to discover these additions during the year, whenever they had time and weren't busy playing their reindeer games.

Rudolph's nose blinked three times, and being the lead reindeer, he took a turn to the right, and dove down in a long winding spiral. Buildings were coming into view as the sleigh broke through the cloud cover and neared the town below.

Santa noticed an unusual amount of activity in the town center. What was going on down there he couldn't make out just yet. This was more than late minute shoppers taking advantage of midnight madness sales to save a buck. It was more than a few die-hard carolers, having no one else to annoy with their off-key voices. And more than a bunch of college kids getting their drink on; with the guys trying to get the girls drunk enough to slide down *their* 'chimneys.'

The scene was focusing in and it looked more like a full-blown riot was going down in the streets. People were running to and fro, some committing incredible acts of violence. Fires were burning in a few of the buildings and the wails from fire trucks cut like a razor through the air. Santa and Parko looked at each other, each hoping the other had an explanation.

"What on earth is going on down there?" Santa said with a scowl.

"I'm not sure, sir." Parko wished he had some explanation. He didn't come along just for the ride. He wanted to be useful to Santa; he wanted Santa to be proud of him. All elves wanted Santa—their surrogate father—to be proud of them.

"I had no foreknowledge of this," Santa said, stroking the white hairs of his curly beard. "Never have I not been aware of the obstacles I would have to overcome in delivering my precious cargo."

Parko had never seen Santa in such a state. He was always confident, always ready with an answer when faced with the most difficult of problems at the North Pole. He didn't want Santa to feel alone, if there was a hard decision to make, Parko wanted to take some responsibility, too.

"It looks too dangerous for you to go down there. I think we should skip this town and head for the next one, Santa. We can't risk you getting hurt. The kids down there will eventually get over it. If you get injured, you might not be able to finish the night. Think how much worse it would be if half of the world's kids woke up without a Christmas compared to just a few hundred."

Santa swelled up with indignity, and looked past Parko with the ancient eyes of the immortal that he was. "To deny Christmas to one deserving child is to deny Christmas to them all." The words came out slow and forceful.

Parko felt his bowels rattle and his face flushed a pale white.

"I'm bound by my creation to reward the deserving children of the world. In times past, when I was known by other names than Santa Claus, I was never derelict in my duties. Neither disease nor wars of mankind's past have prevented me from bringing the joy of giving."

Parko scrunched his body lower in his seat as Santa continued.

"Even in 1944 when the German's were launching V2 rockets upon the innocent people of Great Britain, I provided Christmas gifts for needy boys and girls. The danger not only came from the deadly rockets, but from British Spitfire fighters and antiaircraft fire that peppered the air. Volumes of my heroic deeds could be written how I looked adversity in the eye and won, never blinking. And I shant blink this time either," Santa's voice trailed upward in pitch. "By what chance or what evil has clouded my vision on this sacred night I care not. I'm The Santa Claus, and my mission will not be compromised!"

Santa's voice echoed in Parko's head. Never had he seen Santa so serious, so passionate, so driven. The words also stoked a fire in Parko's tiny heart. He had gotten a glimpse inside Santa's soul that few, if any, had ever seen before. Santa's words were power.

Parko sat upright in his seat as Santa gave his mental command to Rudolph to bring the sleigh around to the first house so that Christmas might begin to be fulfilled in the town of Central.

The sleigh landed behind a small house in a neighborhood filled mostly with beginning families of working class people. Snow kicked up behind the thirty-two hooves as they dragged the shiny red sleigh to a halt. Parko handed Santa an empty sack, and the two entered the house the mysterious way that was only known to Santa himself.

The living room was set up as the area for celebration. The real Christmas tree was in the middle of one wall, the aromatic scent from its needles filling the air.

Santa smiled. Looking at the tree with the hanging silver tinsel and glass ornaments, pushed the thoughts of the riot out of his mind. This humble house, making do with its modest discretionary budget, had captured the true spirit of Christmas.

Candles of red and green sat on the fireplace mantle next to Christmas cards from friends and family, the spirit of love and greetings of best wishes bringing everyone together in the common cause of happiness.

Oh, that it could be Christmas every day of the year, Santa thought, as he took the time to look at each card. Reading the hand written notes and seeing photos of family members brought a small tear to his eye. "This is why I do this," he said to Parko.

Santa stood before the tree, found the switch for the lights, and turned it on. The tree came alive with tiny lights all in white, looking like tiny stars giving a warm glow to the green bristles of the branches, and life to the colored ornaments of glass.

The empty sack by Santa's side swelled as the presents for the two children teleported from the larger sack on the sleigh. Little Jenny and Johnny were both going to get one of the nicer gifts from the list they had mailed him. Santa was so proud of them that he put two extra gifts in each of their stockings hung nearby.

Parko was at the kitchen table, where a plate of cookies sat next to a pitcher of milk. Some of the cookies were homemade. In shapes of Christmas trees, Santa faces, snowmen, all covered in red and green-colored sugar. The other cookies were vanilla and chocolate cream filled in the shape of elves.

Parko looked at them with great curiosity. He knew he should consider it a compliment for his kind to be honored in the image of a cookie. But then the cookies were to be eaten. There didn't seem anything honorable about being eaten. And not just elves, some cookies looked like Santa. Why would anyone want to eat Santa? Wouldn't that be the greatest insult? That was when Parko realized he had a lot to learn about humans.

Santa's hand reached down past Parko and grabbed one of the Santa-shaped sugar cookies. He bit off the 'head' and munched it down, the sugar crunching loudly between his teeth.

Parko watched in disbelief, as Santa gave him a wink, finished the cookie, and poured himself a glass of milk. Parko picked up a chocolate cream elf cookie and nibbled on a foot; something still seemed wrong about it. Santa wiped the milk from around his mouth with the back of his hand and rubbed his fingers together to brush off the crumbs.

Suddenly, shuffling noises of little feet came from down the hall and it gave Santa a start. Santa had detected no one awake in the house. One of his many powers was the ability to sense if someone was sleeping or if they were awake, as everyone knows that from the song. *What dark power has befallen this town?* Santa thought. *The people riot and my immortal powers are clouded.*

In his confusion, the two children coming down the hall discovered him before he was able to make his exit. Santa rarely allowed children to see him, exceptions being made from time to time only for those suffering from a terminal disease. Just before he and

Parko made their leave, Santa caught the faces of the children in the warm lights of the Christmas tree.

A little girl four years of age walked in front of a slightly bigger and older boy. Each was dressed in matching Christmas pajamas. The tops displayed tiny reindeer against a red backdrop, and the pants were solid red in color. The insulated footies were made to look like snow shoes.

What had Santa frozen in astonishment was the ghastly looks on their faces; faces that showed no emotion and had dark black circles under their eyes. Even in the dim light, he could tell their skin looked a pasty gray. But most frightening of all, was the blood dripping down their chins to stain their festive nightwear.

Parko let out a squeal of alarm and jumped three feet high in the air like a scared cat. This hadn't been part of his training. He learned navigation and basic toy repair to be of some usefulness to Santa on this night. He wasn't prepared to handle blood-soaked sick children.

"Holy reindeer crap," Santa said out loud. The children continued their slow shuffle toward him, their eyes as black as the coal he left in the stockings of bad children. Parko darted behind Santa, and peered around his knee as they approached.

Santa's mind raced at the speed of a supercomputer, searching the data bank in his mind for a clarification of the situation. This was an unknown. And even though he was repulsed at the sight of the stricken children, with open arms he squatted down to receive them.

The little girl and boy walked side by side, and stopped in front of Santa as he gripped the outside shoulder of both of them. "Children, oh you poor children. What in Yule's name has happened to you?" He knew they needed medical attention, but wanted to offer them comfort first.

The two said nothing, and made no movements to indicate they understood or even heard him. Santa looked in their eyes and felt the icy grip of death reach down his throat and grab his spine. He let out a gasp as he realized that the children looked *dead*, right before their mouths widened and sank crimson-stained teeth into each of his forearms.

Instinctually, Santa jerked his arms back, leaving red fabric dangling from the two pre-schooler's mouths. He was looked at his forearms, seeing the white of his insulated underwear through the holes of his torn suit. The children were trying to bite him, and almost succeeded in puncturing his flesh. Then it struck him. The gray skin, the emotionless faces, the spirit of death, the blood, and the craving for...*flesh*. It was an ancient memory. A memory so hidden he couldn't tell if it was from this world, or another.

The children pushed the red fabric out of their mouths with tongues now sickly gray in color. They advanced on Santa who was forced to defend himself. He gave them both a shove, sending them falling down on their back sides. The little boy came within an inch of biting Santa as he was pushed away.

Once again Parko found Santa in need and was determined to do something that Santa could be proud of. He left his hiding spot behind Santa and ran into the kitchen, where he pulled out a large carving knife from a wooden block on the counter. He then returned and snuck up behind the boy, plunging the eight inch blade into his back.

There was no scream of pain and there was no blood. The girl continued her advance on Santa, as the boy turned and attacked Parko.

The elf fell on his back with the boy lying on top of him. The zombie child's teeth clacked up and down just inches from Parko's face, and he strained with all his might to keep the small, gnashing jaws at bay.

Time went into slow motion for Parko. Each time the zombie's mouth opened and closed, the teeth seemed to move closer. His eyes looked directly into the abyss of the boy's mouth, each tooth and ivory a picket of destruction. Parko turned his face to the side and pushed with strength he didn't know he possessed. The boy's mouth now was close to his pointed ear. The chomping sounds rang through his head. Fear felt like cold ants climbing the back of his neck. The teeth snapped closer and closer, until Parko felt a sting of pain.

Santa was still pulling his blows with the little girl. She was unrelenting in her need to find and eat living flesh. When he realized that Parko was losing the struggle with the boy, he picked the girl up, and threw her against the wall. Then with the boy still on top of Parko, the knife still firmly embedded in his back, Santa picked up the boy and threw him against the wall. The boy landed on the girl, their eyes wide with hunger.

Santa went to Parko's side, who was now sitting up, rubbing his face with his hands like he was trying to wipe off a stench. The two children untangled themselves and stood up. A zombie shows no quarter.

"What do we do?" Parko asked, taking his position behind the heaving bulk of his master.

Santa turned abruptly and headed to the fireplace, leaving Parko alone, exposed as the zombie children closed in. He selected the iron poker from the tool stand and ran behind the two children. He brought the poker up and down as hard and as fast as he could, crashing the heavy metal tip into their small skulls. The sound, akin to bursting melons, made Parko weak-kneed, as he watched the heads of the children cave in, and the gray matter of brains squirt out.

Santa didn't know if the children could still feel anything, as the boy had given no reaction to being stabbed by the knife. If there was even the most remote chance that they could feel on some level, Santa wanted the end to come swiftly, and without pain.

The two children *thumped* to the floor. Two small, frail angles of God, with blood-stained pajamas and bashed in heads.

Santa wept.

Parko looked around the room in disbelief. All the adornments of the season shouted, "Peace, good will toward men." But now, in the center of the room, lay two dead children. Two children who walked no more; taken down by the hands of the greatest giver to ever live.

The familiar sound of feet shuffling came again from the hallway. The heads of Santa and Parko swung around in shock that the nightmare still wasn't over.

The mangled bodies of the children's mother and father dragged themselves into the living room. Both had large chucks of flesh missing from their throats. The mother had most of the meat stripped from her left arm. The father had his left calf muscle eaten, exposed by the bloody and tattered pajama leg. The mask of the living dead covered their faces. Their arms were outreached, teeth masticating thin air, and they were relentless in their quest for human flesh.

Parko shook with fear, "Let's leave now Santa...the kids, yes! The kids! The kids of the world need us. We still have half the world to deliver presents to."

Santa composed himself and looked intently at the dead as they walked his way. Christmas was being threatened. The existence of mankind's most treasured holiday was in jeopardy. Santa's main mission in life was to give. But equally as important, it was to preserve. In order to fulfill his purpose to give, he had to preserve that venue by which the entire world identified him with. This was a challenge that would define him from this day forward.

The empty sack that lay in front of the fireplace swelled in size. Santa dashed over to it while removing his red coat. Emptying the sack to the floor, he moved the rifle aside, and quickly put on the thorium power pack vest. He buckled the straps securely in front, and picked up the ominous looking black rifle. He pushed the *power on* button on the vest and plugged the cable from the stock of the rifle into the power pack. The rifle hummed to life.

Parko watch in amazement as the most loving and caring person in the world has ever known, in seconds had transformed into a warrior of modern times.

Santa aimed the rifle first at the zombie man; a tiny red dot appeared on his forehead. With the squeeze of the trigger, steam rose from the top of his head, and the dead man walked no more. Santa swung the rifle towards the zombie woman, and ended her miserable existence.

Santa stood with the dark rifle at a forty-five degree angle across his chest. "Snap to it, Parko. The time left for us this Eve of Christmas is waning. We must take care of the good town of Central, and then the rest of the world."

In a flash Santa and Parko were back on the sleigh. Rudolph and the other reindeer received mental communication from Santa about the dire situation they now faced, and to be prepared.

Santa set a tuning in his mind to detect the living dead. Now he knew if they were sleeping, awake, or a zombie. At each house visited they made haste in setting out the presents, no longer any time to enjoy the ambience of the season or goodies left for them to eat.

Santa acted with the speed of a storm trooper in frying the brains of all the zombies found in the houses. Parko would leave gifts for those unaffected, if there were any, while Santa eliminated all threats.

After the last gift was delivered, Santa and Parko took high in the sky and passed over the town center. Pandemonium still ruled as the walking dead now wandered up and down the streets, looking for the warm flesh of a breathing human.

Circling overhead, the reindeer leveled out at a height for Santa to get his best aim. It was like shooting ducks in a barrel with the aid of a headset equipped with night vision and automatically-focusing binoculars. The zombie's simply fell to their knees as whatever it was that reanimated them in their brain vaporized. Sometimes his finger would linger too long on the trigger and the head would burst into flame.

Santa lost count at the number of living dead he released back into the prison of death. Certainly it could have been even worse, but now he feared there would be other towns where the dead now walked.

He wasn't defeated yet. He knew he would be able to handle whatever obstacles Fate or some other diabolical source threw at him. He commanded Rudolph to head to the next town.

Parko's little heart beat unusually fast. He wished he had brought a flask of eggnog laced with rum to calm his nerves. His left eye started itching a little and he rubbed it gently. The skin on that side of his face felt sensitive. He touched the side of his head with his fingertips and felt the back of his ear. It felt warm and wet. As his fingers followed the outside of his ear, a little scab had formed where the tip had been nipped off by tiny teeth.

*   *   *

To Santa's and Parko's relief, the neighboring towns and the rest of the world were free from the plague of the living dead. With super determination, Santa went into full work mode, pushing the reindeer to full speed, and working little Parko until—when the last present was shoved under the tree—the faithful little elf collapsed in what appeared to be a mysterious ailment.

When they had returned to the North Pole, Parko was put right to bed. The bed was in a room in Santa's workshop, that way Santa wasn't far from the stricken elf, and he worked feverishly to find a cure for his stricken friend.

There were no doctors in the North Pole. Human doctors would be unable to treat elves, their physiology being alien to human beings. Being immortal, elves were immune to harmful bacteria and viruses. No elf ever knew what it was like to get a cold or to be stricken with a disease.

On the occasion of an industrial accident, or clumsiness, when an elf was injured, Santa would bring them to the Matrix Room.

The Matrix Room was off limits to everyone, even Mrs. Claus. The few that had to be healed over the years brought back stories of large computers humming and clicking that lined the walls. Robots of living metal roamed the hall and maintained the power facility of the North Pole, the energy source coming from the hot magma within the Earth itself. The robots took mental commands from Santa and the injured elf would sit in a chair in a clear tube. After a few minutes of treatment, which amounted to radiated colored lights filling the tube, the elf would exit fully healed.

Parko lay unmoving, his bed sheets soaked, his face a pale gray with dark circles under his sunken eyes. Scores of his friends were gathered around his bedside, fretting and wishing they could do something to help.

Santa could feel their eyes staring at him as he worked with technology that mankind wouldn't invent for hundreds of years. A probe inserted in the back of Parko's neck sent information to a computer that Santa was working on. Parko's vital signs were alarmingly low, and Santa was powerless to do anything to stop the elf's DNA as it mutated into something unidentifiable.

The silence of grief was penetrated by the solid alarm of the computer announcing that Parko's vital signs were no more. Santa's eyes welled with tears. When he turned to look at his departed friend, all eyes were on him.

Their eyes said, *Do something!*

He was Santa Claus, wasn't he? In all the years of their existence he had been their leader, provider, and father to them all. Now one of their own was lost to death. Now the other elves felt they too were no longer safe from the cold clutches of the Grim Reaper.

While all eyes were turned to Santa, pleading for him to do something, Parko arose from the bed, sitting straight up. Yips of surprise went up from the surrounding elves at the sight of their friend making a miraculous recovery.

Parko's eyes darted left and right, and his teeth clattered together like a pair of toy windup chomping choppers. He sprang to his feet, still on the bed, running in place and spinning around.

The elves backed away as they watched their reanimated friend acting as if he was crazy. Santa could only stare, his mind racing to get control of the situation.

Parko leapt from the bed and on top of two elves, knocking them to the floor, his teeth sawing and gnawing at whatever they came into contact with. Blood splattered through the air, and on the walls and floor. The other elves screamed and ran out of the room, taking Santa down at the knees as they haphazardly crashed into him, swarming over him in their haste to flee.

Santa picked himself up and adjusted his right pants legs to clear it from the back of the heel. As Parko fed in Christmas day gluttony, Santa reared back his leg and kicked the zombie elf in his tiny ribs. Bouncing him off the wall, the little bugger hit the floor running, and headed straight for Santa.

Whatever it was that made humans slow and lumbering ghouls, it had mutated in the elf and made him fast and furious. Santa again forced the elf to taste the might of his boot, this time aiming for the head.

When his boot struck the elf's forehead, Parko's head flew back and his feet lifted off the floor as he tumbled backwards, spinning through the air.

Parko hit the ground and jumped back up, his head now dangling upside down behind his back, between his shoulder blades, his spine severed from his neck. He turned backwards to see Santa, small eyes colored obsidian, and teeth clacking their unholy rhythm.

Santa took the elf down at the back of the knees as he attacked, and sent him to the floor. Bringing his heel down as fast as he could, he managed to crush the head of the elf with one blow. Brains shot out of Parko's ears and nose, leaving a horrid mess of his beloved friend.

Santa looked at Parko, and then at the gore covering his boot heel and what had squirted up his pant leg, and vomited. Parko had been so bright and worked so hard to please him. Killing the humans had been hard enough. To kill someone he knew, someone he loved was more than Santa's heart could bear.

His spiral of depression was interrupted by the snapping sounds of teeth. He looked up to see the two elves that Parko had been feeding on had reanimated. They too were running in place and spinning around wildly, then ran full speed past him, out the door, and into the North Pole complex.

The complex itself was thirty acres square, hidden underground below the ice. A unique construct that mimicked the more habitable portions of the surface above. An artificial sun would light the day and in the night holograph images of stars would speckle the night. The industrial area with its flat hard ground covering was separated from the living area by a crystal clear warm water river. The living area had real dirt and green grass and trees, with elf huts dotting the rolling hills.

The two zombie elves darted out of the workshop and on to the industrial streets outside. Word had traveled that something strange had happened to Parko and a large number of elves were waiting outside for news of their sick friend.

The two little zombies hit the awaiting crowd like guided missiles hitting a target, taking down the closest elves to fill their mouths with fresh meat.

Most of the elves screamed in panic and ran for safety. A few, the brave ones, tried to pull the undead off of their screaming brothers. Their attempts were met with bloody-toothed snarls and snapping teeth. And once within striking range, the zombie would leave an old victim for a new one.

Within minutes, eight more elves were lying in the street dying, various parts and pieces of their bodies missing and covering the street in blood. The grayness of reanimated death consumed their bodies, and one by one, each came back to life as one of the walking dead.

Two had become ten, and now ten would become a hundred, and more.

Santa exited the workshop in time to see the small horde of zombies run in all different directions. There was no way he could single-handedly stop the madness from spreading. His heart told him to stay and help any wounded elves, but his head told him that he couldn't do it alone, and had to end it quickly.

He ran as fast as he could to the Matrix Room, arriving out of breath. Being immortal only meant you never died, not that you didn't need to keep in shape. Santa gathered the six organic-metal robots with a mental command and opened a door that hadn't been opened since the robots' creation. Proton beamed rifles hung from the wall, and each took one and turned the power on.

The OM robots were fashioned as the most athletic of human men. Clothed only around the loins, the garment hid little of their perfectly sculptured body. To an elf, their god-like statuesque struck awe and reverence.

Santa knew it would only be by force that he could end this plague of the dead unleashed upon his home.

The seven of them left the Matrix Room, proton rifles in hand, the command to fire at will. To Santa's left a zombie elf was feeding greedily on the back of a fellow female. He looked at his target and pushed the button on the stock of the rifle. The proton gun read the target from Santa's eye and automatically aimed itself, discharging its beam of death. The zombie elf dropped to the ground, the artificial life snuffed out forever.

The six OM robots spread out in all directions. Santa watched as one was overwhelmed by a horde of the gray, pointed-ear elves. The robot took several of them down, but eventually some made it through and began biting at will. It was a futile attempt. Even though the skin of the robot was as pliable as human skin, it was as tough as hard plastic. Teeth broke and ground down to the gums. The robot used its superior strength and speed to pull each of the elves off of it with one hand as it continued to fire the rifle with the other. Removing the final undead elf from itself, the robot tossed the body straight into the air, the rifle finding its target. When the beam hit the elf, it sliced the small form in two, blood and internal organs falling in all directions, to splatter on the ground like red rain.

Santa left the robots to fend for themselves. He had no worries for them, and knew he couldn't stand up to a similar attack. He thought about calling the robots back for protection, but decided to go it alone. Santa knew it would be selfish, the robots needed to save as many of the elves as they could, and he needed to make it back to his home, to Mrs. Claus; he needed to be by her side to protect her.

"I am Santa Claus, damn it!" he said with a roar, and fought his way from the industrial area and crossed the bridge over the river into the living area, proton gun blasting all the way.

He was near exhaustion when he made it to his house. Elfin zombies surrounded the outside, teeth chattering and tiny nails scraping on the windows and doors. They were too distracted to notice him, and with a blink and the press of a button, he took them down one by one as fast as his eye could focus and his finger could press the button.

Death took the elves all once. Santa's heart now beat rapidly in his chest out of concern for the safety of his wife. Was he in time? He sprinted to the front door, hopping over the pieces and corpses of dead elves in his path.

The door was locked, but he had a key, and in seconds he quickly entered the house and scanned the living room for Mrs. Claus. A bashed-in head of a zombie elf poked down from the chimney and out of the fire box, a pool of dark blood below it on the hearth.

But where was Mrs. Claus?

Santa cautiously moved to the kitchen, and saw her standing in front of the stove, her back to him, holding a rolling pin covered in elf brains by her side. He felt a weight lift from his chest. The woman he'd loved through the ages was safe!

Mrs. Claus turned and faced him, her face colored in the life-lessness of death, her teeth clacking for warm flesh.

"Oh, honey, not you, too?" he gasped in horror.

She lunged for him with a low moan filled with hunger.

It took the proton gun a little longer to fire, thanks to the tear in his eyes, but it found its target in time, and dropped her to the floor with half her head missing.

"Sleep in heavenly peace, my love." Santa left with his head held low in sorrow; he didn't want to remember her this way.

Outside the house, on the front lawn, Rudolph staggered by. "Rudolf my boy, come see Santa," he called. Rudolph's head drooped, his walk uncertain. Santa took the reindeer's head in his hands and could see the pain in the animal's eyes. Believing Rudolph was overwhelmed with grief over the dead elves, Santa put his arms around Rudolph's neck, and patted the reindeer on the back.

"There, there my boy, we'll get through this together." Santa's thoughts were still with Mrs. Claus, and he didn't notice the blasts of the proton guns going off in the distance.

Rudolph let out a long sigh, similar to a death rattle, and Santa let him go, taking a step away so Rudolph was now standing behind him. So he didn't see when the reindeer's eyes shifted to black.

"Ouch!" Santa stepped back, feeling a hole in his neck and warm blood pouring out. Rudolph gulped the chunk of meat down and leaped forward for more. Santa fell on his back, pleading for Rudolph to stop, but the reindeer's hooves were on Santa's chest, pinning him down, and chomping away at exposed flesh.

The blast of a proton gun ended Rudolph's ravenous urges, and the reindeer fell over to land beside Santa Claus.

Santa didn't move, but laid still, trying to catch his breath, though he never did and his eyes closed as he slipped into the void of death.

No sooner did he stop breathing, then Santa shot up like a geyser, his legs running in place, teeth animated in search of live flesh.

The OM robot hesitated for only a moment, then brought death to Santa Claus, this time for good. It looked down on Santa with no emotion, for the robots weren't programmed to feel emotion. Still, the death of an immortal didn't compute.

Then, somewhere inside its computer brain, a new subroutine was triggered. The robot broke through the ribs in Santa's chest using its fingers only, and pulled out a small blue crystal embedded in the heart.

*　*　*

In the Matrix room, the OM robots had the collection of the life crystals of all the immortals of the North Pole that had died. Only a handful of elves had survived the attack, and they waited patiently as each crystal was put on the conveyer belt and sent inside a mysterious machine.

Emerging from the machine was an identical copy of the loved one who owned the crystal. The crystal itself recorded all that the person was, and returned all the memories to the blank consciousness of the newly created minds.

One by one, every elf, every reindeer, and even Santa and Mrs. Claus, each came back to life and were welcomed with hugs and tears.

It was Christmas day at the North Pole. The magic of Christmas had returned life to all, and the world could be sure to know again the love and joy of Christmas.

Santa and Mrs. Claus, the elves, the reindeer, even the OM robots, gathered in North Pole Circle and sang praises of thanks.

An OM robot stood next to Santa, its perfect body glistening in the artificial sunshine. No one noticed that a small tooth was sticking out from an imperfection in its organic skin, on its left calf.

No one noticed that the skin had started to turn a sickly gray around the wound.

HIGH PRICE FOR HOPE

REBECCA BESSER

Jerrold Brown sat by the small fire burning in a fifty-five gallon barrel that had been cut in half, a makeshift duct system above it to take out the smoke. He watched his wife across the room, tucking in their son and daughter. Sighing deeply, he looked into the fire, thinking about Christmas. It was hard to believe it had been a year since the zombies had arrived. It was the worst Christmas Eve he'd ever experienced. He still remembered tucking the kids in *that* night—trying to get them to fall asleep so Santa Claus would come. But Santa had never arrived, just the rotting corpses of the animated dead.

With another sigh, Jerrold rubbed his face with both hands.

His wife, Dawn, drew the blanket curtain they used to partition off the kids sleep area, and joined him by the fire.

"What're you thinking about?" she asked quietly, her voice barely above a whisper.

"I'm thinking that Christmas will be here in a couple of days," he mumbled.

"And?"

"I think it's sad we don't have any presents for the kids. Last year they didn't get to open the presents we bought for them—we were too busy fighting for our lives. After a year of being sequestered in this basement, we've lost all sense of hope."

"What are you getting at?" Dawn asked, a suspicious look on her face.

Jerrold dragged his fingers through his hair, closed his eyes, and bowed his head. He knew she wouldn't like what he was going to say next.

"I'm going to go out and get the kids some presents. They deserve to have a decent Christmas, no matter what the condition of the world."

He heard her gasp, but he didn't look up, just rushed on.

"We need food, too. I should have gone a week ago. You know it as well as I do, Dawn. I might as well see if I can find some presents while I'm out there. Who knows, maybe all the zombies are gone, moved on to somewhere else in search of people to eat."

Jerrold looked up at his wife, dreading what he might see in her expression. Tears were sliding down her sallow cheeks. It hit him again just how much they'd suffered—how much they'd had to go without. Clenching his jaw, he decided be damned all danger, he was going to make this Christmas special for all of them, no matter what she said.

Dawn's eyes were trained on the fire. The shifting light from the tongues of flame licking at the wood feeding it sent shadows dancing over her features. She was upset. He could see that from the tightness of her jaw.

"Sweetie," he said, caressing her wet cheek. "I have to do something. I can't bear them not having some joy in their lives. What kind of existence is this for a child?"

Closing her eyes, she pressed her face into his hand and took a shuddering breath. "It's too dangerous. I don't want to lose you."

"You won't lose me," he said, taking her into his arms and kissing the top of her head. "I'll be careful. I promise."

"I can't handle even the thought of losing you," she whispered and wrapped her arms tightly around him. "It's not worth the risk. I don't want you to go. Stay for me. Please."

Jerrold took a deep breath and rubbed her back, tears coming to his eyes at her pleading. His eyes fell on two sticks that were jutting out from beneath the curtain to the kids sleeping area. They were crudely carved to resemble a human being. He remembered making them for the kids for their birthdays. Their eyes had lit up and it was the only time he remembered seeing genuine smiles on their faces since they'd been down here in the basement.

Squeezing Dawn tight, he whispered, "I have to do it—for the kids. They should have some real toys to play with, something to enjoy. All they play with are those damn sticks I made, or what they can draw on the cement floor with charred pieces of wood from the fire. They should have more. They *deserve* more. What kind of childhood are we giving them?"

She pulled back and looked him in the face defiantly.

"We're giving them the best childhood we can under the circumstances," she hissed. "It's not like we have a choice. We're doing the best we can with what we have. Those damn zombies took everything from us, but we have our lives and we have each other. That should be enough."

"Believe me," he said. "I *am* grateful we're all alive and together, and I'll never be able to express how glad I was we found somewhere that had a good supply of food and water, but it's Christmas. I really need you to understand and support me in this. I need to do this...for all of us."

Dawn clutched at the front of his threadbare shirt, kneading it in her almost skeletal hands. Tears ran freely down her face and dropped on her shirt, also threadbare and almost sheer in its overuse. Choking back a sob, she buried her face in his neck and whimpered. She took a few seconds to get herself under control before she spoke in a pained whisper. "When will you go?"

Wrapping his arms around her and rocking her gently, he mumbled into her hair, "In the morning. It'll be Christmas Eve. I'll arrive back just in time to put the presents under the tree, just like Santa."

He laughed at the irony of the thought, as he choked back sobs, too.

She nodded against his chest and clutched at him, not wanting to let go, not wanting to think about what the morning would bring, when her husband would leave their den of safety and venture out into the world that held who knew what.

They sat by the fire, crying and holding each other for hours before they added a couple more pieces of wood to the fire and went to bed.

Even though they'd been careful about sex, using condoms to make sure Dawn didn't get pregnant—which they'd run out of a couple of weeks ago—they made love that night, throwing caution to the wind. The action was full of desperation. They spoke to each other with their bodies, conveying their love and need to be with each other, hoping the bond they created would be stronger than the separation facing them in the morning, and stronger than the fear of never seeing each other again.

*   *   *

The next morning Jerrold was up and dressed before the kids woke. He kissed them gently on their foreheads, brushed back their hair, and said a quick prayer for them. Behind him, he heard the sound of Dawn's bare feet padding softly across the cement floor. She paused at the curtain and sighed heavily. He could feel the tension radiating from her. Turning, he stepped up to her and wrapped his arms around her, burying his face in her hair.

"I'll be careful," he whispered. "I promise I'll come back."

With a quivering breath, she nodded and pressed her face into the side of his neck. "I love you."

"I love you, too," he said, pulling back and kissing her.

Wrapping her arms tightly around his neck, she stood on her tip toes and put her soul into the kiss, making it clear to him one last time how much he truly meant to her.

Breaking away reluctantly, Jerrold picked up his 30/30 rifle and his bag, and headed for the door.

"Make sure you put these back up as soon as I'm through the door," he said, taking down heavy pieces of lead pipe and angle iron jammed at different levels on the door. "I'll padlock the door at the top of the steps from the outside, instead of the inside. Do you remember the knock I'll use when I come back, so you know it's me?"

Dawn nodded, but he was facing the door and didn't see her.

Turning, he looked at her. "Do you remember?"

"Yes," she said. "Three fast, two slow, three fast."

He smiled and nodded, stepped back over to where she stood, and kissed her one last time. Looking deeply into her eyes, he said, "I'll be back tonight."

She smiled weakly, nodded, and closed the door behind him as he picked up his rifle and bag again, and stepped through the door.

Jerrold stood in the shadows of the apartment building basement, waiting to hear the scraping of metal as Dawn replaced the bars against the boiler room door. They'd been lucky to find such a place to stay. They had heat, and had been draining the water out of the building's pipes for months. He'd also fed them on what the building had to offer. Each apartment had provided canned goods and everything else they needed to survive. The zombies had left the building after the people who lived there had died or been turned into one of the walking dead. Now their supplies were getting low, which after a year, they couldn't complain. But this time he would have to venture beyond the safety zone and into the unknown.

Satisfied after he heard the last bar being placed against the door, ignoring the sobs he could hear from his wife, he mounted the steps to their second defense—a padlocked metal door leading into the main lobby of the building. Withdrawing a small, silver key from his bag, Jerrold quickly and quietly unlocked it. Taking a deep breath, he pulled the door open slowly. The hinges screeched loudly and he froze for a moment.

Deciding it would be better just to get it over with, knowing the sound would have already alerted anything in the area to his presence, he jerked the door the rest of the way open and jumped through. Whipping his rifle around from where it hung on his back by a shoulder strap, he held it ready and spun in a semi-circle to check the room around him. Seconds passed and all he heard was his panting breath. No danger presented itself.

Turning back to the door, he quickly closed it and attached the lock to the latch he'd installed when he'd gone on his first 'raiding' trip. They kept it locked from the inside when they were all at 'home', and when he went out, he locked it from the outside.

Surveying the room again, he noticed the only thing that had changed since the last time he'd been here, was that more plants were growing through the openings of the vacant windows, which had been shattered long ago.

It was still dark, the sun just beginning to rise, casting a light-yellow glow to the backdrop he could just make out beyond the vines in-between the buildings. Stepping carefully, holding his rifle in front of him, ready to pull it up at any moment, he advanced to the busted-out glass door that had once been a grand entrance. Pushing aside the greenery, he stepped out into the world, breathing deeply of the fresh morning air, something that seemed almost foreign to him since they'd sought shelter in the haven below.

The sweetness and crispness of it almost made him cry, and at the same time it overwhelmed him with joy.

A bird flitted past and called to its mate, which soon joined it in a tree that once neatly graced the sidewalk of the city, but was now growing wild. Old Christmas lights hung from the branches, providing a ladder for the vines to climb—the tiny, twinkle-light bulbs looked like alien berries waiting to be picked.

With a grin on his face, Jerrold shivered as a strong wind blew, cutting through his worn-out clothes. He'd forgotten how cold it was outside when fall gave way to winter.

"First things first," he said to himself, heading down the street to where he knew a man's clothing store used to operate, knowing he needed a coat, gloves, and a hat if he was going to stay warm long enough to hunt for gifts and food.

The sound of his voice startled a black squirrel that was searching through the weeds for the last of the nuts from a small walnut tree. It chattered at him angrily as it ducked inside a faded blue BMW parked at the curb.

Bending down slightly, Jerrold could see the squirrel had made itself a nice little nest in the interior, where it had dug into a rip in the seat and was now living lavishly in leather and insulation.

Chuckling and shaking his head at the absurdity, yet genius, of the upside down world he now lived in, he continued on in search of warm clothes.

Soon he reached the store he was looking for. But to his chagrin, he noticed that all the showcase windows of the front of the men's store were intact. Smeared on the inside was a dark-brown substance he knew was dried blood, which meant someone or something could still be inside.

He stood there for a moment, indecision warring in his mind of the possible dangers of breaking the glass and alerting any zombies that might be lurking nearby, and the possible danger of going in period, when something could still be in there. A strong gust of wind penetrated his clothes and bit into his skin with tiny, pin-like teeth, and made the choice for him. He had to have something more to wear, and if he didn't go in there, he could waste hours searching for the right items, and then hope they would fit him.

Looking up and down the street, seeing no movement, he lifted the butt of his rifle and broke one of the windows. Glass hit the pavement with a tinkling of accusation, as if angry for having been broken and disturbed after so long in silence.

Jerrold held his gun at the ready and waited for a ghoul to jump out at him. He'd had it happen plenty of times before and had always come away the victor. Nothing happened.

No one and nothing came from the new opening. Glancing up and down the street again, not seeing any movement, he started knocking away the jagged remains of the glass so he could enter the store. His hands were so numb from the cold he didn't feel it when a small sliver penetrated his palm, breaking the skin and letting out a small trickle of blood.

Entering the store, he hurriedly located what he needed. He found himself a new pair of jeans, a shirt, underwear, socks, boots, a coat, gloves, and a hat, piling it all in the center of the store, where he could see all around him.

Quickly, he shed his worn-out clothes, donned his new apparel, and took out his old hunting knife, adding it to his new outfit in case he did meet a zombie. Leaving his old clothes lying on the floor, he grabbed some more clothes and shoved them into a shopping bag he found behind the counter. Knowing he couldn't carry them around all day because he would be collecting more items, he decided to jog them back down the block and leave the bag outside the door to the basement sanctuary.

While Jerrold had been searching through the racks of clothing, the small sliver of glass had come free from his hand, but he still hadn't noticed. Unknowingly, he began a blood trail, starting with the glass, to the racks, to the clothes he left on the floor, and then to the counter where he'd gotten the bag. The gloves he'd chosen were thick, and they absorbed the red liquid, only to start dripping around the cuff after he'd left the bag at the basement door. He didn't think anything of it, as now his hands were warm and his palms were sweating.

He decided that clothing and food should be top priority for this trip, even though he wouldn't return without presents. He just knew that finding appropriate gifts would take longer, and if he got his 'duty' done first, then he would have more time to 'shop.'

Turning to the right this time when he left the men's clothing store, he went to a department store he knew would have clothes for his entire family. There were plenty of shopping carts sitting around, so he used one to procure clothing for his family. Having not seen any zombies for a while, he started to let his guard down. He assumed they'd moved on to where they thought people might be more numerous.

Christmas decorations and fake snow were on all of the displays, some still standing and some destroyed. Strings of lights dangled drunkenly from cash registers, and plastic Santas that had been placed close to the windows had faded from red to pink, where the sun had bleached them through the summer months.

Seeing these relics reminded him of last year—of what a disaster Christmas had been.

After getting all the clothes the cart could hold, he paused to think of anything else his family might need. Batteries came to mind. He searched around the counters where he remembered having seen batteries when he'd shopped there long ago, but there were none. The empty racks stared back at him menacingly, as if mocking his stupidity for thinking he'd find something there.

All the snacks and candy bars were gone as well. There was nothing of use or value.

Pushing the overloaded cart out of the store was harder than he first thought it would be. There was so much debris in the way that the wheels kept getting stuck and he continually had to clear a path.

It was at one of those times, while he was bent over and pulling a long deflated inflatable snowman out of the way, from beneath the wheels, that a noise from behind him alerted him he wasn't alone.

Slowly he stood erect, sliding his rifle strap off his shoulder as he prepared to fire. Spinning suddenly, he brought the butt of the 30/30 tight into his shoulder, and looked down the sights with the ease that only came from practice.

Standing no more than ten feet from him was an old woman and a young boy, but they were no longer human. The wasting of their flesh released a stench he should have noticed and probably would have if he hadn't been constantly moving. But the fact of the matter was, he was used to the smell of death. He'd been living with it for a year now, and it wasn't something he noticed anymore.

They stared at him, the little boy holding the old woman's hand like they still thought they were living and he was going on a shopping trip with grandma.

The stand off ended when the old lady hissed and her dentures fell from her gapping, rotted mouth. Her cheek split and her bottom jaw slid from its socket to dangle below her face by loose, flapping skin.

She darted forward at Jerrold, as if it was his fault she was falling apart. Not seeming to realize she was still holding the boy's hand, she ripped his decaying arm off as she came for Jerrold, the only fresh meat she'd seen in months. It didn't matter that she didn't have any teeth, or that she could no longer bite him, she attacked anyway.

Not wanting to draw unneeded attention, Jerrold quickly side-stepped the old woman, and grabbed the long knife strapped to his thigh. As he spun, he brought the blade down into the back of her head, penetrating the skull with a sickening squish. She was so rotten she was literally falling apart.

Amazed at how easy it had been to kill her, for a moment Jerrold just stood marveling at the corpse, and didn't pay any attention to the boy.

Suddenly, a shriek sounded—it was high pitched and angry. Turning toward the sound, Jerrold saw the boy had climbed up onto an empty rack and was about to propel himself at him.

Jumping back and losing his balance when he slipped in the black blood that had oozed out of the old woman, he landed hard on the marble-tiled floor. The knife fell from his grasp and slid a few feet away. For a few moments, he couldn't move; the breath had been knocked out of his body, and he'd jarred his back.

In those precious moments, the boy took advantage of the situation. Hissing and clawing, he jumped off the rack and crawled across the floor on all fours. He was a wild beast and he smelled blood.

No sooner did Jerrold get his breath back, then he saw the small zombie leap into the air above him. He frantically searched around for his knife. With the boy in the air, merely two feet from landing on him, Jerrold gripped something and brought it up at an angle in an attempt to knock the boy sideways. He succeeded, hitting the boy directly in the head.

The boy fell to the side with a whimper and didn't get up. Jerrold looked over at the small body, slowly sitting up, forcing his back to stretch. He saw that he'd picked up a large plastic candy cane, and by a miracle, had stabbed the boy in the temple with it, killing him.

Sadness gripped his heart. He was here to get things his family needed to survive. He knew the boy was a zombie and there was nothing he could have done to save or help him, but he still felt regret about ending his existence.

It took him precious minutes to get his back to stretch enough to allow him to stand. After that, he hobbled his way out of the store. By the time he was halfway home with the cart, his back had almost returned to normal, with only a few spasms every now and then.

Pushing forward and through the pain, he made it back and dropped off the cart, leaving it beside the bag of clothing he'd left earlier.

Now that he'd seen a couple of zombies, his guard was up again. Slipping off his glove, he wrapped his hand around the padlock, giving it a swift tug. Looking back over his shoulder when he heard a rustle in the rubble, he slid his hand back into his glove, not seeing the blood he smeared all over the padlock. Holding the rifle in front of him like a combat soldier creating a perimeter, Jerrold snuck over to where he heard the noise. A rat jumped up from a hole in the pavement and scurried away. Startled by the sudden appearance of the rodent, he almost pulled the trigger.

With a deep sigh, he bent over and closed his eyes for a moment, still thinking about the undead boy he'd just killed. Mentally shaking off the thought, he reminded himself why he was out here, and left the apartment building, this time going straight across the street, heading into a residential area, where he had the best chance of finding food and presents.

Ten minutes later, the first house he entered was small, and it looked like it had been the home of a young couple with a small children. Baby toys were strewn about the decaying, dirty carpet, looking as if a small animal had decided to play with them. Having become brittle over time, the soft plastic and plush toys now sported holes and teeth marks.

Quickly doing a check to make sure there was nothing moving around upstairs—where he found a crib and a toddler bed in one of the rooms—he ventured back downstairs. Sitting under the dust-covered, fiber-optic Christmas tree were many presents. Jerrold knew his children would be too old for the toys, but he knew he could use the bright red wagon to haul food and gifts. Digging it out from beneath the packages, he was about to leave, but thought he better check a couple of the woman's presents to see if there would be anything Dawn might like.

Kneeling down, he tore open a small, somewhat flat, rectangle box. The paper came off easily as the weather had broken it down. He discovered it was a new cell phone. With an ironic smirk he tossed it aside. The once vital piece of technology no longer had a purpose.

He dug through more of the pile and opened a few more packages, finding CDs, DVDs, and all kinds of other things that needed batteries or electricity to function. He was about to give up when he came across a small box far under the tree in back. It held a dainty opal ring. He slid it into his coat pocket, knowing Dawn would love it. Deciding to open one more item and then check the kitchen, he found a collection of children's books. They were too young for his children, but they hadn't had much experience in reading and he knew they could use them to practice. He hoped he would find more age appropriate books at another house. It would be great for what little schooling and teaching he and his wife tried to provide.

A quick check of the kitchen cabinets yielded a couple cans of soup and vegetables, but not as much as he was hoping for. A door on the far wall of the kitchen was slightly ajar, and Jerrold decided to check it out, and was glad he did. It was a pantry, and all kinds of canned and dry goods were stored on the shelves.

Feeling like a kid at Christmas time, the thought of which made him laugh, he pulled the wagon close to the door and began filling it.

He wasn't paying much attention to what he was grabbing, and when something warm and furry slithered across his hand, he screamed and dropped it. He looked down at a box of corn flakes that had a hole chewed through the side. The light tan flakes inside moved and wiggled. He knelt down and gently brushed the cereal aside to see a rat's nest.

Standing, he kicked it off to the side and was more careful while loading the wagon. Once it was full to the point of overflowing, he set out for another house. Pulling the wagon down the sidewalk with his injured hand caused it to bleed more profusely. Blood ran down the handle and dripped onto the cement, but he didn't notice, he was still on a high from finding so much food in one place. Now all he had to do was find a few more gifts and he could go home.

Gazing up at the sun, he saw there was plenty of time before sunset.

The next house he entered smelled like muscle cream, even after the time it had sat vacant and open to the elements. He knew immediately that an older couple had lived here; it was a smell no other dwelling would have possessed. It reminded him of his parents, and what it had been like to visit them. He didn't look through the presents under the small, four foot Christmas tree, but he did take the time to look through the medicine cabinet, taking anything he thought might be useful. When he finished searching, he moved on to the next home.

Three houses later, he hit pay dirt. After quickly securing the house, he found out that a boy and a girl had lived here—there was a room for each. He took some of the decorations from each room for his children, so they could decorate their sleeping area, but he was mostly happy with the books he found on the wooden shelves. After carrying the books downstairs and putting them in the wagon with everything else gathered, he knew he would have to find something to make sides for the wagon or if he hit one bump on the way home everything would tumble free.

With a little bit of thought and some quick innovation, he fashioned sides for the wagon out of shelves from one of the bookcases. He held them together with a roll of duct tape he found in a small tool box underneath the kitchen sink.

The family had purchased a live tree, which was now dry and bare of all needles. They lay on the floor of the room in a carpet of brown strands. Pushing them aside, Jerrold dug through the presents and was disgusted when he had to throw more than half of the items aside. Electronics. They were so worthless now.

Finding a couple more books, he added them to the wagon, along with the other gifts he thought his children would enjoy.

When he left the house a half hour later, he focused his attention on the wagon as he maneuvered it down the front steps. When he turned around to look forward, he noticed there were five zombies stumbling down the sidewalk toward him.

Frowning, he wondered where they had come from. Lifting his rifle, he shot the first zombie in the head. The bullet pulverized its rotting brain and still had enough power to hit the third one back in the neck, taking out enough tissues for its head to fall off—both fell to the ground at once.

The second, fourth, and fifth in the stumbling line-up of ghouls kept coming, ignoring their downed comrades lying in their path.

Jerrold clenched his jaw, hating to fire once, but hating even more to fire again, knowing that if there were zombies around, they would come searching for the source of the gunshots. He now wouldn't be able to search for anything else, and would have to hurry home after dealing with the ghouls or risk serious danger.

Jerking the lever action of the rifle, he released the spent casing and chambered another round, hoping to do intentionally what he'd done by accident with the last shot, but it wasn't to be.

After three more shots and a stab with his hunting knife, the zombies were all down. Hurriedly, he jogged in a round about way back to the apartment building. It took him a half an hour, with all the curbs and debris he had to navigate through.

The sun was beginning to set, as the apartment building came into view. He breathed a sigh of relief and increased his pace, even though he was exhausted. The thought of seeing his wife, of holding her and the kids, gave him the strength he needed to make it back.

Fatigue made him lazy, and he didn't take the time to peer into the lobby before rushing in with the wagon clattering noisily behind him.

Twenty zombies were gathered around the door leading to the basement, pushing and clawing at each other, fighting over who got to lick the blood-covered padlock. They turned, seeming as shocked to see him as he was to see them.

Jerrold stood frozen until the zombies started to cock their heads and sniff the air, inching closer and closer to him.

Raising his rifle once again, he blasted as many as he could. Some of the zombies went down as legs were severed from shots to their knees, in a splash of thick, black blood.

Jumping over the reception desk, Jerrold took cover and re-loaded the rifle, and when he stood, hands that were stripped of flesh reached for him. Stepping back, he let bullets fly. The rotted corpses were so far gone the bullets did almost nothing to stop them. The rounds went through two or three zombies before losing momentum.

He caught glimpses of eyeballs dangling from sockets and grotesque figures with missing or damaged limbs; face after face of hungry horror eager for him to fill their bellies and join their ranks.

After a couple more reloads and attacks, he managed to kill fifteen of them, and the other five were damaged to the point they were no longer a serious threat. Jumping back over the counter, he thanked God they hadn't been smart enough to find the little swinging door for the counter, or the latch that held it shut, otherwise they would have gotten back there with him and he would have been trapped.

He finished off the last five ghouls with his knife, retrieved his bag from the wagon, and attempted to unlock the padlock. His gloves made him clumsy and he dropped the key. Biting one of the fingers of his glove, he yanked it off. Crying out in pain, his teeth parted and the blood-soaked glove fell to the floor.

"That's how they found me," he whispered to himself. "I was leaving a trail of blood."

Knowing now that it was just a matter of time before more zombies showed up, following his trail of blood, he quickly picked up the key and unlocked the door. He threw his bag of clothes down the stairs, and then moved to the cart. Armload after armload of clothes followed the bag.

Heaving the cart out of the way, and dragging his feet in a shuffle so he wouldn't fall in all the blood and guts, he retrieved the wagon.

As he made it to the door, more zombies came through the entryway in search of the fresh meat they'd been trailing.

Rushing and panicking, Jerrold pulled the wagon down the stairs after himself. Scrambling, he struggled to reach around the wagon and close the door. He slipped and the wagon, with all its weight, shoved him down the stairs. He tumbled down, landing hard at the bottom, his head hitting the pavement just beyond the pile of clothes.

Dazed and fighting for consciousness, he was only vaguely aware of what was actually going on. His eyes focused on the door to safety, to sanctuary; it was his only chance. Forcing himself to crawl, he made his way to the door to the boiler room where his family was safe from the danger that hunted him.

Knocking on the door, just like he told Dawn he would, he was relieved to hear the metal bars being quickly removed. He sighed with relief and closed his eyes, letting his forehead rest on the cool cement floor. He was too dazed and confused to understand there were now six zombies stumbling down the stairs after him.

Dawn opened the door and he looked up into her sweet face, smiling, but frowned quickly at the look of fear he saw there—her eyes were focused on something behind him. Half rolling onto his side, he saw what she was looking at—a huge brute of a zombie stood over him.

The zombie growled, with what would have once been a grin on its decaying face. It lunged forward and overpowered Dawn in an instant.

Jerrold cried out weakly, holding his hand up as if pleading with reality, asking it not to be real. He cried out again, this time from physical pain as two of the other zombies bit into his legs, tearing flesh from bone.

As he bled out, Jerrold stared into the eyes of his dead wife who lay on the floor in front of him. When death was about to overtake him and his eyes drifted closed, he heard the chorus of screams as his children were eaten alive.

THE GIRL WITH THE SNOW-CONE HAIR

KELLY M. HUDSON

The girl with the snow-cone hair danced through the crowd of holiday shoppers like a delirious fairy fluttering through a woodland blanket of flowers. Her name was May but Dwight always thought of her as 'the girl with the snow-cone hair.'

It was because of the colors she wore in her hair—a strip of blue, a stripe of red, and a slice of green, alternating strands all around her head—and the way they glittered in the fluorescent lights of the shopping mall. He thought of a rainbow-streaked snow-cone, and thus her name.

She worked at a couple of different eateries in the Food Court; Goldman's Deli, Christine's Bakery, and Amplas Pizza. She worked them on alternating days, six days a week, always taking Sundays off.

Dwight knew this because he kept his eye on her, not in some psycho-stalker kind of way, but simply because whenever he saw her, she brightened up his day. He worked as Santa's assistant in Santaland, right smack dab in the middle of the mall Food Court. He was a tall, skinny man with the face of a bird and the physique of a scarecrow. He had to wear a lime-green elf suit and was the bearer of the clipboard, the one who would usher the next child up to Santa's lap. It was a thankless job, and one of many he'd worked at the Crystal Lake Mall. He was a seasonal employee, which meant he had a job for a month or so before whichever season he was working was over and then he was unemployed. That lasted about two hours before the next season started and he would be hired again for whatever menial job the next season required. He always had work, but it was never continuous, so he was never given health insurance or all the other benefits that come with a steady job. He didn't mind, though, because most of the time, he got to see May.

There was something about the way she moved. She reminded him of girls he'd seen in old movies and documentaries about Haight-Ashbury, the girls from the sixties with the flowers in their hair and the wonderful smiles on their faces.

But he was no fool. He knew those grins were because they were bombed out on some kind of drug, but there was a peace there, a harmony with the world around them, a joy he could almost taste when he saw them. The day he first laid eyes on May, he had the same feeling about her, only she wasn't on any kind of drug. She was the real thing.

And today was the day Dwight was going to approach her. He was going to introduce himself, ask her to sit and share a coffee with him, and he was finally going to meet the woman of his dreams.

Too bad the man playing Santa had a heart attack. Too bad because it was at that precise moment, that something in the reality of the world flipped and the dead came back to life to eat the living.

Santa, a man with an authentic, bowling-ball belly and a two-pack a day habit, reeled up from his throne and spat a wad of foam, clutching his chest and gasping in agony. He flipped forward and fell face first, shattering his nose with a crack that sounded like a candy cane flung against a wall.

Dwight stumbled, mouth open in shock, watching Santa writhe on the floor. The kids behind him screamed and he heard one say, "Mommy! Santa's sick!"

The parents swarmed over their kids, grabbing and hauling them away even as one of them—a father with fading hair, a skinny body, and terrible breath—yelled at Dwight. "Do something, man!"

Dwight couldn't move; he was rooted to the spot. Santa raised his head, his face dripping with blood, and Dwight knew instantly something wasn't right. It was in the eyes. They were rolled back into his head like a shark, all whites and no pupils. There was also the guttural growl gasping from between Santa's ragged, torn lips, and the broken teeth inside his mouth, gnashing together like gears grinding in a machine.

Dwight shirked back and it was this action that saved his life, because another one of the elves, a clever girl just out of high school named Clarice, stepped between them.

"Oh, you poor thing," Clarice said. She was a blonde, with a voice like a mouse crying from having its tail tugged on. "Let me help you."

Santa slapped Clarice so hard her green elf hat went flying, smacking Dwight in the face and blinding him for a moment. In the second it took him to snatch the hat away, Santa buried his teeth into Clarice's right shoulder, tearing out a hunk, followed by a spray of arterial blood. Clarice couldn't even scream before Santa's fingers found her mouth and yanked down, tearing her lower jaw clean from her head. She stumbled and fell, her tongue loose and lolling, glistening in the fluorescent lights of the Food Court.

Behind Dwight, the screams of the children and the adults mixed so you couldn't tell them from each other, but it didn't really matter. Everyone was afraid now, and they were all equals in their panic, be they old or young.

Clarice gasped, shuddered, and died from shock. She sat up a few seconds later, her tongue hanging down, limp like a dead snake, her eyes white and dull. She clambered to her feet and she and Santa stood side by side, him chewing the meat he'd torn from her arm, and her dripping blood and spit from the crater in her face. They both turned their pale eyes on Dwight, the nearest person.

Behind the zombies, a woman screamed and tried to run. It was another of the helper elves; a girl who'd started just yesterday, a girl whose name escaped Dwight. She ran headlong into the clawing fingers of Clarice. The elf tripped and fell, careening to the side as Santa and Clarice descended on her. Dwight blinked twice in the time it took them to rip both arms off the elf, holding them up into the light like champion bowlers raising their trophies in adulation.

The elf bled out quickly and after dying, rose armless, her eyes white and her teeth clacking together.

Dwight wasn't ashamed of his next move, nor should he have been. He turned and ran. He was no coward, but he also knew he didn't stand a chance alone against the three of them, so he fled, hoping to find some safety in the number of others also hightailing it. Unfortunately, what he ran into instead was a mass of desperation and death.

A number of people had already been trampled and died, and they sat up or rolled over, their fingers digging into the ankles and calves of those trampling them. More people fell and more were stepped on; arms breaking, necks snapping, fingers smashed. Only a few minutes had passed since Santa had died and come back to life before there were thirty more zombies, each rising and attacking those fleeing, carving deep gashes into flesh and bones, their teeth tearing out soft chunks wherever they found them.

Dwight was lucky; because the pandemonium had already led to a number of deaths and resurrections, he bounced off the back of the fleeing crowd, stopped now because of the carnage in front of them. He stumbled away and dashed in the opposite direction, back towards Amplas Pizza. He dove over the counter and collided head-first with a rack of empty trays, spilling them across the floor.

When he rolled over, sitting next to him was the girl with the snow-cone hair. She nodded grimly at him and he smiled back, star-struck.

If he thought May was beautiful from afar, he understood now just how wrong he'd been. Up close, she was gorgeous: dimples dug in deep in each cheek, bright blue eyes sparkling like diamonds under a tropical sun, and a cute nose sitting atop puffy lips, red and full of promise.

Dwight swooned. He would have sat there forever, in her thrall, if not for the zombies coming over the counter to attack them.

May and Dwight moved as one, like twins, their actions mirroring each other. Both of them stooped and swooped up the big metal trays he had knocked down, the ones that went into the ovens and were used to bake with. They were rectangular and flat, with slight raised edges and were the size of an extra-large pillow. They were solid, though, unlike a pillow, and when May swung hers, the side of it cracked the head of the closest zombie, the sound it made like a rifle shot.

The zombie she hit wore a flower-print dress and was a woman, except now she was dead and missing her face, which was torn off and hanging in shreds. Long slices of skin dangled down like wet confetti, dripping with blood and shimmering in the light. The tray slammed the side of her head and caved it in with the precise edge of the corner. The zombie fell to the side, its body shaking violently and spilling to the floor, never to move again.

Dwight raised his tray over his head and crashed it down onto the head of a farmer, some yokel wearing overalls and a flannel shirt beneath. The yokel's throat had been slashed open and blood was still pouring from the wound, even though the man was dead. The tray shattered the top of his skull and the zombie spat out a bloody wad of chewing tobacco as it fell to the counter, shaking and then dying for good.

The tobacco splattered on Dwight's chest and dribbled down, thick with blood and juice. He shuddered in disgust but barely had time to react before two more zombies were scrambling over the counter, their hands clawing the air and their teeth clattering with such furious impact he thought they might shatter.

Dwight glanced over at May and they locked eyes for the briefest of moments.

In that moment, he lost himself in the ocean of her beauty and would have died if not for her sudden spring forward. She slashed her tray like it was a sword across the back of a male zombie leaning over the counter, about to bite Dwight's hand. Her blow cracked the ghoul's spine and it froze in place, unable to move.

The tray blasted from May's hands from the impact, and Dwight could see the shock of the blow reverberate up her arms and shake her head. She stumbled back and he returned her favor by battering the head of an old lady zombie as it slid over the counter, dentures clacking inches from May's right arm. The tray smashed the lady's nose up into its brain. The old lady slumped and slipped to the floor, blood pouring from its mouth and nose.

May looked at Dwight and back at the zombies. There were too many of them, at least a dozen, if not more, and some of them were over the counter now and stumbling toward them.

"Follow me!" May yelled and Dwight smiled, chasing after her as she bolted to the back of the kitchen. He would follow her just about anywhere.

They dashed past a series of giant ovens, still hot from cooking pizza and the other dishes Amplas served. Two of the ovens were pouring out black smoke, whatever was inside now reduced to burnt husks. The stink of the smoke filled his nose and he was happy for it because it drowned out the other smell, the stench of the dead pursuing them.

The smell wasn't one of rot because there was no time for these freshly dead to decay. No, the stink was where they'd vacated themselves, pissing and crapping until their pants were full. It was enough to make a man gag, and when they were in such overwhelming numbers, it was too much to handle.

Dwight stopped and spun to the side and vomited what was left in his stomach. Half-digested tacos and nachos splattered the side of one of the ovens. The puke sizzled from the heat of the range, making him wretch again. Only the cool, calming hand of May on his shoulder kept him in check.

"It's okay," she said. "I'm parked just outside. We'll get to my car and leave."

Dwight nodded, feeling retarded. He wondered what he must look like to the most beautiful woman in the world, standing there, a grown man in a green elf costume, spatters of puke on his face and a big wad of tobacco juice staining his chest. Something awful, he reckoned.

Contrary to his appearance, May looked like the most gorgeous thing he'd ever seen. Her eyes shone and her grin was magnificent and even the grim, little details, like the gobs of blood and flecks of human skin in her hair, couldn't ugly her up.

"What?" she asked.

"Nothing," he said. "I just always wanted to talk to you. Funny we ended up meeting like this."

"You work with Santa, don't you?" she asked. His heart blasted in his chest like a jackhammer.

"You know me?" he stammered.

"No," she smiled. "But I've seen you."

Dwight thought he might die right there.

Of course, an ugly zombie with a face full of pimples stumbled between them, moaning and groaning. Dwight shrieked and jumped back as May spun, grabbed a butcher's knife off the counter behind her, and slammed the blade into the zombie's face. It split the flesh open, horizontally, just under the nose. A dozen zits popped, their pus mixing with the blood now pouring from the wound. May had slammed the knife in so far it got stuck above the teeth, somewhere in the sinuses, but not deep enough to puncture the brain.

Zit Face groaned and turned towards her, the knife embedded like a silver mustache. It grabbed her arms as she tried to shrink back, and pulled her to him.

Dwight leapt forward, a fire extinguisher in his hands. He slammed it into the back of Zit Face's head three times until the skull crumbled and its brains spilled out and slid down its slick, black hair. Zit Face sighed and slumped to the floor, dead again.

Four more zombies shambled into the kitchen, only three feet away from them. May tried to pull free of Zit Face's dead grasp but couldn't, her wrists locked in its death grip. She screamed and wrenched and kicked at its dead face, hoping to pull free, but it was all for naught.

The closest zombie, a holiday shopper with foam antlers for ear muffs, bit May's arm, tearing out a chunk of her triceps. May screeched and shook, her blood spraying from the open wound. Antler zombie bit her again, this time in the tender flesh of her inner arm, and ripped free a hunk of soft skin, its teeth grinding the meat and gulping it down in a quick second.

Dwight was too late to save her, he realized, but the anger burning in his heart wouldn't hear of it. He lunged and swung the extinguisher, battering the zombie in the face, crushing the skull inward with one swift blow. The ghoul fell back, the piece of May's arm falling from its mouth like bubblegum, hitting the floor and rolling under one of the ovens, leaving behind a slug's slime trail of greasy blood.

He spun and grabbed another knife from the counter and hacked at Zit Face's dead arms until they were slashed enough for May to finally pull free, the zombie hands still attached to her wrists like awkward bracelets.

The other three zombies closed in, but Dwight was still full of fury and he made short work of them, bashing their heads with the extinguisher until none of them stood. When he was finished, he slumped against the table, breathing hard.

May sat next to him, crying. He slid an arm around her. Things didn't go as he'd hoped and now it looked like there wasn't much left to say or do. He heard the other zombies, still in the front part of the restaurant, stumbling around and knocking things over. Their moans and their gnashing teeth were growing closer by the second, and he knew it wouldn't be long before they were back in the kitchen, surrounding him and May, bringing certain death.

Dwight felt a hand on his crotch and looked down to see May, her crystal eyes rolled into the back of her head and her teeth grinding together. He knew what she'd become and his heart broke in his chest. There was only one way now for them to be together, and this way would mean forever.

He closed his eyes and listened to the music the mall pumped into all the stores, blaring out a salsa version of Jingle Bells. He unzipped his pants and waited, then screamed as May's teeth tore into his balls, chomping them in two and gobbling them down.

Dwight opened his eyes and looked at her, the girl with the snow-cone hair, and smiled as she chewed on his manhood. Very soon, he would join her in living dead life, and even though it wasn't how he always imagined it would be, his dreams were about to come true.

He closed his eyes again and felt his tears, hot against his cheeks, as his eyes rolled up into the back of his head.

He couldn't believe how truly lucky he was.

KIDNAPPING SANTA

D.B. REDDICK

"Is everyone in place, Roger?"

"Yes, Master, exactly as you planned it," Roger replied as he gazed up at his tall, slender boss, who was standing near the center atrium inside Somerset Mall. "They're waiting for your signal."

"Good," Master Z said, a tiny smile forming at the corners of his mouth. "The exchange should happen any minute now."

"Tell me again why we're doing this, Master?"

The Master slowly unfolded his crossed arms and looked down at his assistant. "Because I've dreamed of this day for a very, very long time. I hate Christmas. Always have. My parents were so poor when I was growing up that my sisters and I ended up with practically nothing in our Christmas stockings each year."

"That's truly a very sad story," Roger said, nodding his head. "So, that's why you want to kidnap Santa Claus?"

"My parents never brought me here when I was young. I hated them for that. And I also hated Santa Claus for never bothering to show up at our house on Christmas Eve."

"Never got over it, huh?"

"No!" Master Z screamed.

His sudden outburst startled several shoppers who were walking by at that moment. The shoppers stopped dead in their tracks, turned and began to stare at the strange young man in the ankle-length black trench coat and the fedora pulled down over his face, and at his tiny companion, who was standing next to him dressed in a green elf outfit.

"Enough about me," Master Z said, quickly regaining his composure so as not to draw any further attention to himself. "We've have work to do."

As he spoke, Master Z glanced ahead and noticed that Santa had just gotten out of his high-back chair on the giant stage in the middle of the atrium. He was about to take a twenty-minute break, along with his elves. Master Z knew that because for the past week, he'd quietly stood at different spots around the perimeter of the atrium, closely watching every move the pudgy man in the red, crushed-velvet suit made.

"Put the zombies in their places as soon as Santa and his elves walk away," Master Z whispered to his assistant. "And tell the zombie playing Santa not to ooze too much. I don't want his makeup dripping off his face and scaring kids to death."

"Yes, Master."

"I'll follow Santa to the break room and kidnap him there."

It took Santa and his elves four to five minutes to make their way through the crush of holiday shoppers and reach the break room. It was located along the back wall of Nordstrom's. The elves had abandoned Santa along the way. Three headed straight for the food court, while two others stopped to flirt with some high school girls.

Santa swung the break room door open and walked inside. Master Z slipped in behind him.

"Hey, you can't come in here," Santa said when he realized he wasn't alone. "Didn't you read the sign on the door? This is for employees only."

"Shut up, Santa Claus. You're coming with me."

"No way, mister," Santa said, placing both hands on his wide hips in a show of defiance. "I'm on break. It's bad enough I only get one every four hours. The last thing I'm going to do right now is run off with some skinny looking stranger."

Master Z pulled a handgun out of his trench coat and pointed it at Santa's large midsection. "You're coming with me," he said, slowly repeating his words.

Santa threw up his hands in disgust and followed Master Z out of the break room door. Once back in the mall corridor, Master Z spotted an emergency exit door not far from the department store. He walked up to it and somehow managed to disarm the alarm system without summoning the mall's overweight security guards.

When they were outside in the cool December air, Santa turned to Master Z and asked, "Now what?"

"Put on this blindfold," Master Z said as the two men approached a rusted-out florist's delivery van. "I'm taking you to my secret hideout."

"Now, hold on a second. What's this all about?" Santa asked as he fumbled with the blindfold. "Do you really expect me to ride around in this piece of junk? Does it even run? I'll ruin my suit if I have to sit next to a bunch of cruddy old flower pots. I just got my suit back from the cleaners yesterday. And second of all, why do you want to kidnap Santa Claus anyway? Are you some kind of modern-day Scrooge?"

"You'll find out soon enough, Santa," Master Z replied as he pushed aside some flower pots and shoved Santa into the front seat of the van.

The vehicle sped out of the mall parking lot. They'd driven only two blocks when they came to a red light. Master Z used the stop to reach into his flannel shirt pocket and pull out his cell phone.

"What's going on, Roger?" he asked after reaching his assistant.

"Everything's fine, Master Z," Roger replied. "The zombies assumed their designated positions without much prodding from me. The one playing Santa Claus really seems to be enjoying himself. He keeps shouting 'ho-ho-ho' to anyone who comes within twenty feet of him."

"Good. I'll check back with you in half an hour."

As Master Z put away his phone, Santa Claus leaned in and asked if he could bum a cigarette.

"I know I should quit smoking, but it's my nerves," Santa said. "They're always frazzled at this time of year what with kids jumping up and down on my lap all day, and their mothers screeching in my ears while the elves take pictures of me with their little Johnny's or Suzy's. It's a wonder I don't have migraines. Been doing this for thirty years, you know. I'm beginning to wonder how much more of this I can take."

While Santa continued to rant, Master Z reached inside his coat pocket, pulled out a pack of smokes, and passed it and his lighter to his passenger.

"Thanks, buddy, you're a real life savior," Santa said, taking a deep drag on his cigarette. "Say, I heard the guy on the phone call you Master Z. How'd you end up with a crazy name like that? Are you one of those rapper fellows?"

"No, I'm preparing myself to become the next master of the universe."

"Master of the universe, huh?" Santa said, taking another long drag on his cigarette. "Say, how's that working out for you so far?"

"I'll know in a few more minutes."

"By the way, the name's Lewis Swartz, but you can call me Louie if you'd like," Santa said, extending his hand. "I usually don't let people call me by my actual name while I'm still wearing the suit. It's actually against department store policy. Management doesn't want us traumatizing some kid and having his parents end up suing us."

It was another five minutes before they arrived at Master Z's hideout. He quickly shuttled Santa inside an abandoned office building and closed the door.

"Any chance I can borrow another ciggy from you?" Santa asked as Master Z ordered him to sit down in a straight back chair.

Master Z handed Santa his smokes again. "Now shut up for a few minutes while I make an important phone call."

"Whatever you say, pal," Santa said as he removed his blindfold. "Say, you wouldn't happen to have an extra cold drink lying around this dump of yours, would you? I'd really prefer a Diet Pepsi if you've got one. I gotta watch my waistline, you know."

"Shut up, Louie. I really need to make this call."

"No reason for you to yell at me, most Masterful one. I was just asking. It's just that I get real thirsty talking to kids all day. And the last thing I need this time of the year is to lose my voice."

Master Z walked over to the corner of his hideout so he could make his call in peace. It took a few minutes before the receptionist at Somerset Mall connected him to Christine Murphy, the mall's special events coordinator.

"I've kidnapped Santa Claus," Master Z said in a low voice when Ms. Murphy answered the phone.

"What?" she asked.

"Santa Claus. You know, Louie Swartz. I kidnapped him about an hour ago."

"You're mistaken, mister. I'm standing in the middle of the atrium right now, staring at Louie talking to a bunch of snotty-nosed kids."

"That's my Santa. I've got Louie."

"Really? But your Santa looks so real. And he's so polite to all the kids. To tell you the truth, he's actually a whole lot nicer to them than Louie is, even on one of his good days."

"That's nice to hear," Master Z said. "But can we get back to Louie."

"What about him?"

"Like I told you, I kidnapped him a little while ago. I want you to pay me a ransom for his return."

"A ransom?"

"Yes, fifty thousand dollars."

"Fifty thousand bucks? You've got to be kidding me. Is this some kind of a sick joke that you and Louie are playing on me?"

"I'm not joking, lady. I want fifty thousand for Santa Claus, and I want it before the end of the day."

"In your dreams, pal." She hung up.

Master Z stared in disbelief at his cell phone for a few seconds. He couldn't believe she had hung up on him. Master Z threw his cell phone against the wall before walking back to where Santa was still sitting.

"What's up, Z?" Santa asked.

"The mall doesn't want to pay a ransom for your return."

"A ransom, huh. How much were you asking?"

"Fifty thousand bucks."

"Wow," Santa said, slapping both of his knees. "Fifty big ones, eh? Gee, I never thought I was worth that much money to anyone. That's very kind of you to think of me like that."

"Don't mention it, but now I need to come up with another plan to get the money."

"Let me help you, kid. As I always like to say that two heads are better than one. Say, did I already ask you for something to drink? I'm really dying of thirst."

Master Z wandered into another room to find Santa a drink. When he returned a moment later, Santa was stomping back and forth across the already thread-bare carpet in the tiny hideout. "I've got a plan," he shouted as he grabbed the bottled water out of Master Z's hand and took a gigantic swig.

"What is it?"

"Didn't I hear you mention earlier that you left a bunch of zombies at the mall?"

"Yeah, so what?"

"Call Christine back and tell her that if she doesn't pay you fifty big ones, you're going to turn your zombies loose in the mall."

"I was hoping I wouldn't have to do that."

"I know, but you gotta remember this, kid. Christine's an all-American bitch. I think she was born that way. Anyway, you've got to get in her face, or she won't listen to you."

Master Z nodded and walked over to where his cell phone had landed on the floor. After putting the battery back in it from where it had fallen out when he threw it, he called Christine Murphy back. A minute later, she answered the phone.

"Ms. Murphy, it's me again. You know, Louie Swartz's kidnapper. Either give me fifty thousand by five o'clock, or I'm going to turn my zombies loose on the mall."

"Zombies?"

"Yes, the Santa Claus and elves now working in your mall are actually zombies. All I have to do is send my assistant a text message and he'll turn them loose. They'll scare the mall's shoppers to death. You don't want that to happen, do you?"

"Zombies, commies, whatever. These guys don't look very scary to me. Sorry, but I'm not interested," she said. She hung up.

"Did she buy your threat to turn your zombies loose?" Santa asked when Master Z put down his phone.

"No, she hung up on me again."

"Damn, that's too bad. Maybe, you're not being forceful enough with her. Christine's one hard-nosed broad. She has to be to handle all the crap that comes her way every day. Give me the phone. I'll talk to her."

Master Z handed his phone to Louie after he dialed again.

"Hello?"

"Christine, honey," Louie purred into the cell phone. "It's me, Louie Swartz. Listen, we seem to have a bit of a situation here that I need you to help me resolve. This master of the universe wannabe is holding me hostage. And he wants fifty thousand for my return. He seems like a nice guy and all, but I'm afraid he could go postal on me if he doesn't get his way. Can't you get the owners of the mall to come up with some cash for his ransom demand?"

"No way, Louie, you know the owners aren't going to go for that."

"Well, then, what about me? How am I getting back to the mall if you don't pay him? What's going to happen to me?"

"I don't know, Louie. By the way, your replacement is really doing a terrific job. He's got the kids jumping up and down on the stage. They're in such a good mood and their parents and grandparents are buying extra photos of their little devils. You take care of yourself now, Louie." She hung up.

"What did she say?" Master Z asked when Louie handed the phone back to him a second later.

"She doesn't care about me anymore," Louie said as he slumped in his chair. "She's in love with your Santa zombie."

"Great. Now what should we do?"

"Turn the zombies loose on the mall," Santa said.

"What?"

"Listen, kid, it's one thing for Christine Murphy to blow you off on the phone, but she's not going to do the same thing to me. I was playing Santa Claus when she was still in diapers. The hell with her and everyone else at Somerset Mall. We're going to show them that they can't treat us this way."

Master Z and Louie high-fived each other and then wandered into an adjoining room where they spent the next hour working on their plan. When they finished, the two men jumped into Master Z's van and headed back to the mall.

The parking lot at the mall was full of cars and trucks when they arrived, so the pair spent the next ten minutes cruising through the massive lot looking for an open space. They finally found one at the opposite end of the lot, far away from the main entrance. They slowly started making their way toward the entrance when a kid tackled Santa around his legs and wouldn't let go.

"Not now, kid," Santa said as he reached down and tried to loosen the kid's death grip. "Santa has to get inside the mall."

"Why won't you talk to my son?"

Santa looked up in the direction of the deep voice he just heard. He found himself staring at a guy twice his size. Getting to the mall entrance would have to wait. Louie jumped up on the nearest car hood he could find, and motioned for the humongous dad to lift his son onto Santa's lap.

"Okay, kid, let's have it, what do you want for Christmas?"

"That was such a nice thing you did back there," Master Z said to Santa after they left the father and his son in the middle of the parking lot.

"You've got to learn to pick your battles," Santa said.

A minute later, Master Z and Santa walked through the main entrance of the mall and headed straight for the center atrium. As they approached, Roger stepped in front of them.

"Where have you been, Master?" he asked. "I was beginning to worry about you."

"It's a long story, but we're here now."

"Everything has been running smoothly since you left. I see you've brought back the real Santa with you. Did the mall decide to pay the ransom?"

"Afraid not, Roger, but Santa and I have a Plan B." He turned and began walking away.

"Where are you going now?"

"To confront Christine Murphy."

It took another a few minutes before Master Z and Santa could make their way to the mall's administrative office. They walked through the front door and asked the receptionist to page Christine Murphy for them. A moment later, Christine entered the office and directed the two men to her office down the hall.

"I see you've made it back, Louie," Christine said as she sat down behind her oak desk. "Is this the Master of the Universe guy?"

Master Z nodded and shook her hand.

"Now that you're back, Louie, does this mean this whole ransom thing is over with?" she asked.

"Not exactly, Christine," he replied. "You see, Master Z here thinks that even though he brought me back as a sign of good faith, his zombie friends should be compensated for their troubles during my absence."

"I don't have any problem with that," Christine said, leaning forward in her chair. "In fact, Master Z, I'd love to hire your Santa, but I'm under contract with Louie through the end of this holiday season. But come back and talk to me at the beginning of the new year, and we'll see what we can work out. In the meantime, how much do you need for your troubles today?"

"Is five hundred dollars too much?" Master Z asked.

"It beats fifty grand," Christine said, reaching into her desk drawer and pulling out a checkbook. "Who do I make the check out to?"

"Peter Simmons, please. That's my real name."

"No problem," Christine said as she quickly wrote out the check and handed it to Master Z. "Anything else?"

"No, ma'am."

"Christine, I still have a few personal issues I'd like to discuss with you. I believe I should be compensated as well for the time that I was in this man's custody. Who knows what would have happened to me if he hadn't come to his senses and drove me back here."

"Nice try, Louie, but I don't think so," she said flatly.

"Perhaps this will change your mind," Louie said, pulling out Master Z's gun and pointing it at Christine. "Master Z, run out to your van and get the package we brought with us. Bring it back here as soon as you can."

It took Master Z about ten minutes to make the trek to his van in the mall parking lot, retrieve the package, and return to Christine's office. The package was about five feet tall and two feet wide and he wheeled it in on a dolly.

"Leave the package and wait for me in the hallway," Louie said. "I'll only be a few more minutes."

Master Z did as he was told. Two or three minutes later, Louie emerged from Christine's office with a wide smile on his face.

"Did you finish the job like we planned it?" Master Z asked.

"Sure thing, kid. While you were at the van, I tied up Christine and locked her in the closet in the corner of her office. Then, I set the Christine zombie look-a-like that you brought in from the van at her desk."

"Won't people be suspicious of what we've done? The zombie replacement doesn't look too much like her."

"Nah we'll be fine," Louie said. "Most people who work here look for ways to run away from Christine. I'll wait until Christmas Eve before I release her and give you back your zombie."

"Won't she fire you?"

"Naw, that's our biggest day of the year. She couldn't afford to fire me. Besides, the bad publicity would be too much for even her to handle."

"Well, Santa, I'm glad I could help you out. Now, I need to find my assistant, round up my zombies, and go home. It sure has been nice getting to know you."

"Same here, kid. I hope that universe thing works out for you. Say, before you leave, can I bum another cigarette off you?"

I SAW MOMMY EATING SANTA CLAUS

R.S. PYNE

The best part about Christmas in Cardiff is a trip to Winter Wonderland: ice skating in the open air, a two hundred foot high Ferris wheel and lots of rides for the kiddies. The Gorsedd Gardens by the National Museum becomes a magical fairy grotto with twinkling lights strung on every tree.

Jolly plastic snowmen loom around every corner from the middle of November to the first week of January. Drifting smells of festive food and drink fill the air: freshly brewed coffee, German sausages, hot mulled wine and gingerbread; even a herd of live reindeer at the weekend.

That is where I would rather be, anywhere but the new John Lewis store—otherwise known as the third level of Hell reserved for those who leave their shopping to the last minute.

It was predictably crowded, people shuffling around like distracted sheep with too much on their minds. All I wanted was a Candy Bears Mega Play set, this year's 'must-have' toy.

Not too much to ask. True, I had left it until Christmas Eve, but my darling wife made it very clear what she would do to me if I came home without one.

Loud and over-jolly festive music flooded the store, a relentless reminder as if anyone could forget the season. Before all hell broke loose, there was a lot of shuffling and vacant stares but that was still the shop assistants. When you've watched an elf tear the throat out of a John Lewis Santa Claus and then a child having a tantrum—you've seen it all.

I snatched the last Candy Bears Play Set from the well-gnawed fingers of a woman who didn't need it any more. In life, she was morbidly obese, wore far too much makeup and bleached her hair with peroxide. It was hardly surprising that the elf bit her first. She screamed like a stuck pig, dying messily among a display of synthetic wigs. Then she got up again and savaged the person next to her. It got a lot worse from there, spreading through the shop floor in minutes until the un-dead outnumbered the living. Survivors stampeded in all directions, every man for himself and to hell with everyone else.

A cashier trampled in the rush dragged himself across the blood-slick tiles and begged for help; the only one to answer that call was more interested in eating his liver. One of the managers managed to shut himself in a changing room cubicle, only to find that the half-dressed woman in there had already changed.

"What's happening here?" a purple-haired teenager screamed as three corpses took the invitation on her t-shirt literally. When all is said and done, wearing the words **Bite Me** is a bad idea during a zombie apocalypse.

They spread her entrails over two rails of designer dresses and fought over every scrap of flesh. A human being's large intestine was never meant to be viewed from the outside.

I made it down an escalator, narrowly avoiding the out-stretched arms of an elf coming up the other way. He chewed on a child's arm like a turkey drumstick, stripped the last shreds of meat from the bone, and went looking for more.

The music continued to play over the public address system. Bing Crosby dreamt of a White Christmas and Peggy Lee rang those Christmas Bells while John Lewis lost a fortune. The customers now had no interest in last minute panic buying.

A shop assistant ran headlong into a display cabinet when the CD got stuck on repeat. Perhaps she was driven mad by hearing one too many renditions of *I saw Mommy kissing Santa Claus.*

She struggled to her feet, blood streaming from a nasty looking head wound. On any other day, she would just have been another unapproachable beauty behind the perfume counter.

My wife had gone to bed with a migraine, all doors and windows bolted, but even Julia would feel sorry for the girl. I caught her by the shoulder to steady her, as I breathed in the expensive scent tempered by the stronger smell of fear.

"We have to leave." I thought about a slap and shook her instead. "It's not safe here."

Her eyes cleared, becoming almost steely. "No shit, Sherlock," she said, staring at the high definition widescreen television set up to watch the Winter Wonderland. It was one of the department store's latest gimmicks to stop customers thinking there was more to the season than shopping. "It's not safe anywhere."

The brightly lit Ferris wheel still carried its passengers round and round in a ride that would not end for hours, if anyone was left to get them down—a 360° panoramic view to die for. The wheel's operator was on an unscheduled dinner break, the controls abandoned while he savaged a screaming Japanese tourist. Small knots of activity marked where other unlucky visitors had been hunted down; a bench where I had eaten lunch so many times now hosting the worst kind of al fresco meal. Worse still was the open air ice rink; most of the skaters chasing the few still left alive.

They had nowhere to go, an eager wall of other undead reaching out whenever they tried to leave the ice. Exhaustion and a painful death accompanied by Christmas carols could be the only outcome. I shook my head to clear the terrible image of a small boy holding tight to his mother's hand. The rest of her was not attached and he looked straight at the camera, staring eyes cloudy as spoiled milk. The television was linked in to more than one live feed across Gorsedd Park, but it showed only the dead.

"Turn it off," said a blood-soaked man with teeth marks on his face, as he dragged himself across the room, the stump of one arm wrapped in a silk dress that had once been white. We had exchanged season's greetings in the toy section less than an hour ago and he seemed pleasant enough. He certainly didn't deserve this—I had seen the movies, once-bitten, good as dead, but he was still at the conversational stage and determined to go down fighting.

He took a cigarette from a battered packet, picked up a can of hairspray and a lighter, and used them to set the nearest zombie on fire in a jet of flame. Another two came at him and got the same treatment, walking torches that had started the day in a festive mood and ended up as charcoal.

"You'd better go, I'll try to buy you some time." He angled his head towards a pair of revolving glass doors. "Merry Christmas."

I watched him fit batteries into an electric carving knife as twenty-five shambling figures came down the escalator. Not all of them used it though; more than one stepped over the edge to let gravity take its course. He seemed to know what he was doing and we left him to it, the smell of burnt flesh overpowering when mixed with expensive perfume.

The street outside was deserted, blue lights glittered on every lamp post, giving the restaurant quarter a charm of its own. A glass of red wine sat on a table, a slick of lipstick on its rim contrasting with the puddle of blood that covered the overturned chair. Twenty yards further on, we found a man lurching down the pavement. At first, I thought he was a zombie and almost smashed his head in with a chair leg when he got close, but then I smelled his breath. He wasn't one of the walking dead, just dead drunk, and he objected to being told what to do by someone carrying a Candy Bears Mega Play set, even if it did have extra-snuggle accessories.

"Go away," he slurred as the shambling figures finally made it through the revolving doors. Their leader was a huge woman with bleach-blonde hair, and fatty ribbons of flesh hanging off her shredded cheeks. She reached out with a hand stripped to bare bone and sinew to point at the box in my hands.

"*Mine.*" The single word escaped from a horribly mangled throat, the sound little more than a low moan, but I knew what she wanted.

"You can't have it." I pulled the girl from the perfume counter forward, assuming she was frozen to the spot with fear. I was wrong. I looked down and saw a bread knife in one manicured hand, and a heavy beech-wood rolling pin in the other, as well as a cleaver.

"From the kitchen section," she explained, passing me the meat cleaver. She brought the rolling pin round in an accurate strike that broke bone and sent teeth scattering across the paving slabs.

What was left of the zombie child reached for me before a second blow caved in its head and destroyed its brain. The teenage girl with the purple hair and **Bite Me** t-shirt shuffled with the rest of them, threads of tinsel and glitter foil showing through a gaping hole in her midsection. The Christmas elves were there, too, in their garish red and green livery; Santa's Little Helpers with snarling mouths rimmed with crimson. Bloody spittle ran down their chins; they were drooling and still hungry. The great man himself was not far behind with a gutted human torso over one shoulder instead of a toy sack. An unconvincing fake beard hung on a string around one ear; the other ear was missing-in-action and presumed eaten, his throat a gaping ruin.

Not trying to find out if we had been naughty or nice, he simply wanted to know if we were tasty. The waiter screamed as a middle-aged woman in the uniform of a Salvation Army Captain ripped into his back. She worried the wound, burying her teeth still deeper, her carefully wrapped gifts dropping from her basket like ripe fruit. They no longer interested her, the drive to buy things replaced by the lust for living flesh. A sweet-faced, silver-haired grandmother came in from the other side, her false teeth proving as effective as the real thing.

"Help me," the waiter begged but we had to leave; no other choice but to stay there and die with him.

It was the night before Christmas. My daughter would play with her Candy Bears tomorrow, even if I had to kill every last zombie in Cardiff to get back to her.

"My car is just around the corner," the girl said after telling me that her name was Liza. She wiped congealed brain matter off the rolling pin with an old copy of the Metro newspaper. The bread knife was gone, left embedded in an undead security guard's chest. A long smear of blood brightened her pale cheeks as she curled her fingers in the time-honored battle invitation. In that moment, she was more beautiful than ever.

"Do you want a lift?" she asked.

I wanted to kiss her then, to taste the cherry red lipstick and lose myself in the limpid gray-blue of her eyes. For the first time in twelve faithful, unremarkable years of married life, adultery didn't seem so bad. I managed to croak a reply and then there was no time for kissing. One of the elves lunged forward, sinking its carrion-laden teeth into my shoulder. The thing tried its very best to bite me but couldn't get through my mother-in law's Christmas jumper—last year's hand-knitted offering. The cross-eyed red nose reindeer on the front had a nose that started red and ended up purple because my wife's mother never wastes wool. Her knitting could almost stop bullets, and for the first time since I married into the family, I was grateful for that. The elf spat out a mouthful of triple-ply wool and tried again. If you have ever wondered what it's like to decapitate one of Santa's Little Helpers with a brand new meat cleaver—don't bother.

It's a whistle and a thud, a few flakes of optimistic snow drifting down onto a red and green clad body that refused to stop moving, however finely you chopped it. I used the Candy Bear box as an offensive weapon and hoped that blood and brain would wash off laminated cardboard. The fat woman reached out for it, her muddy, spoiled-milk eyes hungry, what was left of her mind fixed on what had once been hers. Not that she had been particularly bright before but now she had the IQ of an eggplant.

"*Mine*," she hissed.

"No it isn't." I brought Mr. Cleaver into the argument and her right hand dropped to the sidewalk, every small bone visible through the chewed mess as it skittered along on its own accord.

Five painted talons tapped on the gray slabs until I stomped on it, just to stop the noise.

The memory of dispatching an overweight zombie piece by piece will stay with me until the day I die. She refused to lie down and stay decently dead until I split her skull into three pieces and impaled what was left on a convenient spiked railing.

Liza and I fought our way down the street together, falling into a rhythm that was almost like a mad dance lit by street lamps. We killed the last of the pack by throwing it through a Pure Rugby shop window and then beating its head to a pulp with a pricing gun.

Her talents were wasted on John Lewis; the ability to use any object offensively is not usually part of a perfume seller's job description. She flicked a piece of human tissue off my shoulder and helped herself to one of the least blood-stained Wales shirts and a ball-shaped alarm clock.

"Didn't get time to finish my shopping," she said by way of explanation. "Shall we go?"

She pulled a mobile from her pocket and punched in some numbers, her face showing increasing worry when the person she called didn't answer. She tried again and got a busy signal, then straight to voicemail. No sooner did she hang up then her phone rang.

I watched the relief make her beautiful once more and felt glad when she finally got through to her fiancé and made certain he would live long enough to walk her down the aisle. Their wedding invite was happily accepted even though I couldn't contact my wife to ask her about it—our phone was still off the hook, no way to know if she was dead or alive. More devout men would have prayed, but I wasn't a fan of organized religion. Nothing to do now but hope, and try not to think about what might wait for me at home.

Liza escorted me to her car and helped me wipe the blood off the Candy Bear Play Set box before it dried. The cardboard cleaned up perfectly well, leaving no trace of the slick, dripping mess that had coated it.

We stopped to pick up a hitchhiker at the top of Tudor Street, the first living person in more than twenty minutes of driving. The streets were clogged with roaming dead, some side roads barri-caded and impassable. Liza slowed the car, releasing the door locks as the well-dressed young Asian man stuck out his thumb and grinned hopefully. He wore sharply creased trousers, polished shoes and a winter jacket. He had a trendy haircut and wore designer thin lens eyeglasses, only the gore clotted baseball bat in his hand spoiling the image. If not for that, he might just have been a successful executive leaving an office party.

Ironically, as it turned out, that was exactly where he was. He made himself unemployed by killing his boss, his manager and twelve other colleagues when they tried to eat him, but he was still alive, which was all that mattered on a night when so many couldn't say the same. His voice was perfectly calm as he told the story, the truth of it showing only in his ghost-haunted eyes. He smiled his gratitude and didn't seem to mind the clutter of weap-ons on the back seat.

"Jimmy Nguyen." He introduced himself as he wiped other people's blood off his face with a wet wipe, threw it away, and rolled up the car window before anything showed up to bite him. "Man, am I glad you showed up."

"Where are you going?" Liza asked as she swerved, running over another zombie to score double points in a game we had only just invented. It helped to pass the time, even if she was winning. The zombie had been a gangly fitness freak with a shiny bald head and bright yellow Lycra shorts—un-death was too good for him.

Jimmy took one look at the horde following us and reached a decision. "Anywhere but here is fine by me. Do you mind if I smoke?" He waited for permission with a perfect sense of comedic timing before he delivered the punch line. "Now, has anyone got a cigarette?"

I watched Liza clench her jaw with the effort of mowing down three zombified Father Christmases and a group of carol singers in Victorian fancy dress. A fat woman in a bonnet and crinoline nearly broke the windshield before disappearing under the speed-ing wheels. Tires screeched as my perfume Valkyrie reversed and did it again, a quirky smile on those cherry red lips.

We heard on the local radio that the twin tragedy of Winter Wonderland and the John Lewis department store were not isolated incidents; breaking news reports as we sped away from the infected centre. City Hall was a slaughterhouse. Cardiff University's entire Salaries and Human Resources section had been eaten alive, but that couldn't happen to a nicer bunch of people. Geological curators had survived, barricaded into a storeroom in the National Museum while the hungry dead roamed the galleries. The less said about the massacre at Ysgol Mynydd Bychan's Nativity Play the better.

We dropped Jimmy Nguyen off at his front door, and watched in the rearview mirrors to see that he got in safely before the zombies arrived.

It was snowing heavily by the time the Army tanks and troop carriers trundled through the streets. They took the same route they had used for the homecoming parade on June 26th when soldiers from 1st Battalion Welsh Guards returned from Afghanistan. Nearly six months later, the convoy passed down St. Mary's Street, past the Castle and Millennium Stadium, disgorging a hundred, grim-faced men in uniform with telescopic sights and high-powered rifles. They had direct orders to shoot only the turned and infected but I suspect that more than one survivor ended up riddled with bullets because it was easier to fire first, and ask questions later. The soldiers funneled the tide of dead flesh into four designated killing grounds and shot them full of holes. They poured gasoline over the mounds of still-moving body parts and burned what was left.

When the last oily-black flames died, the soldiers sang Silent Night—an impromptu carol service I'm very glad to have missed. As they sang, a silent invading army of snowflakes dropped out of a starry sky and Cardiff would have its white Christmas after all.

"I wish I could say it was fun," Liza said as we pulled up outside my house. The curtains twitched on the next door but Mrs. Evans could think what she liked. The neighborhood gossip and self-appointed busybody lived on scandal, and spread it wherever she could because she had nothing better to do. I was too tired to care.

"Have a good day tomorrow," she said. "Merry Christmas."

I wished her the same and waved goodbye. Walking up the stone walkway, I opened the front door to my home. The cleaver dropped onto the mat as I wiped my feet to avoid treading blood and brains on the carpet. It was the night before Christmas and all through the house, I double checked the doors and windows and let the mice get on with it

Our little daughter slept peacefully upstairs; everything was right with the world—wasn't it?

Julia met me on the stairs, a little pale and still showing the effects of a three day migraine. She glanced at the box that almost killed me and cursed under her breath, the corners of her mouth turning down in a disappointed but not surprised look of resignation.

"She wanted the blue one."

MIDNIGHT RIDE

BRANDON CRACRAFT

"I took a huge chance hiring a sixteen year old," my twenty-year-old assistant manager said, trying to look and sound more mature. I glared at the schedule, wondering who wanted fast food on Christmas morning.

I forced a smile, frustrated at having to prove myself to that burger joint again. "Rosie and Marisol both have kids too young to understand the excuse 'Mommy has to work.' I guess it's up to us kids to pick up the slack," I said as I clocked out, causing the twenty-year old to wince at being called a kid.

I hopped on my bike and raced home as quickly as possible. Even though I pretended like I was fine working on Christmas, the truth was that I was pissed off. I knew I was never going to get any respect at the job, but I figured it would be the same all over.

I wanted to get home as quickly as possible. Taking a deep breath, I decided to take the shortcut across the cemetery. The caretaker posed warnings on the gate that anyone caught there after dark would be prosecuted, but I didn't care. Cutting across the graveyard shaved twenty minutes off my ride.

I scaled the six foot chain-link fence, balancing my bike under my right arm. When I heard the rip, I dropped my bike on the grave of a man who died fifty years before Arizona became a state. I ended up tumbling on top of my bike, the spokes and chains ripping into my left leg. I felt graveyard dirt in my boxers, and felt the entire seat of my uniform pants tear open.

"Damn it!" I screamed. "These cost me thirty bucks!"

"That looked like it hurt," said a voice from a nearby, empty grave. Every scary story about people disappearing in the old cemetery rushed back into my head. Despite its size, Tucson was still an Old West town filled with ghost stories and tales about bogeymen carrying off people in the night.

"Who's there?" I called out, my voice stuttering and high pitched. I reminded myself there was no such thing as ghosts, before the realization that Satanists and cannibals both hung out in graveyards.

A small head peeked out of the grave. It was a little boy rather than some psychotic killer. "I'm hiding," he said. "Go away."

He was dressed in a military uniform, probably believing the camouflage made him appear invisible. I looked at the young boy, figured he was about eleven or twelve years old, and was positive I had seen him before.

"Who are you hiding from?" I asked. "They'll call the cops if they catch you out here. I saw a bunch of cops arrest a bunch of kids last Halloween. They were trying to find some witch's grave or something like that. They weren't doing anything but walking around with candles, but the cops picked them up."

The boy tried to shrug off my warning despite his nervousness. "Shows what you know. The caretaker went to visit his daughter for two days. He won't be back until Christmas morning."

"Whatever," I replied, trying to hop back on my busted bike. It immediately toppled over and I got a mouthful of dirt and grass. I swallowed my frustrated scream.

I started walking the bike away when I heard the kid right behind me. "Where are you going? You going home?"

"Why are you following me?" I asked.

"I'm not following you," he said defensively. "I'm just going home. We live in the same trailer court, so I'm not really following you…just kind of…going in the same direction."

I let out a sigh. "You can walk with me if you want. My name's Conner Blake. So we live in the same trailer court? Yeah, makes sense, I thought I recognized you."

"I know who you are, too," he said, speeding his pace to keep up with me. "My mom thinks you're all responsible and stuff, because you got a job and your mother doesn't work."

I smiled, happy that someone realized I was mature.

"My name's Boris. Mom loved Fu Manchu, so she named me after Boris Karloff. A bunch of white guys played Fu Manchu, but Boris was her favorite."

The boy loved to talk, and he made me feel a lot less nervous and superstitious. I decided to let him ramble.

"What were you doing out here?" I asked.

Boris opened his mouth to speak, but he began to trip over his words. "Could you help me with something, Conner?" he finally asked.

Even though I was pretty sure I was going to regret it, I shrugged. "What do you need help with?"

Boris' eyes lit up. "I need help finding a grave." He looked around and then whispered the name, "Algernon Arthur Anderson." From the look on his face, he expected me to know who that was. "You know, the 'Christmas candy kid.' I'm supposed to put some candy on his grave at midnight, just before it becomes Christmas morning. A bunch of kids at my school told me that it was my turn."

"I think they were screwing with you," I said, putting a hand on his boney shoulder. "I lived in Tucson my whole life, and I've heard all kinds of stories about this cemetery. I never heard anything about a 'candy striper kid.'"

"'Christmas candy kid,'" he corrected.

"I thought they only did crap like this to kids on Halloween," I said with a laugh. "I give your buddies credit for branching out. I wonder if they have stories for Arbor Day or Columbus Day, too. Lots of Indians buried here."

"Algernon Arthur Anderson was real," Boris said. "I looked him up on the internet. Do you think I'm an idiot?"

We walked in silence for a few moments, and I watched Boris' eyes read every gravestone. Curiosity seized me. "Why do you have to put a piece of candy on his grave? Is his ghost..."

"He's not a ghost," Boris interrupted. "Ghosts can't hurt people. We got this ghost in our trailer, and she just turns on faucets and breaks dishes and such. Algernon Arthur Anderson's a zombie. If he doesn't get a piece of Christmas candy, he has to...you know...eat someone." He bit his lip. "Normally it's the kid that forgot to give him the candy."

"And you're worried that he's going to eat you if you don't put a candy cane or something on his grave?"

Boris nodded.

"Don't you think something would be on the news if a little kid got eaten?"

"That's because everyone always gives him his Christmas candy," Boris replied matter-of-factly.

I started to say something before I realized that I couldn't argue with his logic. "Can you help me find his grave? My Christmas sucks enough without getting eaten."

I rolled my eyes. "You don't know anything about having a bad Christmas. I have to work on Christmas day. I was supposed to spend Christmas with my mom over at her boyfriend's house. I know she isn't going to change her plans because I have to get up at three in the morning. I'm going to be stuck home alone on Christmas."

"You get along with your mom's boyfriend?"

A disgusted sound escaped my throat and I spit on the ground. "I hate the son of a bitch! Mom thinks he's going to start looking for work. If someone paid him to sit on his ass and smoke cigarettes and watch court shows on TV, he would complain that it was too much work and quit after a day."

Boris smiled smugly. "Sounds like it's a good thing that you're not going if you ask me. My new stepfather brought every one of his relatives up from Mexico, about a thousand girls who don't speak English. There's barely room for my mom, my little brother, and him. They have me sleeping on the floor, crammed into a corner with the dust bunnies next to my brothers. The only thing they eat is Mexican food. You would think they would get tired of eating Mexican food. What else do you eat in Mexico? When I suggested that my mom make something else yesterday, they acted like I asked her to dump rat poison into the beans." He scratched his chin thoughtfully. "That might not be such a bad idea. My stepfather and his brood actually threw away my favorite pajamas, because he decided that I was too old for them. Whenever I watch cartoons, they start laughing at me. Have you ever watched a 'novella'? I don't know how they can call anything I watch stupid!"

I threw my bike to the ground. "Look at that piece of crap." I kicked it a couple times.

"That sucks," Boris said. "You probably depend on it to get you to work. You got money to buy another one?"

I swallowed, realizing that he was winning the contest for worst Christmas. "My dad's boyfriend bought me a new bike for Christmas," I said. "But I'll have to spend all morning before work putting it together so I can go to work on Christmas morning." I kept repeating about my work obligations, because it trumped any little kid problems Boris had. "I guess it'll give me something to do. I'm going to be completely alone on Christmas Eve."

Boris snapped his fingers and his face lit up. "I got an idea, Conner. You don't have to be alone on Christmas Eve. I'll spend the night with you. My mom thinks you're a saint. I'm sure she'll agree. I think she'll be glad to have one less kid in the house for the evening."

"I've got work Christmas morning, remember? I have to be up at five a.m. I probably won't get more than a few hours of sleep."

"That's perfect. I'll come over and get a little shut eye then wake before midnight so I can put the piece of candy on Algernon Arthur Anderson's grave. There's no way that I could sneak out of my house. Those girls managed to booby trap the house with dolls and clothes. I can't walk anywhere without stepping on something pink and hearing a girl's voice cry and whine about it." He grabbed me by my work shirt. "Show some mercy, man. I can't take it anymore. You're my only hope."

I laughed it off. "Okay, fine. Don't be so melodramatic."

Boris suddenly stopped, and I looked as his body began to shake. He tried to talk, but his teeth chattered. He grabbed my arm, fingernails digging into my skin. He pointed to the ancient gravestone. Irrational fear grabbed us both. The wind seemed to howl louder, and I expected a freak strike of lightning in the sky. I felt my spine shake and my testicles crept higher.

"We found it," he whispered. "It's his grave."

Algernon Arthur Anderson died a hundred years ago on Christmas day when he was twelve years old. Printed under his name were the words,

May his crime never be forgotten.

Someone scattered expensive candy bars around his grave, anchoring them to the earth with kitchen knifes. Chocolate oozed around the base of the tombstone, congealing into slime.

"This is freaky," I said.

"We try to make the grave as easy to find as possible," a voice said from behind us. Both of us jumped out of our skin and turned around. The woman looked to be around seventy and covered in makeup. She scratched at her gray wig and gave us a cigarette-stained smile. "You boys look hardy. You'll make the midnight ride fine." She pushed past us to place a chocolate on the grave.

"This has to be some kind of a trick," I said. "A hidden camera show or something."

The old woman shook her head. "The survivors always come and bring chocolate to him, even though we know Little Al can't eat it." She started crying, her mascara streaking her face with clumps of black. "My older brother should have just put the candy cane on the grave, but he didn't believe it. I begged him to go to the cemetery but he wouldn't listen."

Boris and I exchanged nervous looks.

"When I woke up that morning, I ran to his bedroom. I wanted to make sure he was awake, because I knew Santa had brought me the doll I wanted. I was an especially good girl that year. His sheets were soaked, and I was about to make fun of him when I realized that the entire bed was covered in my older brother's blood. When I pulled back the blankets, the only thing there was a skeleton.

Algernon Arthur Anderson ate every piece of meat on my brother's body."

"That can't be real," I said, stepping back when I saw fury in the old woman's eyes. "I mean, I've never heard of anyone being eaten recently."

The old woman wiped her face with her sleeve. "That's because everyone remembered to feed him these last twenty years. I hope you boys don't screw it up." She looked Boris up and down. "You look just like the kind of little boy that he likes to eat." She pointed a bony finger at me, the fingernails painted orange. "If that little boy dies, it will be your fault."

I pointed to myself. "My fault? Lady, I don't really know this kid. I've probably seen him a couple times…"

"We're just neighbors," Boris added. "We're not brothers or anything. I've got a little brother."

"Then you two better hope that Little Al doesn't eat your little brother by mistake," she warned. She walked off into the darkness and seemed to disappear.

I swallowed loudly. "All right, Boris. You can spend the night at my place, but don't bother me. I have to put my bike together early if we're going to ride out here at midnight."

We kept looking behind us as we walked home; it seemed to us that we kept hearing someone following us.

Later that night, there was a knock at my front door, and when I went to answer it, Boris and his mother were there.

Boris' mother made him wear his new red, wool pajamas over to my house. She gave me a disapproving look when she saw that I was covered in grease and my ash blond hair matted down with sweat. She quickly smiled when she realized I was working on my new bike. She handed me a French manicured hand to shake and I accepted the chubby fist as politely as possible, ignoring the fact that the sweat running down my face and into my eyes and lips was driving me nuts.

"I'm Mrs. Rodriguez, Boris' mother." She gave me a smile then cast a disgusted glance toward the stuffed triceratops under her son's arm. "He's almost twelve years old and still sleeps with that.

You should have heard the fuss when we threw out his dinosaur pajamas. I swear, his seven year old brother acts older than he does."

"Pleased to meet you," I said, uncertain what else to say.

"Thank you very much for looking after Boris. He's been so weird since all of his cousins came up from Mexico." Her laugh sounded insincere. "The truth is, my son has been driving us all nuts. He refuses to speak Spanish. I know he speaks Spanish. He learned it in school and speaks it all the time."

Boris rolled his eyes and said something under his breath.

His mother stomped her high heels against the floor. "If you're going to get smart with me, we can just go home right now."

"Apologize to your mother," I said, trying to play the mature older teenager. His mouth dropped open and I gestured that I was serious.

"I'm sorry, Mama," he said, finally. The young boy looked at me like I'd betrayed him.

Mrs. Rodriguez smiled at both of us. "I don't suppose I could convince you to look after my other son tonight as well." Boris shook his head, terror in his eyes.

"Not tonight, ma'am," I said, keeping up my image. "I would be happy to look after both your sons on a later date, but I have to be up very early to go to work tomorrow."

Mrs. Rodriguez kissed and hugged Boris several times. He turned dark purple from embarrassment, and I hid my laughter until after I heard her leave. I fell back with laughter, causing Boris to fume.

"She's so embarrassing!" he screamed. "Does your mom ever do anything like that to you?"

"No," I said, swallowing my giggle, "but I think my dad still thinks I'm a kindergartner. Whenever I spend the night over at his house, he picks out my clothes for the next day and sets them out for me, even my socks and underwear."

Boris went and looked at himself in the bathroom mirror, sticking out his tongue. "I think my mom wants me to become an old man. Whenever we go shopping, she stops by the ties and khakis." He looked at his triceratops and asked it, "Do you think I look like

Grandpa?" He shook the stuffed animal up and down to make it look like it was nodding.

I stood the bike up and admired my work. "It took me most of the day but she's beautiful."

Boris looked it over, kicked the tires, and squeezed the breaks before nodding.

"I'm going to hit the shower. I was gonna make some burgers. You want one?"

Boris smiled so wide I thought his face was going to split open. "Boy food!" he exclaimed as dramatically as possible. "I'd almost forgotten what boy food tastes like. Mom started putting pink salsa on everything. I don't even know what you use to make pink salsa. Unicorn blood?"

"Relax," I said pulling out my ponytail and stripping for the shower, "this is a dude's night."

I turned the water on and drowned out whatever Boris said next as he waited in the small living room. I looked at the clock on the bathroom wall and saw it was almost eight o'clock. I put on my version of pajamas, an oversized black concert tee-shirt and sweats, and started dinner.

"So how did he die?" I asked between bites a few minutes later as we sat at the small kitchen table.

"Who?" Boris asked, talking with his mouth full and letting the catsup and mustard drool down his chin.

"Who do you think? Alistair...Albert...you know... Little Al? I'm assuming there's a gruesome story behind his death."

Boris wiped his mouth with his sleeve and nodded enthusiastically. "He was killed at the stroke of midnight on Christmas morning. He snuck out of his bedroom early to check what Santa brought him, because he still believed in that kind of stuff. His parents told him Santa arrived at midnight, and he wanted to get to his presents as quickly as possible."

I nodded. "I remember staying awake to catch Santa when I was seven years old. When he wasn't there, my dad tried to make an excuse. He even dressed up like Santa the next year. Mom let me in on the bad news."

"The person in the living room wasn't Santa but a man by the name of John Bludgeon."

"Bludgeon? What did he kill Little Al with, a hammer or something?"

Boris looked at me confused since he didn't know what bludgeoning was. "No, he used a knife, actually a lot of knifes. John Bludgeon liked to carry his knives in a belt like a chef. The only thing he ever cut up was little boys. No one knows why he killed kids. I guess he was just sick in the head."

I nodded and prompted him to continue.

"He grabbed Little Al and tried to slice the skin off his face. The little boy started screaming but no one came to rescue him. No one knows why his parents let him scream like that, because it took John Bludgeon nearly an hour to kill him. When his parents came down on Christmas morning, they found their son lying in a pool of blood under the tree...unwrapped." He made a disgusted face as he pictured what Little Al looked like that morning.

"What happened to John Bludgeon?" I asked.

"No one knows how he died, but..." Boris looked around and spoke very softly. "They say he was buried right on top of Little Al. The second they did it, it woke the little boy up. Every Christmas he wakes up and freaks out, goes all psycho like only a zombie can. He has to stare at his killer's face every Christmas. The only thing that can quiet him down is a piece of candy. If he gets a piece of candy, he just goes back to sleep for another year after his snack."

"A lot of people seem to believe that story," I said. "Even if I heard it for the first time yesterday."

"Do you believe it, Conner?"

I thought a moment then nodded. "I think I do. That old woman was pretty creepy."

Boris let out a relaxed breath. "I was afraid you thought I was just some stupid kid."

"We're both stupid kids," I said, giving him a playful punch in the shoulder.

"Be careful," Boris warned, taking several different colored candy canes out of his pocket. "I'm carrying precious cargo." He studied the candy for a few moments. "I have all kinds of flavors, even old fashioned peppermint. Which flavor do you think is Little Al's favorite, Conner?"

"You have anything that is stupid kid flavored?" I asked, trying to make a joke. The two of us laughed, but it was hollow. We were really terrified.

The alarm blasted in my ears, and I pulled on my cargo pants and combat boots without opening my eyes. Halfway though my cup of hot chocolate, I gathered enough of my senses to wake Boris up. He kicked and flailed, resisting any attempt to get him up until I rang out a wet washcloth over his eyes.

"I was about to wake up," he whined.

I changed from my sleep shirt to a turtleneck, then threw his clothes at him. "I tend to be a little impatient when I'm worried about being eaten alive," I said.

Boris jumped up and practically ripped off his pajamas as he changed. "How much time do we have, Conner?"

"It's eleven-twenty, and it's a fifteen minute ride to the cemetery. Hopefully we won't stumble in the dark too much trying to find Little Al's grave again." I peeked outside. "Lots of Christmas lights around here. Should make finding it a lot easier, especially now that we know where to look."

"Just follow the smell of chocolate," Boris reasoned. "I think someone actually dumped hot fudge on his tombstone once."

I made sure to watch Boris put the candy canes in his jeans pocket. The boy was flustered and scared. It took him three tries to get his arms in his shirt. I was thankful he remembered the important thing, like the candy, as he tried to run out the door without any shoes.

Boris had stashed his bike at my place the night before. We pedaled so fast that we made it to the cemetery in less than seven minutes. Boris climbed the fence with the grace of a spider and I handed his bike to him. I fell on my butt, but I didn't rip my pants this time and I kept my bike from crashing onto the ground.

"Are you all right, Conner?" Boris whispered.

"Nothing broken," I replied, ignoring the bruise on my hip. "Both the bike and I are fine."

All the wreaths and poinsettias made it difficult to navigate the graveyard. Each row looked like the last with the markers covered in garland. When we finally found Little Al's grave, it was two minutes to midnight.

"What should I do?" Boris asked. "Just put the candy on the grave?"

I shrugged. "I guess. I never heard anything about Little Al until yesterday. What did the kids tell you to do?"

Boris thought back a moment. "They just told me to give him the candy."

"I don't think we want to be here when he wakes up," I said. "Just put the candy on the grave and we'll go home. I want to catch a little more sleep before I take you home and go to work."

He nodded and took the candy canes from his pocket. "I hope you like it, Al," he said, reaching down. "Please don't eat us."

Boris dropped the candy as the ground began to shift and move. He backed up, and I placed a protective arm around him. Fear and curiosity kept us from running away. I held my breath and hoped I would hold down my dinner.

The figure that burst out of the ground was much bigger than any twelve year old, even an undead one. Boris screamed. I got so scared that my body began to ache. My eyes went toward my new bike, and I tried to will myself to take Boris on to the handlebars and ride away as quickly as possible. My feet gave out, and I fell to the ground, barely conscious. Boris' frantic crying kept me from fainting.

Roaches, worms, beetles, and maggots crawled out of the various wounds on Al's arms, face, and bare chest. He wore nothing but jeans, revealing a myriad of deep cuts from various wounds. I figured he had been lynched, and the mob made sure he had died of suffering and blood loss. Graveyard dirt added bulk to the muscular frame. We both knew the monster by the belt of knives he carried.

"John Bludgeon," I whispered.

The zombie moved like a predatory plant, slow but so methodical and ferocious that we seemed to be moving in slow motion as we tried to escape. He grabbed Boris by his shirt before the boy could run away and lifted him to eye level. His white eyes saw nothing, but his black tongue probed the air like a snake.

John Bludgeon lifted the blade for a killing stroke, and I forced away all of my flight instincts. I used my bike as a weapon and slammed it into the zombie's torso. It let out a nasty sound that fouled the air with the reek of the creature's breath. I followed up the initial attack with some fighting moves I learned from the internet. When those didn't work, I grabbed Boris by the legs and pulled him away. The boy slipped out of his shirt, and was no longer in the zombie's grasp.

I pushed him ahead of me. "Get out of the cemetery! Maybe he's like the Headless Horseman and he can't cross the cemetery gates!" I yelled.

Boris started to panic, so I forced myself to remain calm for him. "Don't think about it. Just ride off."

The zombie moved to attack, his knives slicing the air. I ducked and dodged as I tried to get back on my bike. I felt the heat of steel and a searing burn as my leg erupted in pain. John Bludgeon twisted his knife against my leg, before he pulled the blade out for a deadlier swipe at my face.

The sound of candy being crunched stopped the knife before it pierced my eye. We both looked back at Little Al's grave. The small zombie sat on his tombstone, eating his Christmas candy. Instead of skin, the little zombie had a hardened purple exoskeleton that was once his blood.

When the killer approached the zombie boy, I saw terror in his lidless eyes. "Please don't kill me again," Little Al said. As the knife slashed into the zombie boy's throat, revealing his bones, Little Al said, "It's all right. Everyone runs away when they see him. Even my parents ran away. They locked the door and hoped he would go away after he was done killing me."

I looked down at the wound on my leg and realized that a sane person would have limped away and let the zombies play out their little Christmas play. Boris rode in circles, scared to get off his bike.

"I hope this works like in the movies," I said, stumbling over to a large rock and picking it up with both hands. "In the movies, you kill a zombie by destroying its head." I tried to forget that most zombie slayers used guns.

John Bludgeon leaned over his victim and started to pull out Little Al's ribs. I summoned as much strength as possible and smashed the rock into the giant zombie's skull. The monster turned toward me, scowling with broken teeth.

"You should have just walked away," he hissed, vomiting up slime and mud as he spoke.

I closed my eyes and hit him over and over. He tried to strike me with the knives, but Little Al grabbed his arm. The monster used his free hand to grasp my long hair and shake me. I felt everything lurch as Boris, teary-eyed, rammed his bike into John Bludgeon's back.

"Kill him, Conner!" he screamed.

Taking a deep breath, I strained every muscle in my body to get maximum strength. John Bludgeon's skull smashed like jelly as I brought the rock down one last time.

"Teach you to pick on little kids," I said.

The giant zombie disintegrated into crimson and yellow ooze before sinking into the ground.

"You rescued me," Little Al said, dumbfounded. "No one's ever rescued me before. They just left me...with him."

"Dead or not, you were still human once. It wouldn't feel right to leave you with him." I turned toward Boris. "How 'bout you? Are you all right?"

Boris nodded. I put my arm around him, and he clung to me tightly. I let him cry for a few moments as he regained his strength. "Thanks," he said, wiping his tears and trying to look tough.

"How about you, Little Al?" I asked.

Al grinned at me, more teeth than mouth. "I waited forever for someone to finally free me." He pointed to my leg. "Sorry about that."

"It's fine, I'll live," I replied.

"I think you ended a curse, Conner," Boris said. "A lot of zombies and ghosts are under curses. He probably had to keep repeating that Christmas until someone finally rescued him."

"Merry Christmas," Little Al said one last time before turning into ash and blowing away on the wind.

I smiled to myself, feeling like an adult for the first time in my life. "Merry Christmas."

13 DAYS OF CHRISTMAS

JODY PAGE

*D*ecember 14th

On the first day of Christmas my true love gave nothing to me other than a break-up. This was also the first day I found out about the zombies. I went to her condo to beg for another chance, forgiveness, or even mercy, and they were there. I thought I might find another guy there, as she had been distant of late, but I didn't think I would find that. They were eating her in the doorway to her condo. Her scalp was hanging off, arms twitching, and they were gnawing on her face. The flowers I had stolen from a graveyard and left on her step earlier were strewn about and the glass vase shattered on the floor. As it was she that had broken up with me, I left.

December 15th

I didn't sleep much last night. It was now the second day of Christmas. I drank. I showered repeatedly to get the smell of blood off me. I watched the news. The zombies were all over it. Initially they were reported as murders, but as the night went on, the confirmation was broadcast on the news. The pangs of guilt I initially felt for not calling the police at my ex-girlfriend's were gone when I realized there was nothing that would have come of it anyhow.

December 16th

The zombies must be more of a problem than everyone realized—I don't go out, so I can't be sure—but some of the TV stations have gone off of the air today. I saw a couple of the zombies on my street, while looking out the window, and they were the first I had seen since the other day.

They stumble about, seemingly incoherent, apparently in search of food, and in this instance made the mistake of bumping into an Escalade and setting the car alarm off. The owner of the vehicle, a drug dealer from a couple of doors down, came out with one of his friends and shot them in the head after first taking target practice on them. I don't know if shooting them repeatedly was intended, but the hits to the torso and arms didn't do anything other than knock them down. They would continue to get up until they were shot in the head. The police arrived at the end, and another shootout ensued, which isn't all that unusual for our neighborhood. After a brief exchange, the police killed the dealer and his friend, and left all four of them in the street like road kill.

December 17th

I haven't been out at all, and it's driving me crazy. I'm not sure why, because before this all happened I had no problem staying home. Not having a job, my mornings were quiet, my afternoons the same, and the evenings pretty much like that as well. Why is it when I shouldn't want to go out I suddenly feel compelled to do so?

I can see very little when I peer out the front door. Nobody is out, and for that matter I haven't seen any of my neighbors for some time other than the annoying ones across the street who continue to look out the windows of their homes.

I recall from the other day that the zombies had to be hit in the head to die, to destroy the brain, so I grab my two pound sledgehammer to take with me. Since it's cold, and for practical reasons, I dress in my outdoor gear, including a thick winter coat and a ski mask with the intention that if any of them do try to bite me, they won't have any skin to find.

I walk outside and the winter chill seems that much worse since I haven't been out in a while. The streets are empty, but not quiet. I can hear sirens of all varieties off in the distance and a few stray gunshots. Down the street, beyond the zombie and drug dealer corpses littering it, I can see what looks like the remains of four bodies. There are two large and two small, both lying in a driveway, with a minivan parked behind them with open doors.

I walk to the drug dealer and his dead friend. They're both frozen, their skin bluer than the tattoos that adorn their arms, and the blood pooled near them is now crimson ice. I wrench the guns out of each of their hands. They might come in handy. Having watched enough action films, I know enough to figure out how to check the magazines and chamber to see how many bullets remain. Both are empty, which makes sense with the resulting one-sided gunfight with the police. It's hard to win when you've already wasted all of your bullets on zombies.

I throw the guns to the ground and turn to walk back to my house, but before I can take a step, I realize that a zombie is headed toward me. It doesn't move fast, or straight, but I sense it sees me and I'm why it's coming this way. Its black eyes stare straight ahead at me. I tighten my grip on the hammer in my hand, realizing I'll have to use it. I admit, I'm a petty criminal, generally not a good person, but violence was never my thing. I might steal something, commit fraud, or do something else for my personal gain, but hurting someone isn't something that comes naturally to me.

The few times I was in jail I was lucky enough to avoid any of that stuff due to the low level of the prison or the people I knew in there.

When the zombie closes, I swing with an overhand arc. Steel meets flesh, and the forehead caves in. A sickening sound accompanies the impact and the zombie falls right in front of me. I stop and look at what I've done. There's electricity moving through me that I haven't felt before. The zombie is on its side, looking up at me with dead eyes and a forehead that could double as a glove box. The generic blue work uniform of the gas company reminds me it used to be a person. It doesn't matter, though. I didn't think it would be that easy to kill, and even if I did really kill it, I have to wonder: if it's already dead, is it still killing?

December 18th
There were a couple of more that came around today, so I decided to practice on them. This time, in addition to the sledgehammer, I also took a ball-peen hammer. One for each hand is probably more efficient.

December 19th
Christmas is getting closer. While one normally might be overwhelmed by television specials, advertising, and mall Santas, this year is a little different. Well, really, a lot different. I was watching television today, on the last local channel, and it went off the air. It wasn't that it went off the air that shocked me, as they all have, but that it was while I was watching when it happened.

The news anchor, despite the continuing chaos of society being eaten as a whole, appeared his usual plastic self while detailing the day's carnage. A distraction appeared in the studio—obvious by the background noise—and the anchorman strained to see something that might have been off to the side. He didn't see the zombie approaching from his right. It saw him, though, and it grabbed his hair and bit into his cheek, spraying blood at the camera. Two more appeared from the left and set upon him. The greenish gray of their skin, tattered clothing, and dirty hair provided quite a contrast to a spray-on tan and hairspray addiction. They fell to the floor, out of sight, with the microphone still on. The screams and gurgling were quickly replaced by gnashing of teeth and tearing of flesh.

I, in turn, am left with another black screen on my television. There's nothing to do now but watch and wait for some more zombies to kill outside.

Today I made my own fun. There were two zombies outside, and I had a can of that stuff you spray in the windows to simulate snow. One looked like Cher, tall and female, and the other appeared to be a male. I called him Sonny Bono—he was shorter and probably a little greasy before he was undead. They walked as if they were on a '70's variety show, with poor choreography and out of sync head-bobbing. They didn't get too far apart, and when one moved, so did the other. I waited until they were far enough apart for my purposes, and then ran out of the house to the nearest one, Sonny.

They move slowly, so I was able to spray the fake snow in their eyes without fear of being bitten. I wasn't sure if they actually move by sight, but the random flailing of arms and abrupt changes of direction told me they did. The other, upon seeing me side-stepping the now-blinded zombie, moved towards me, and I did the same to it.

Now, with two of them blinded and close together, it was only a matter of kicking one from behind and sending it crashing into the other. The two collapsed to the ground and fought for my entertainment. I ran back to the safety of my house and watched out the window as it continued. A fight is probably not the most apt description, but the constant gnawing on one another while they rolled around really defies any other. It lasted about ten minutes before Cher was accidentally pushed up by Sonny and regained her feet, staggering off down the street. I guess the relationship was over.

December 20th
I never liked my next door neighbor. For that matter, I didn't like the other ones, either. Not in the least. When I saw this particular one become a zombie, I wasn't too concerned—I didn't really think much had changed. Actually, though, it had. He became more preoccupied with shoveling his walk, which is interesting. They said on the news how those that turn are left with very basic

memory, and something that they did often is one of the few things they recall. I'm not sure how he recalls this, since he didn't shovel when he was alive.

Now he wanders around outside, plastic snow shovel in hand, making half-hearted and uncoordinated attempts at trying to shovel randomly. One-handed, with the wrong end pointed down; he doesn't get it. He seems to know his home, as well, because he stays close to it, which is a problem.

I watch as he shuffles around out front. A string of lights and the electrical cord of a plastic snowman have become entangled with his leg, so he drags these around as well. He didn't move too well before that, but now he barely gets around. His gait is somewhere between a one-legged hop and an intentional fall as the debris trails along behind him.

The cord gives me an idea.

I take an old chain and collar I used with my dog, since passed, and a large red Christmas stocking hanging on the wall. In addition, I put a ball-peen hammer through the back of my belt and a padlock in my pocket.

The neighbor is the only zombie on the street, so it appears to be safe for me to venture outside. I know the neighbors four houses down and across, who I like even less, are still around as I see lights on in their house periodically. They seem to be the only ones. I also catch them looking through the cracks in their blinds, as well, which now perhaps one can excuse, but they did it constantly before as well and were quite the annoyance. They were the kind of people who would call the police on you for washing your car on the street.

I rush out my front door when I see the zombie's back is turned. The distance between him and my door is easily covered before he turns around, and I subsequently pull the stocking over his head so he can't see. He tries to flail his way out, but only succeeds in falling on his face. I then put the collar on him, attach the chain, and pull him over to the home of the neighbors. Their wrought iron railing serves a good purpose as I wrap the chain around it and lock it on so the zombie can't go anywhere. I pull the stocking off as it flops around on the ground and retreat back to my home.

Merry Christmas, neighbor, I think to myself.

December 21st, 22nd, and 23rd
These days seem like one long one. Lack of food, along with higher zombie traffic, and all of the sudden it has become hard to remember the day. I've become very proficient at killing them, though, and this has passed the time out of boredom, necessity, and a seemingly new-found cruel streak.

December 24th
Knock. Knock.
There is a soft knock at my front door, barely audible. It's heard just above the Christmas carols playing on the last remaining AM radio station. A few seconds lapse and another round of knocking is heard, this one with more pause, and a complete lack of rhythm.
Knock... ...Knock... Knock.
I know it's one of them, and I grab my pickaxe from the front hall closet. Are they getting smarter?
Through the glass, I watch as it stands there in its brown uniform, looking even more stupid than it probably is, and waiting for the unsuspecting to answer their door. If people chewed their cud, like cows, we would look like him save for the brown parcel delivery uniform and graying ulcerated flesh.
It's interesting that they're coming to my door now. Rumor had it the whole thing started with the mail delivery service. Something in the packages did it. It affected them, the postal service and other private delivery services like this one, first, and it spread from there. When they got it, they were left knowing a few primal things—their job, and eating flesh.
Unfortunately for humanity, the two blended together for them and not a lot of people knew better until it was too late. After all, it is the Christmas season and everyone is expecting parcels. Most doors were opened without a second thought until a chunk of flesh was ripped out.
Thankfully, I happen to live in a poor area, and delivery people don't often make their way here. We were okay for a while. Problem is, though, is that other zombies, such as collection agents,

police officers, and social workers, do occasionally. I have a few of them stacked in the backyard. At this time it isn't bad, because they're frozen as a result of winter, but come spring it isn't going to smell too good. Of course, who is to say that I'll live that long?

When they come to the door, the routine I have now is a standard one—I open the door, hit it in the forehead with the large end of a five pound pickaxe, and then drag them into the house with the axe still attached. I then pull it through the house, dragging it across the cheap linoleum, and toss it out into the backyard onto the growing pile. I guess you could say I take *No Soliciting* to a whole new level.

Before opening the door I pull my Santa Hat down onto my head firmly and take one last look out through the peep hole. It's still there, waiting patiently, but I can see over its shoulder an army of them also clad in brown.

This changes things.

I run up to the second floor and look out the window onto the street below. There are at least thirty zombies; all in parcel delivery uniforms, except one, who appears to be Santa Claus. It appears they're traveling in packs now. They move in random directions, slipping on black ice periodically, around the small circular road as if part of some deranged roller derby exhibition. Every home has one at its door, just like my house, and some have more. The Santa stands in the middle of the others, ringing a bell as they move around him. Arguably, it appears to be more of a spastic flailing, but slow, and occasionally hitting the others as they walk by.

I was all right to this point. Like I said, they hadn't really come here yet, as this is a little out of their usual routine, but perhaps we're it now. The well-to-do have all been eaten and there never was a middle class to begin with. The poor is it. I would need to do something a little different to work this out. This wasn't just a stray zombie neighbor. Do I stay or go? Is it safe to run, or is it better to maintain where I am in a controlled environment? I decided I'm better off to stay, but need to get rid of the zombies.

They know their job—that much is clear. There's no way they're simply dressing up as delivery men and knocking on doors as a premeditated way to attack. This is what they do. If they were smart, the one chained up out front of my neighbor's house would have figured a way to escape by now. But then again, as I look out at him eating an arm in a snowflake sweater, perhaps the food situation was too good there to leave. The elderly can't run well, and apparently are about as smart as the zombies. I'm not sure why they would have tried to go out their front door when the zombie was there waiting, and even then, all they had to do was give it a wide berth.

Maybe distractions will help. If they know their job, and their job revolved around envelopes and signing for things, perhaps I can distract them with those items. The Santa is pretty fat and even slower than the rest, so he's not a worry, but if he becomes a problem I can probably do the same thing with him using pennies and nickels since he was always looking for change in his previous life.

I slide the ball-peen hammer back into my belt, along with a large butcher knife on the other side, and take the two pound sledgehammer out of the front closet. I like the pickaxe, but it has a tendency to stick, which can be a problem with so many out there. My back pockets are full of pens, and the front pocket of my sweater is full of blank envelopes, junk mail, and previously stolen mail I haven't gone through yet.

I rush out my front door and go for the first two on my left. They don't move quickly enough to respond and one blow to the head of each is all that's required. No distraction necessary. Others see me, though, and begin to move toward me. The first wave approaches within several feet and I throw some pens. They hit them in the face, but don't provide the distraction I hoped for. I have to swing the hammer in retreat. They fall as fast as I hit them, but the strikes aren't all on target, so some continue to approach even after being hit. There are more visible in the background, and they're heading my way. I drop the sledgehammer and throw a handful of envelopes in the air. They float in the air, and it seems to work. They stop and look long enough for me to get a little ahead as I smash their heads with the smaller hammer. Seven fall quickly, and I'm able to get some distance. Moving forward, as the next wave approaches, I do the same. The envelopes are caught in the wind again, and the zombies stop long enough for me to drop the next group. Eight more fall. The others, at least the last main grouping, are looking at the envelopes as well. I run to them, in the middle of the street, but lose my footing and fall. The hammer slides from my hand and skitters through their feet. I reach for the knife and sit up from my back. Their attentions have turned from the envelopes back to me and I'm barely out of arm's reach of the closest one. An uppercut with the knife goes up into the flesh just behind the chin of it, but the blade sticks. When I pull, it pulls the zombie with it.

It's stuck!

I have to let go. Without a weapon I have to return to my house. They're dumb and slow, but there are too many.

December 25

Merry Christmas. I haven't eaten in two days, and the food is gone, and there are too many zombies outside to fight through to try and get more. Their numbers have doubled, even tripled, and that's just since I was out yesterday. That doesn't include the undead group singing carols on my front step.

There's nowhere to go. There's nothing else I can do. I'm resigned to my fate, which isn't good, either way. I can kill myself, or let them have me. Unfortunately, I don't have the guts to kill myself.

So I turn up the radio, let Rudolph the Red-nosed Reindeer play loudly, and in the spirit of the season, I let the Christmas carolers into my home.

Maybe it won't hurt too much.

December 26

I want flesh.

THE LAST CHRISTMAS

JEREMIAH COE

Santa's sleigh flew high in the sky over Portage, Michigan. He flew lower than usual, but then it had been far from being a usual Christmas Eve.

Looking over the side of his sleigh, Santa said, "It's the same here. They're everywhere."

In all of the millennia that he had made this yearly flight, the most he had ever seen, except in times of war, were a few cars that were out late for one reason or another.

This Christmas Eve however, it seemed that everyone was outside. More than that, everyone appeared to be angry and rioting for some reason he was unaware of. It was unlikely that he wouldn't have been aware of something this important considering that the North Pole received every single news broadcast around the world thanks to Claus One, a satellite the Americans had placed in orbit back in the 1960's.

"What's happening, Santa?" an elf named Lester asked from the back of the sleigh.

"I wish I knew, Lester. Something down there isn't right," Santa answered.

"Santa, I think we should cancel Christmas this year. We don't know what's happening down there and that makes things dangerous," William, the second of the three elves accompanying Santa this year, said.

Santa laughed, a sound that always came out 'ho-ho-ho' and said, "There's no way we're canceling Christmas. Could you imagine all of the sad faces when all the little boys and girls around the world wake up in the morning and discover there isn't anything under their trees. No, we're most definitely not canceling Christmas."

Jose, the third elf, said in a voice that was almost begging, "But Santa, the danger. Think of how disappointed all of those little boys and girls will be if something were to happen to you."

Again Santa laughed his ho-ho-ho laugh and said, "Danger? I've lost count of how many war zones I've flown into over the years to make my deliveries. Sure, this is the first Christmas in history with Christmas Eve riots, but it was bound to happen eventually. I've survived antiaircraft fire, I can survive this. Not to mention that the riots are happening outside and we'll be inside. The danger is acceptable if it means happy boys and girls in the morning."

With the matter settled, Santa began lowering his altitude and brought his sleigh to a stop on top of a house.

"You guys have talked me out of stopping everywhere else we've been. We have to start somewhere if we're going to finish before kids start waking up. I don't want to hear any more about this," Santa said as he climbed out of his sleigh. "Lester, why don't you come with me this time," Santa said once he was out of the sleigh. One elf always accompanied Santa into the homes to assist him with placing gifts under the tree.

Without a word, Lester hustled out of the sleigh and followed Santa to the chimney. When Santa waved his hand with a slight twist, the chimney's size increased enough to allow Santa's considerable size to slide down it at once.

He didn't feel any hesitation after so many lifetimes of doing this, when he placed his boot into the chimney and pushed himself off into it. Lester followed suit.

In the fireplace, Santa's slide ended with him landing gracefully on his feet. He quickly moved out of the chimney so that Lester wouldn't land on him. It was an experience he'd had before and wasn't in a hurry to repeat.

The two of them set to work placing presents under the Christmas tree and stuffing the stockings of the family that lived in the house. Only a few seconds passed before they heard the sound of feet shuffling in the kitchen, coming closer to the living room where they were.

A seven-year-old girl appeared around the corner and stopped, looking at Santa and Lester.

Santa gave his ho-ho-ho laugh and said, "Little Michelle Miller, what are you doing up this late? You should be in bed so that I can give you your Christmas gifts."

As Santa spoke to Michelle, Lester thought, *Her eyes are foggy. There's something very wrong with this girl.*

Outwardly, they couldn't see anything wrong with Michelle, but Lester's fears were confirmed when her mouth opened and issued the worse scream either of them had ever heard. Then, with her arms extended forward, Michelle ran straight at Lester, who was too stunned and confused to even consider moving out of the way.

She wrapped her arms around his neck, as if to hug him. Only instead of hugging him, she sank her teeth into the pointed tip of his left ear and bit it off.

Even though he was shorter than Michelle, Lester pushed Michelle away from him and, with his hands attempting to stop the blood flow, began running for the chimney to go back up it.

Santa was aghast at what Michelle—who had chased Lester to the fireplace and dumbly still trying to get to the elf—had done right in front of him. Santa pointed a finger at her and said, "You, young lady, have just earned yourself a spot on next year's naughty list and coal in your stocking."

As if on cue, Michelle turned her attention back to Santa Claus and hissed like an annoyed housecat. She then gave the same blood-curdling scream she'd voiced before going after Lester. Immediately after screaming, Michelle charged at Santa.

He avoided her attack by spinning to the right as she neared him, and leaving his bag of gifts behind, he ran for the fireplace. The second he began his magic induced journey back up the chimney, Santa looked down just in time to see Michelle dive into the fireplace as fast as she could and run into it, her head whacking the back of it.

Before he could see what she did next, Santa was back on the roof of the Miller house. He saw that Lester had already climbed back into the sleigh and that Jose was bandaging the bitten ear.

Santa joined them in the sleigh and didn't waste anytime taking hold of the reigns. He jerked the reigns and said, "Christmas is canceled this year. Now Dasher! Now Dancer! Now Prancer and Vixen! On Comet! On Cupid! On Donner and Blitzen! Take us home!"

With the command phrase said, the reindeer lurched into motion. They ran across the roof, and as they stepped off it, they took flight.

Later, Santa gazed over the side of his sleigh as they flew over the North Pole. All he saw was the frozen tundra that made up the wasteland of the farthest northern region of the world.

Then, as if it came out of nowhere, they passed into the magical oasis that was Santa's Village. There were many unexplainable things in the world and how Santa's Village managed to exist in such an inhospitable environment was one of them. The sleigh flew over the entire village, circled around, and came in for a landing.

Once they were down and the reindeer were no longer moving, thirty of the elves that took care of the reindeer approached.

Santa turned his head to Jose and ordered, "Take Lester to Doctor Lapre right away."

Fester, the elf in charge of Santa's flight plan, walked up to Santa as he climbed off his sleigh.

After turning around and seeing Fester, Santa said, "Fester! What's going on out there? Why didn't you tell me there were worldwide disturbances?"

Looking truly apologetic, Fester said, "Santa, I can't begin to say how sorry I am about what's going on out there. As I prepared your flight plan, my staff and I paid close attention to the world situation just as we have for the last four hundred years. There weren't any indicators that there were any problems on that scale until after you'd left, and by then I couldn't get in touch with you."

"What's happening out there exactly?" Santa asked.

"Santa, it would be much easier if you watched the news feeds yourself than it would be for me to try and explain it to you," Fester answered. "Besides, you wouldn't believe me if I told you."

"Okay. Lead the way," Santa said with a quick nod of his head.

Hours later, Santa sat in his house, which had started off as a simple log cabin hundreds of years ago but had slowly grown into an impressive and stately mansion. He had stripped down to his undershirt, red Christmas Eve pants and socks. He sat in his favorite chair with his feet up on a footstool and Mrs. Claus stood behind him, massaging his shoulders.

"Papa, you're so tense," Mrs. Claus said.

"Of course I am. This is the first time I've ever had to cancel Christmas." He shook his head sadly and said, "All those poor little boys and girls who made it a point to be good all year, and what are they going to wake up to? Nothing."

"Don't be too hard on yourself, dear. You did try to make Christmas happen. You did land; no one can fault you for stopping when you realized things were too dangerous."

Santa groaned, half out of depression, half out of relief as his wife worked the tension out of his shoulders.

"Kids don't understand that kind of thing. All they'll understand is that Santa Claus didn't keep his promise to show up and reward them for being good," he said.

His hopelessness built to the point of eruption. To release it, Santa balled his right fist and slammed it into the arm of his chair.

"Riots! Why did they have to riot on Christmas Eve of all nights! Why!"

"I know, Papa, but it happened and it isn't your fault. You can't hold yourself responsible."

Santa leaned forward and pulled his shiny black boots back on. He then stood and put his jacket on. He kissed his wife and said, "I'll be back. I have to go and check on the reindeer."

While Santa checked on his reindeer, Doctor Lapre stood with his nurse Marsha in a corner of Santa's Village's Infirmary. Just because Santa's elves could live forever didn't mean that illness or injury didn't affect them and on occasion even end their long lives. The infirmary and the two elves that manned it usually weren't busy, but were necessary to have around for the times when they were needed.

Looking at the unconscious Lester, Dr. Lapre shook his head slowly. "I don't know what I can do for him. I didn't have any idea that a human bite could prove so deadly to us."

"Deadly?" Marsha asked.

Dr. Lapre nodded slowly in confirmation. "There isn't anything I can do for him. I've tried everything I know. His vital signs keep dropping and it won't be too long until they stop. How nasty does the human mouth have to be to have this affect on us?"

There were three separate reindeer barns in Santa's Village. Since they lived in such a cold environment, those who lived in Santa's Village were unable to grow the feed that the reindeer needed. In addition, a great distance separated Santa's Village from anyplace that did grow what they needed, which made getting more feed a difficult task. Because of this, reindeer breeding was strictly controlled. Male and female reindeers were housed in separate barns and the third barn was for the selective breeding they allowed to happen. The male reindeer that were the biggest, strongest and fastest but had grown too old to pull Santa's sleigh, were retired to the breeding barn.

Eugene, the elf taking care of the male reindeer, looked up at Santa as he walked in. "They're all bedded down for the night, Santa. Snug as a bug in a rug," Eugene said cheerfully.

"Good," Santa replied.

Eugene looked at Santa questioningly. "Are you okay? You seem sad."

Santa nodded his head. "I'm down about having to cancel Christmas, but I'll be fine."

"What happened anyway? Out here in the barns, we don't hear very much." Eugene said.

"Riots. Worldwide riots on Christmas Eve. What's the world coming to? It's really too bad, because this was Blitzen's last trip. Next year a new buck will be in his place and he'll be in the breeding barn."

After leaving the reindeer barns, Santa walked to his toy workshop, where all the toys that he had planned to deliver that night were being put into storage for the following year.

His workshop, which started as a one room woodworking shop, was a massive complex with entire wings dedicated to plastics, metal, mold making, painting, quality control and so on.

Standing next to Yancy, the elf he'd chosen to be in charge of the entire workshop's production, Santa sighed sadly and said, "It's a shame. The way kids change their mind, most of these toys won't be wanted next year."

Not knowing what to say, Yancy didn't say anything.

Sighing again Santa said, "Oh well, it was bound to happen sooner or later."

Santa, you're needed in flight operations. Santa, come to flight operations please, was heard in every room of Santa's Village from hidden speakers.

Looking at Yancy, Santa said, "Well, I'd better see what's happening there. You're doing a good job, Yancy, keep it up."

Santa turned and walked out of the workshop without saying another word to the elf.

Flight Operations was another large building. In it were rooms full of communications; radios, televisions, and computers. The elves in flight operations monitored every single television station, website and radio station that had the potential to carry information that would impact Santa's yearly flight.

Santa walked up to an elf, whose name he wasn't sure about, and asked, "Where can I find Fester?"

"Hi, Santa," the elf said, in a voice that wasn't very cheerful. "He's in television bank five."

Santa nodded his head to the elf and said, "Thank you." He then walked towards the room named television bank five.

Once there, Santa walked right up to Fester and asked, "What's the problem, Fester?"

Shaking his head in disbelief, Fester just pointed at the television screen he was watching. "Just like when I told you earlier, you're better off watching it first hand, Santa."

Santa turned his head and saw a news anchor sitting at his desk.

"Well, I don't know what to say," the American news anchor said. "You heard the President speak. It appears that the rumors are true. It appears that the dead are returning to life and feeding on the flesh of the living..."

Turning his attention away from the television, Santa said to Fester, "Why did you call me away from the unloading of this year's toys for? Please tell me it wasn't to listen to this drivel."

"Santa, it's true. Every television station, every internet website, everything worldwide is saying the same thing. What you saw wasn't Christmas Eve riots, what you saw was the dead walking."

Disgusted, Santa turned away and started walking off.

"Santa, please wait. You need to hear what they have to say," Fester said, his voice on the edge of begging.

Santa turned back around and pointed at Fester. With the first anger Fester had ever heard Santa Claus speak in for over fifty years, he said, "Listen to me, Fester. I've been around for a long time. The dead have never walked, the dead will never walk. Call me back once the world media is finished peddling sensationalism and start talking about facts."

"Santa, I know it's hard to believe, but..."

He didn't hear the rest of Fester's words, nor did he want to. Santa turned his back and finished walking out of the flight operations building without speaking another word to anyone.

That night, long after most of the residents of Santa's Village had gone to bed; there were elves awake in only two areas. The first was the workshop, where an unfortunate crew of elves—who would have much rather been in their houses in Elf Town—were stuck unloading toys from Santa's sleigh. The second area was the infirmary, where Nurse Marsha was attending to their only patient.

Usually, the only activity the infirmary ever saw were the practice scenarios run on a regular basis to keep Dr. Lapre, who was an actual medical doctor in several of the world's nations, and Nurse Marsha's skills sharp.

On the occasions they did have an actual patient, they weren't allowed to leave the infirmary and took turns sleeping in a small apartment that was added onto the medical building.

Lester, who had slipped into unconsciousness many hours before, began to convulse and Marsha sprang into action.

She did her best, but it wasn't good enough. A few seconds later, Lester's convulsions ceased, his eyes rolled up into the back of his head, and his last breath escaped his lifeless lips.

Marsha checked Lester's neck for a pulse and when she didn't find one, not that she expected to, she covered Lester's corpse with a blanket and left the room to wake Dr. Lapre.

When Marsha and Dr. Lapre returned to Lester's room, there wasn't a blanket covered body on the bed. Instead, they saw the blanket half-on and half-off the bed. Lester was standing, looking out the only window.

With a puzzled look on his face, Dr. Lapre said, "I thought that you said Lester was dead."

Looking even more puzzled than Dr. Lapre, Marsha replied, "I...I thought he was. No pulse, no breathing, no reflexes. It all says he was dead."

Lester began turning to face them. They way he turned looked more like a blind man turning towards the sound of voices than the way Lester normally would have.

Not realizing that their patient was turning to face them, Dr. Lapre continued. "Please, Marsha, the next time you wake me up to tell me a patient has died, please make sure that the patient is actually dead."

Without so much as a look back at Lester, Dr. Lapre turned and began walking back to the infirmary's apartment. When he took his fifth step away from Lester's room, Dr. Lapre heard a hiss. He turned back around to see what had made the sound and heard the worst, almost demonic sounding scream he had ever heard in his long life.

The next thing he saw was Lester, who came running out of his room so fast he almost appeared to be flying. Lester, or what had once been Lester, grabbed a hold of Marsha and kept running, driving the nurse into the wall.

Even though Marsha's back was to the wall, Lester continued to run forward, as if he didn't realize that she couldn't be driven back any further. Less than a second later, the embrace the two of them shared looked more passionate than life threatening.

Dr. Lapre's eyes widened to the size of golf balls as he witnessed Lester's mouth open as wide as it could and then bite into the side of Marsha's neck. Lester pulled his head back, and with it took a mouthful of Marsha's flesh.

Marsha screamed briefly and then passed out from fear. She would bleed to death before she ever regained consciousness.

Dr. Lapre had always been very protective of females. As soon as his shock at the dreadful sight passed, he ran at Lester in a misguided attempt to save Marsha's life.

The dead have a sixth sense that only they have and which the living couldn't comprehend; they can locate warm flesh—their food. It was that sense that allowed the walking corpse that was Lester to notice that Dr. Lapre was running toward him.

In the same blind man way that Lester had turned around in his room, he began to stand from the cooling corpse of Marsha. He wasn't able to do so before the doctor slammed into him, taking them both to the floor.

Functioning on his most primal instincts, Lester wasn't the fighter he once was, which considering that fighting was unheard of in the North Pole, didn't say very much.

On their way to the floor, Lester sunk his teeth into Dr. Lapre's cheek. While he failed to rip free the desired flesh, Lester succeeded in breaking the skin and leaving a bloody bite mark on the doctor's face.

Confused by his patient's behavior, Dr. Lapre put his hands in Lester's mouth and on his chin and began pushing the elf's face upwards and away from him. Lester's mouth closed hard and Dr. Lapre lost three fingers from the knuckle forward.

His pain caused what little reasonable thinking Dr. Lapre had left to leave him. He pulled both of his hands away from Lester's face, and without missing a beat, Lester lunged for the doctor's neck. Lester's mouth opened again and his teeth sank deep into the front of Dr. Lapre's throat. When Lester pulled his head back this time, it wasn't only flesh that came with him but also some of the doctor's trachea.

Unaware of what was happening in the infirmary, Dr. Lapre's wife, Bernice, walked up to the front door with a late night snack for both her husband and Marsha. She opened the door and it was her bad luck to have all three of the walking corpses standing there. Instead of the steamed duck eggs she had lovingly prepared for her husband, Bernice became the late night snack for Dr. Lapre, Marsha and Lester. It didn't take long until she became one of the walking dead as well.

With the barrier between them and the rest of the village's residents removed, all four of them made their way out of the infirmary and went their own way into Santa's Village in a search for more food.

In the breeding barn an elf, named Gene, led a young female reindeer that had just reached breeding age, named Ruby to the stall of the oldest buck in the barn, Dreamcatcher.

"Oh yeah, Ruby, you're gonna like old Dreamcatcher, yes you are," Gene told Ruby.

Before he could get her into Dreamcatcher's stall. Bernice rounded the corner, in the same blind man way that all of the reanimated dead were moving, and walked into the barn.

Facing Gene, she hissed and then immediately bellowed the same blood-chilling scream that they all gave off right before attacking their prey.

Gene was too surprised to react, and before his mind could function enough to do so, Bernice had passed him and had her arms wrapped around Ruby's long neck. The reindeer, who had no natural predators in Santa's Village, panicked, but Bernice kept her hold on the bucking deer as she sank her teeth into Ruby's face.

Although they didn't understand what they were seeing, the scene caused a panic among the bucks at the smell of blood, and many of them kicked through their stall doors and escaped from the barn. Some of them would fall victim to the dead and come back to attack the living. Some of them would avoid that fate by escaping into the frozen wasteland of the North Pole, where they would freeze to death. Either way, all of the reindeer were doomed.

Gene wrapped his arms around Bernice to restrain her as he yelled, "Help! Help in the breeding barn!"

The shock from everything that had occurred so unexpectedly caused a heart defect in Ruby to rear its ugly head and she died of heart failure.

In a matter of seconds, her fog-covered eyes reopened and she pulled herself to where Gene and Bernice were struggling against each other. The reindeer bit Gene's ankle and even though her bite didn't make it through his boot, it drew his attention away from Bernice long enough for her to turn around and renew her attack on him.

Ruby and Bernice fed on Gene until he also reanimated.

After a short nap, Santa returned to his workshop to supervise the final toys being unloaded.

Another elf that Santa didn't know the name of, burst into the workshop, and in a flat out run, ran to find Santa.

"Santa! Santa! Santa!" The elf yelled in near panic as he ran.

"What is it?" Santa asked the elf.

"There are disturbances being reported in all of the reindeer barns and in Elf Town."

"Disturbances? What kind of disturbances?" Santa asked, concern thick in his voice.

"I've never seen one in person, but from what I've seen on TV, I'd say they're rioting," the elf answered.

"Rioting?" Santa asked in disbelief.

"Violent ones," the elf confirmed.

"There has never been violence or riots here. I think you're greatly mistaken, my little friend. We're all upset over Christmas being canceled for the first time in history, but please don't exaggerate the problem."

"Santa, please listen to me. Something is very wrong in the village. The infirmary, it's empty, as in no one's there, and there's blood all over the place," the elf replied, standing his ground.

Realizing the elf truly believed everything he was saying, Santa said, "Okay, okay. I'll go and see what's going on in Elf Town. You get the other elves and check out every other building in the village. Once you have, we'll all meet back here and you can give me a status report of everything that's going on."

Santa walked down the main street of Elf Town and everything appeared as it should at this time of night.

Just as I figured, Santa thought as he walked. *No signs of life because everyone is sound asleep just like they should be.*

He rounded a corner and saw a sight that brought him to a complete stop. He saw Rudolph standing over the body of an elf child. His lead reindeer was actually eating the child's body.

Stunned and unsure of what was going on, Santa didn't make any attempt to intervene. Instead, he just walked through Elf Town in another direction.

He didn't have to walk far before he came upon another grisly scene. This time he found an elf eating another elf. Unlike Rudolph, this elf realized Santa was there and looked at him.

When he locked eyes with the elf, Santa felt more fear than he ever had in his entire, long life. The elf stood and hissed. Then bellowed the same scream, more of a battle cry, and charged at Santa.

Not sure of what to do, Santa just stood where he was, dumbly, and watched the horrific looking elf charge at him. When the elf reached him, bloody teeth bit into Santa's left hand, which shocked him back to reality.

For another first in his life, Santa punched the elf. His punch landed with enough force to knock the little body to the frozen ground.

Santa took off running with the elf not far behind him. The elf was in much better shape that the bulkier Santa, but his longer legs prevented his pursuer from catching up to him. Santa ran until he reached the workshop and slammed the door closed behind him.

Santa looked around his workshop and noticed that of all the elves that had left to see what was happening around the village, only he had made it back.

"Where are the others?" Santa asked Shaun, another elf.

Shaun shook his head in bewilderment and said, "I don't know, Santa. They haven't come back yet, nor have they communicated with me in any way."

Worry filled Santa as he asked, "Will you please go to my house and check on my wife. Don't worry her about anything, but get her to join me here. I don't want her on her own until we figure out what's going on around here."

In the most comforting voice that he could manage, Shaun said, "Certainly, Santa. I'm sure she's fine."

As Shaun walked up the steps to the front door of Santa's house, he was filled with a sudden sense of dread. He stopped just long enough to regain his emotional center, and even though he really didn't want to, he continued on.

He put his hand on the doorknob and pulled the door open, asking, "Hello? Mrs. Claus? Are you here?"

He walked into the house, wondering why he hadn't told Santa to go and check on Mrs. Claus himself. He heard noise in Santa's den and went to investigate. He called, "Mrs. Claus. It's Shaun. Santa sent me to find you. Are you here?"

A noise from Santa's den caught his attention and Shaun followed the sound. "Mrs. Claus? Hello?" He called as he went.

Immediately after walking into Santa's den, Shaun saw Mrs. Claus standing in the middle of the room. She appeared to be completely clueless as to what was going on around her.

Within seconds of Shaun entering, Mrs. Claus' demeanor changed entirely and her head repositioned itself to face him. That was when Shaun noticed the flesh missing on her right cheek and that her throat had been torn wide open with the trachea protruding out.

She hissed at Shaun and then sounded off with the exact same scream that was becoming all too common of a sound in the North Pole this Christmas Eve.

Surprising Shaun with her speed, the walking corpse of Mrs. Claus ran towards him. Shaun responded by turning around and running as fast as his little legs would carry him in the other direction.

But before he could get far, the ravenous beast that was once Mrs. Claus had her hands on his shoulders and she used her considerable weight to force him to the floor.

Mrs. Claus landed on top of Shaun and she immediately began taking mouthfuls of flesh and hair off the back of his head and neck.

Shaun fought with what was for an elf, a Herculean effort, but Mrs. Claus's superior weight won out and within minutes, Shaun was dead. Soon he would return as one of the walking dead.

Hours went by with the living dead running amuck. Things in Santa's workshop weren't going much better than they were anywhere else in Santa's Village. Santa's health was deteriorating badly and he had lost consciousness an hour ago.

With great effort, the elves that had returned had been able to move him into the quality control section of the workshop, and they laid him out on one of the inspection tables. Santa hadn't so much as moved a muscle since.

His elves, being loyal to Santa, remained in the quality control section with him. Ten of them stood in a circle.

"They say the dead are returning to life, but I don't believe it. What we have going on is some sort of chemical infection that the humans concocted and it has somehow made it here and is driving some of us insane. That's all there is to it, pure and simple," an elf named Bruce said in a matter of fact way.

"What do you propose that we do?" another elf named Carl asked.

Bruce shrugged and said, "Look around us; we have everything we need to make weapons. I say that we go out and get things back under control."

In a voice that was well past condescending, Carl replied, "Oh yeah? Why don't we make ourselves some machine guns. Maybe some hand grenades while we're at it. Maybe we can make a nuclear missile or two. Come on, Bruce, no elf has ever used a weapon against another elf. Never."

Disgusted with Carl, Bruce fired back, "We can't make those weapons. I wasn't referring to those kinds of weapons, as you well know. But bladed weapons are well within our means. We make toy swords and axes all of the time. Why can't we make the real thing?" Bruce looked around but no one said anything to dissuade him. Finally, in a voice that sounded far too reasonable, Bruce said, "Well, I'm doing it. By a show of hands, who's with me?"

Slowly, hands began to go up. Finally, only Carl's hand remained down.

"Carl? You aren't with us?" Bruce asked.

Shaking his head, Carl said, "No, I'm not. No elf has ever used violence against another elf and we shouldn't start now."

Bruce didn't see the point in illustrating the fact there were elves attacking elves already. He thought it would have been nothing more that a waste of breath and instead said, "All right, everyone except Carl, who will go down in elf history as a coward, follow me to the metal shop."

The elves decided to bring things under control in Elf Town first, since that was where they lived with their families. In the first militaristic action the North Pole elves had ever participated in, the nine elves from Santa's workshop walked in a straight line carrying their hastily made swords.

They moved down Main Street and it didn't take long for their presence to be noticed. Hundreds of their dead friends and family surrounded them. This was followed by a long series of hisses and demonic sounding yells.

Nine against hundreds weren't even close to being accurately called 'bad odds,' they were impossible, and the nine elves were quickly devoured before what was left soon joined the ranks of the living dead.

Back in his workshop, Santa's breathing became short and labored. It continued to grow increasingly shallow until his breathing completely stopped. His eyes rolled into the back of his head and Santa Claus died.

A few minutes later, Carl, who had been walking aimlessly around the workshop, returned to the quality control section and saw Santa, who was now standing up, though he swayed slightly, as if he was drunk.

"Santa!" he said happily. "I knew you'd pull through, I just knew it!"

In reply, Santa hissed and roared. This was immediately followed by Santa running towards Carl, whose short legs didn't give him any chance of escape. Santa tackled Carl and immediately began taking bites out of the elf's exposed flesh. Santa's feeding continued until Carl's life escaped him and he too joined the ranks of the reanimated dead of the North Pole.

Carl died being completely unaware that he was the last living being in the entire world.

In a world that was ruled by the dead, Christmas was truly over.

A CHRISTMAS TO REMEMBER

KEVIN MILLIKIN

The roof creaked beneath the sounds of a thundering footfall as someone treaded their way across Betty-Lou's bedroom. She smiled, her heart flopping about excitedly in her chest. She wasn't scared. You see, Betty-Lou was a smart girl. She knew there was no boogeyman, no monsters and no ghosts, and with those aside, she knew exactly who it was.

"It's Santa," she whispered, throwing the covers off her and on to the floor. In a blink of an eye she was gone, running across her bedroom in a flash, her pink nightgown flapping behind her like a cape as she flung open her bedroom door.

Above her, the monstrous footfalls followed, occasionally losing ground behind the anxious child.

Her bare feet slapped the hardwood floor, making it sound as though someone was knocking on the front door with every frantic step she took.

Passing her parents' bedroom, she caught the gargled rasp of her father's snores, accompanied by the hushed chatter of her mother's television as she dozed to her favorite, late-night talk show. Betty-Lou made no attempts to be quiet. Her parents could sleep through almost anything and tonight would be no different.

Betty-Lou's pace never slowed, the excitement in her chest pushed her forward. Rounding the bend from the hallway into the living room, she cut the corner quick, but never lost step. The gentle glow of red, blue, green and white lights twinkled, beckoning her forward.

The living room was large, as one would typically expect a living room to be, with a couch, a TV, and a fireplace. The glow from the Christmas tree lights softened the room, giving it an angelic sense of perfection. In the corner of the room was the large, Christmas tree her father had chopped from Mt. Shasta. It now sat solemnly, radiating its light and guarding the presents.

On any given night, Betty-Lou would sit by the tree and let the colorful lights warm her face, as she gazed upon the wrapped presents and ponder what sorts of magic and wonder were contained within their fancy bows and colorful paper. Tonight, she wanted none of it—at least not yet. The small child could barely contain her glee as she ran across the room towards the fireplace where her mother had hung up their stockings a few weeks prior.

There, on the mantle, sat a plate of cookies and a large glass of milk. Betty-Lou picked up the plate and was careful not to spill the milk as she plopped down on the floor a few feet from the fireplace. The plate of cookies and the glass of milk were laid out before her like an offering of peace and goodwill.

Somewhere overhead, she could hear the approaching footsteps and couldn't help but feel an overpowering sense of joy wash over her, after all, she had just outrun Santa Claus!

She listened as the jolly fat man's footsteps stopped just short of the chimney stack, causing the child to squeal with excitement as the house began to shake. Betty-Lou pictured him as he climbed into her chimney, heaving one massive leg upon the other, all the while balancing his massive sack of goodies all the way down. She wondered what treats he had in store.

A gentle *poof* of dust trickled down from the chimney, and small, pebble-sized pieces of chipped brick fell along with it, making little *popping* sounds as they hit the bottom, signaling Father Christmas' arrival.

As she waited, her smile never faded.

"Come on, come on." Her whispered words becoming a fevered mantra, as her mind spun with the thoughts of all she would receive this Christmas Eve.

The slithering of fabric on brick stopped, and moments of excruciating silence passed and still, the child smiled and she continued to smile as a long, hard, moist cough shattered the night.

Betty-Lou's smile flipped to a frown. *That's not very Santa-like,* she thought as Santa's phlegm hit the bricks with a *plop!* She didn't think twice. Even though it was gross and *un*Santa-like, she still had to lump him into the category of being a boy, and short in years, she still believed boys to be *gross*.

She only started to worry when a feverish groan resonated throughout the mason tomb, followed by what she thought to be some curse word, but she wasn't sure.

"Santa?" She jumped to her feet and rushed quickly to his aid.

Betty-Lou's words were met by a moment of silence that hurt her ears as the last of the dust fell.

"Little girl?" he finally coughed. The man's voice was deep, loving and warm. "Betty-Lou, is that you?"

She poked her head into the chimney and looked up, seeing nothing but darkness. "Yes!" she cried. "It's me!"

Another second passed with no movement, no other exchange of words, just another wet hacking cough as the man discharged more phlegm. Betty-Lou ducked out just as the sickening glob passed by her face.

"Santa?"

"Yes?" he replied, his voice faltering with every breath lost.

"Are you okay?" Her voice was heavy with concern.

Santa chuckled, his laughs morphing into a poorly constructed *ho-ho-ho* that only managed to worsen her mood.

"Betty-Lou," he said finally, "I'll be straight with you. I'm not feeling so hot right now."

"What's wrong?" she asked.

Santa Claus groaned, and as he did, Betty-Lou could hear him sliding further down the chimney. "Let me..." he struggled, panting wildly as he spoke, "tell you about it when I get out of this blasted thing."

Betty-Lou was surprised. This wasn't the Santa Claus she remembered from last year, and she didn't like this at all. Not one bit.

As he inched his way down, she finally caught sight of his red jacket and flowing white beard, both of which were blackened by soot. Santa's jacket glowed a brackish shade in the faint light of the Christmas tree, the sight of which filled the girl with a sense of horror she'd never felt before; one that rose in her throat like some godforsaken scream.

Santa looked out at her from within the fireplace, his beady little eyes the only bit of purity left on him as they pierced the darkness.

For just a second, Betty-Lou didn't recognize him, but as he emerged from the chimney, she cried out, "Santa!" and rushed to his side. "What happened to you?"

Betty-Lou wanted to help him, but he gently waved her off and shook his head, "Oh, Betty-Lou," he said, still shaking his head as he sat down on the lip of the fireplace.

Catching sight of the milk and cookies, he began to laugh, but before he could say anything, Betty-Lou said, "Santa, you're bleeding!"

It was true, Santa Claus was bleeding. It was a hard thing to miss.

"Oh, this?" he replied, hoping to lighten the moment as he touched his murky hands against the bright crimson flowing across his cheek just above his snow-white beard.

"Nothing to worry about," he sighed. "Just another reminder as to why I should stick to the good list instead of the naughty one."

Before she could respond, Santa Claus held up a silencing hand. "Betty-Lou," he said. "You have always been such a good girl."

Betty-Lou blushed.

"Now, could you please be a dear and get me a towel or a rag? Anything I can use to clean myself up."

She smiled and nodded, willing to do anything to help.

"And while you do that," he smiled, "I think I'll help myself to some of these glorious cookies!"

Together they smiled, and he sent her off with a wink, and in less than a minute she returned to find that Santa had finished off the cookies and was polishing off the rest of the milk.

"Thank you, dear." He washed off his face and then his hands, and after a good scrubbing, he began to look just like the Santa Claus she remembered from previous years. As for the cut that ran across his rosy cheek, it wasn't big, maybe an inch or two in length, and even though she was young, Betty-Lou knew that all of the gunk and dirt wasn't going to do it any good. The wound had scabbed over some, drying into a hideous shade of brown.

Santa winced in pain as he touched the towel to it, the sound of him in pain stung at her aching heart.

"How old are you?" he asked. "Seven? Eight?"

"I'm almost ten," she replied, holding up both hands to show off her digits.

His eyes went wide. "Wow, most children your age don't even believe in me, can you believe that?"

Betty-Lou couldn't but even if she did, she still probably wouldn't want anything to do with it.

Santa coughed, and crimson spittle got caught within the whiskers around his beard. When he realized what happened, he tried to cover it up by coughing into his hand, but it was pointless and he knew it. He'd have to tell her eventually, and for the first time since it happened, Santa felt like he was going to cry and now, the pangs in his stomach were becoming too much for him to handle.

Even in his old age, an age older than the stars themselves, Santa Claus still couldn't fathom why on earth bad things happened to good people.

"Betty-Lou?" Everything he said brought a blinding white pain to all his senses.

"Yes?"

"You know about bad people, right?"

She nodded. Her parents had told her all about bad people and the bad things they did.

"What about that little shit down the street, Jeff Roberts?"

Betty-Lou gasped, she never imagined the day would come when she heard Santa Claus curse.

"He did this to me," he spat. His bloody spittle dribbled to the floor as he pointed towards the cut on his cheek. "Some people are just born naughty. Horrible, horrible, nasty, naughty things, but you knew that."

Betty-Lou nodded.

"You try to help, perhaps *this* favor or perhaps *that* favor. Perhaps that's all they would need to understand, but no, the little bastards have to go and muck everything up."

As he spoke, Betty-Lou couldn't shake the feeling he was speaking *at* her and not *to* her. He began to sweat; it beaded across his forehead and dripped from his nose in ribbons.

"You're about that age when you realize just how horrible this beautiful world of ours really is."

She was lost; Betty-Lou had absolutely no idea what he was talking about.

"Am I right, Sarah?"

"I'm Betty-Lou," she corrected.

"Right, Betty-Lou. Well, am I? Am I right?

She began to worry. What if her parents woke up? What if they came out here and found Santa Claus sitting in their living room in the middle of the night, spitting blood all over the floor?

She shuddered; her mom never let her eat out here. What would she say when she found blood on the floor?

"I...I guess so." She furrowed her brow. She had no idea what was what anymore and the ever-degrading shape Santa Claus was in only managed to crush her spirits even more.

"Damn right you do!" he snapped.

In that moment, Betty-Lou desperately wanted her parents to wake up and come to her rescue.

"Can you believe what he did?"

"Who did what?" she asked.

"The Roberts child," he said, sending more spit her way. It was obvious, he was furious. His once jolly physique was now crippled with tremors as he continued to sweat profusely.

Even though Betty-Lou was young and often times naïve, she knew a serious problem when she saw it.

"Do you want me to get someone to help you?" she asked, her innocence breaking the old man's heart with every word she said.

"No." Santa shook his head slowly; anything more was like a burst of excruciating pain. "I don't think anyone's help will be doing me any good at this point. Just... just call it a hunch." His smile did nothing more to regain her confidence. Together, silence engulfed them before Betty-Lou finally asked, "Santa, what happened?"

He sighed. "Very well." As he spoke, he turned away from her slightly. She caught the reflection of the Christmas tree lights in his troubled, bloodshot eyes.

"Jeff has been having a bad year at home. You know Jeff, right?"

She nodded; he was a teenaged boy who lived a few houses down. Jeff was the stereotypical bad seed that every parent warned their kids about. Once she had even heard her mom on the phone gossiping to her friend about the Roberts' household, about their misfortune, and heard her say that if Mrs. Roberts could control her cheating husband, than maybe she could control her out-of-control son.

"I just thought maybe I would do a little something extra for the kid; give him a boost of self-esteem. I thought that something special would make him want to turn his life around and do something good for a change. But the instant I popped in, something was wrong. I came in through the chimney and found their living room was in complete disarray. The couch was tipped over and ripped open like someone had taken a knife to it, stuffing everywhere." Santa shook his head remorsefully. "Their Christmas tree was knocked sideways against the wall, the lights burned out, ornaments and decorations smashed—and the smell, that God awful smell." He winced as he remembered it.

"I knew something bad had happened there, something *really* bad. I didn't worry about being quiet anymore. 'Is anyone here?' I yelled, walking through the living room, presents crunching under my boots. 'Hello? Is there anyone here?"

Santa leaned forward, his face a few inches from Betty-Lou's face as his eyes went wide. He did so as to prove a point. "I made a big mistake!"

Santa leaned back, his eyes drifting up towards the ceiling as though he was speaking towards Heaven. "That's when I heard them, they were behind their bedroom door, scratching and pounding at the door, and then I heard them moan. At first I didn't know what they were, but the closer I got to the bedroom, the more excited the damn things seemed to become. Finally, I don't know how he did it but Mister Roberts managed to get his gnarled hand around the door knob, and the next thing I knew, it was like I was looking into a freaking vision of Hell!"

Betty-Lou was taken back, her little heart palpitating madly, pumping blood and terror throughout her tiny body.

"Mister Roberts comes walking out of the bedroom all fat and ugly in a pair of gore-soaked slacks and some hideous Christmas sweater that even I wouldn't wear. His face was all but gone, his jaws snapping with no cheeks to keep his teeth in place. His head was cocked to the side, looking at me from an unnatural angle, like his neck had been broken. Then I saw his wife, I don't know how I even missed her to begin with, but there she was, crawling across the carpet at me, dead—dead as a door nail but still moving." He bowed his head. "God rest her soul," he whispered. "She moaned and just looking at her I knew she wanted my hide and I—well, do you know about magic?"

Betty-Lou was so enticed by Santa's story that she completely missed the question.

Finally, after he asked her again, she replied, "Yes."

He smiled. "Good, because you know magic *does* exist. There are just so many things in this world of ours that no one understands and probably never will. What happened to the Roberts family is a perfect example of it. Let me ask you, do you know what zombies are?"

The twinkling lights from the Christmas tree caught his eyes, reflecting darkness upon her as she shook her head no.

"Well, a zombie is…" he said, in-between a violent fit of coughing. "A zombie is a dead person…a walking dead person whose only purpose is to feast upon the flesh of the living."

Betty-Lou felt herself shake a bit. The fear was becoming a bit too much for her to handle, and as though he could sense her fear, Santa chuckled feebly.

"*Ho-ho-ho*," he coughed loudly. "That's exactly what they were—zombies," he said. "All three of them had been stuck in that house for who knows how long—zombies, goddamn zombies!"

She wondered if these *zombies* were the reason why Santa Claus had been acting so strange.

"Then I saw that little shit, Jeff. He came at me from his bedroom when I tried to escape. I punched the little fucker in the face, he goes down and then BOOM—he's right back up before I can even get a few feet away."

She didn't like to hear him curse, it made her feel bad. As she watched him, she realized how badly Santa was sweating, swaying back and forth as he sat on the edge of the fireplace.

Betty-Lou found herself fighting off the urge to giggle. The picture she painted in her mind was a funny one at best: Santa Claus punching a child in the face and the fact that it was Jeff only made it seem funnier. The tale Santa told left her wondering: *what next?*

"He came at me again like I never took a swing in the first place. The little bugger was resilient, so when he got close, I took a swing at him with my bag of goodies, told him to F-himself, and with a wiggle of my nose, I got outta there and well, here I am."

Santa looked to Betty-Lou, his massive belly rising and falling. She could hear him wheeze with every breath he took.

"Let me be honest with you," he said. "I don't know how much longer I have."

"What do you mean, Santa?" she asked

"Well," he sighed, "when Jeff came at me the second time, he managed to do a little number on my cheek." He pointed to the scabbed scrape on his face before shaking his head. "I don't think I'm going to make it, Betty-Lou."

"Why? What do you mean?" she cried, leaping to her feet.

"I mean, I mean..." Santa just couldn't find the right words to tell the child what was going to happen, but he had to. After all, it was the reason why he was there.

"I mean, I'm going to become one of them."

She thought it over; Santa Claus was going to become a zombie?

"But zombies are..."

"Dead," he finished.

"No!" she gasped.

He nodded. "I'm sorry but I need your help."

"What do you want me to do?" she asked with wide eyes.

It was hard for him to say what he needed to say. "I need you to do exactly what I tell you to do."

She jumped at it. "What ever it is, I'll do it. Trust me, Santa, I'll do it!"

He already knew that, but it didn't mean he liked it.

"Very well, then." He could feel his heavy clothes stick to his body. His belly rumbled; it felt like his stomach was eating itself alive but in all actuality it was probably beginning to rot.

"Listen to me *very* carefully, child." As he spoke his eyes grew wide as if to convey the seriousness of the situation. "I'm gonna need you to do me in. Do you understand me?"

She thought about it and was pretty sure that she understood, but the fear of what she thought kept her mouth shut.

Santa Claus never blinked, never lifted his gaze off her as he lifted his hand and placed it against the side of his head. His thumb and index finger made the shape of a gun.

"I need you to do this for me. I need you to kill me," he told the child.

Betty-Lou blinked. There was no mistaking the once jolly man's words. With her eyes wide and her mouth open, she sat there, stunned, as the mystical elf told her to commit homicide.

"Can you do it?" he asked.

She shook her head, tears welling up in her eyes. She couldn't. She regretted even saying that she would help him.

"I...I don't think so, Santa," she said as her little ten-year-old world crumbled down around her.

"Please," he pleaded, his sunken eyes glazed with tears. "For all that's good in this world, for children everywhere, I'm asking you, please bash in my brains."

Santa Claus needed to die and he needed to do it *now*. He had thought about flying back to the North Pole and getting one of his elves to do it for him, but by the time he returned home, the undead virus would have ravaged his insides, turning him into one of the walking dead.

Then what?

Who's to say he wouldn't get his holly-jolly ass back onto his sleigh and spread some Christmas-time pandemic across the globe?

He wouldn't—no, he couldn't let that happen. No matter how naughty the children of the world got, he trusted the child before him. Santa trusted her more than anything and it was because her faith in him was so strong and so pure that he could count on her.

Betty-Lou began to sniffle, but in no time those sniffles turned into full-fledged tears.

She heaved, "I can't do it!" Salty tears streamed down her cheeks. "I can't kill Santa Claus!"

"Yes you can," he consoled, wrapping a loving arm around her. He held on tightly, using her to stop his body from shaking.

"It won't be a problem," he told her as tried to hand off the would-be weapon as he took the fire poker from its stand. "See, you can even use this." Santa tried to hand the poker to the child, but she looked at it as though it were gift-wrapped poison.

"One swing," he begged, turning his words to bribes at a second's notice. "If you do this for me, I'll make it worth your while."

She perked up. "You will?"

"Yes," he lied. "Next time Christmas comes around, I'll make *all of this* worth your troubles."

Betty-Lou thought it over, but something about his words just didn't sound right to her.

"But won't you be dead *next* year?"

"I, uh…" He stumbled over his words like a fat kid on the track team. He was so sure he had her, if only he hadn't left his magic bag of goodies back at the Roberts' residence, he would have been able to shut her up right then.

"I'll get my elves to do it." His lies clung tightly against his teeth. "They'll do it, they'll send it to you overnight, fully insured. All expenses paid," he said, waving it off.

Five minutes from now Santa Claus was sure he would become one of the walking dead, that is, if he didn't get the little girl to act fast.

She shrugged, "Okay, I guess."

He was a little taken aback by how easy it was to convince her otherwise.

"Really? You'll do it?"

She nodded.

"Well, hot-damn!" he laughed as he slapped his knee. His throat felt as if it was about to bleed acid. His health was failing with every passing second, he could feel it.

Betty-Lou took the spiked weapon and stopped, her big doe eyes reflecting the tears that hid behind them.

"Will I go to Hell?" she asked.

He groaned, wondering what next. Santa wanted it over with already. He wanted to die.

"No," he replied. "I have some friends in pretty high places. I'll see to it that *nothing* bad happens to you."

"You will?"

"You bet," he smiled. "Jesus, you know Jesus, right?"

She nodded.

"Well see, there you go. Jesus and I go back, *way back*!" As he spoke, his vision began to blur. "Actually, my friend Jesus was kinda like a zombie." Santa smiled, his world was dimming fast.

The last thing he saw as his life ended was Betty-Lou rising up. The fire poker was raised above her head, and in a flash of white heat his world dissolved to black.

* * *

Santa Claus awoke in a world of white.

Around his jolly frame drifted clouds. It took him a while to realize where he was.

He smiled, realizing the job was done.

Walking forward, the glint of gold broke the whiteness. The closer he stepped, the shape of gates appeared. Slowly, with a metal groan, the gates opened, and without missing a beat, Santa Claus strolled through.

As he did, he saw people he had once known, friends and family, loved ones and enemies, all of whom had long since died. Through it all, he saw his old friend, Jesus.

"Jesus!" he smiled, opening his arms wide for a hug, but Jesus never moved. He never removed his arms from his chest.

"What?" Santa stopped.

"That last part you told the girl, about the zombie," he said. "That *wasn't* funny."

* * *

"Jason, Jason—wake up!" Jackie whispered as she shook her husband awake. "I hear something."

"You always hear something," he groaned, taking half of the blankets with him as he rolled over.

"Yeah, I'm surprised, too!" she snapped. "Especially with you snoring all the goddamn time! Now go check it out!"

"It was probably Betty-Lou," he whispered, still half asleep. "I'm sure she couldn't sleep so she's probably out there waiting for Santa."

Jackie figured her husband was right but still, she couldn't shake the feeling he wasn't. After all, he never was.

"Just check it out, will you please?" she begged.

He groaned again, throwing the blankets off them both and onto the floor. As he opened his mouth to speak, their daughter's screams cut through the night.

"Betty-Lou!" they screamed as they leapt from the bed, their minds racing with the vilest of thoughts as they threw open the bedroom door.

Their hearts raced as they cleared the hallway in a few short steps.

"Betty-Lou!" they cried again, entering the living room.

They stopped, shocked by what they saw.

"Mommy, Daddy!" Betty-Lou cried.

Their daughter stood in the center of the living room, the fire poker firmly in her hands.

She backed up toward them, then to the wall, bumping into the Christmas tree that crashed to the floor with the shatter of glass ornaments.

A fat man with a white beard dressed in a Santa Claus suit lunged for her. He was stark raving mad, and crusted in blood. As he moved forward, Betty-Lou swung the fire poker, striking the man across the face with a *whack*.

He spun around, dazed, but recovered quickly.

Seeing Betty-Lou's parents, Santa Claus turned his sights on them. His face was pale, slick with blood.

His lips peeled back with every drunken step he took, and as his breath escaped dead lungs, it brought with it an agonized, rasping, *"Ho-ho-ho."*

THE END OF CHRISTMAS

ANTHONY GIANGREGORIO

Santa Claus closed the computer laptop and shook his head while taking off his thin, wire-rimmed reading glasses. He walked over to the television and stared at the screen filled with white snow.

"Still nothing, I just don't understand what's happening," he muttered under his breath.

Mrs. Claus entered the room, carrying a silver tray of milk and cookies—Santa's favorite snack.

"It's probably nothing, dear," Martha said as she placed the tray on a table beside Santa. "A solar flare or some such thing."

Santa picked up a cookie and took a bite. As crumbs fell into his white beard, he sighed. "For over a month, Martha? I highly doubt it. No, there's something wrong in the world. No phones, cable television or internet service for almost four weeks. I fear the worst."

"You said it was everywhere, right?" she asked.

He nodded. "As far as I can tell. Well, everywhere but here, and as you know, we're hidden from plain view."

"Well, dear, tomorrow night is Christmas Eve. When you head out to deliver presents to all the good little children, I guess you'll find out then what's been happening to the world."

He merely grunted in response, as he took another bite of his cookie.

Half an hour later, Santa left his small home to cross the town of Santa's Village. His destination was the main toy workshop, a warehouse located at the west side of town. This was where almost all the toys were designed and made.

The village was alive with activity as everyone rushed to finish the last toys so Santa could head out tomorrow night. Everywhere Santa looked he saw smiling faces. He nodded to a few elves and other workers as he walked, but most were so flustered with their chores they barely noticed him.

He didn't mind. While in the outside world Santa was a celebrity, loved by millions, here at Santa's Village—his home—he was just another worker—even if he was the boss.

Crossing the street, he waved to a few people and soon was at the warehouse.

From the outside, the building was rather plain, with snow piled five feet on all sides. Like all buildings in the village, this one was painted white.

Despite the invisibility spell that kept Santa's Village hidden from the outside world, camouflage was still necessary in case the spell ever failed.

Santa stepped through the front door and into a cacophony of busy elves. Tables were lined up throughout the warehouse, each one for an elf. Here, they fabricated toys the old fashioned way, though many of the items were flown in from outside sources by using dummy accounts and false businesses.

Loud holiday music was being blasted through hidden speakers, adding to the merriment and chaos.

The instant Santa entered the warehouse, an elf with thick black glasses appeared, standing right behind Santa.

"Hi, Santa!" the elf yelled and Santa jumped a foot into the air.

"What the...? Who?" Santa yelled as he turned and saw the elf where a moment ago there was no one. "Rufio, what have I told you about sneaking up on me?" Santa asked as he frowned at the elf who had almost given him a heart attack.

"You said not to do it," the elf replied. "But I have big news to tell you."

"Oh, and what might that be?" Santa asked.

"I just got the latest statistic report and it looks like not only are we on time, but we're ahead of schedule in manufacturing all the toys you requisitioned, Santa."

"Wonderful, that's wonderful news, Rufio. Well done. I'll have to make sure to thank everyone personally at the party when I return from my deliveries on Christmas morning."

Santa was talking about the party they had in the village every year to celebrate another successful Christmas. The entire village would relax and have fun, with food and games and joviality. But the next day they would get right back to work, for there would only be a year before the next Christmas and there was always so much to do.

"Excellent, I'll make sure to pen you in for that speech," Rufio said as he pulled a small, computer notebook out from behind his back and began typing into it. "Oh, Santa, any word from the outside world?" Rufio asked. "I still can't get internet service and all the lines seem to be down. I've called Tokyo to Africa, and then Ireland, but it's like the entire network is malfunctioning."

"Yes, I'm well aware of it, and have been for quite some time. At least when I leave tomorrow night, I can see first hand what's going on with communications across the globe."

"Do you think its anything serious?" Rufio asked.

Santa frowned, the gesture seeming out of place on his usually happy, jolly visage. "I don't know, Rufio, we'll just have to wait and see when I get to the United States."

A chorus of yells filled the warehouse and Santa and Rufio looked up to see a five foot, plush teddy bear walking down the center aisle. It had an adorable face, with big button eyes and a smiling mouth. But despite this, the bear looked mad, and as the elves tried to stop it, the stuffed animal would push them away.

One elf tore off his shirt to expose a muscled upper chest, and he pulled a small knife from a hidden pocket. He placed the knife in his mouth and growled like a warrior going into battle. He climbed onto a table and jumped onto the back of the teddy bear, to then hack and slash at the fake fur.

Stuffing went everywhere as the teddy bear tried to yank the elf off, but the tiny warrior was in the center of the bear's back, and the arms wouldn't go that far. Slash after slash, the elf cut and hacked and soon the air was filled with stuffing.

The teddy bear took a few more faltering steps and then fell forward, its fluffy limbs twitching before finally remaining still.

Another elf came running up to Santa. This elf was breathing hard from the exertion of the battle and he had a small cut on his forehead. The bells on his pointed green shoes were missing, having been torn off, and his green tunic was ripped.

"I'm so sorry about that, Santa," the elf said. "Herman sprinkled too much pixie dust into the stuffing and well, you saw the result."

"Is anyone hurt?" Santa asked with a look of concern.

"No, Santa, a few bumps and bruises, but everyone's fine."

"Good, that's good. Well, tell Herman to be more careful, will you? Little Suzie doesn't want to wake up Christmas morning with a killer bear under her tree."

"Yes, Santa, right away, Santa, it won't happen again, Santa," the elf said quickly and jogged away to help with the cleanup. Santa watched for a few seconds as the elves picked up the corpse of the teddy bear and dragged it away. A trail of stuffing trailed behind, an aftermath of the toy carnage.

He turned and looked down at Rufio. "Things seem to be under control here, I think I'll go check on the reindeer."

Rufio saluted like a soldier. "Will do, Santa, just let me know if you need anything else."

Santa left the warehouse, relishing the modicum of silence as the door closed behind him.

With a heavy sigh, he let out a plume of air that coalesced into fog before him, and walked to the stables, where his cherished flying reindeer were housed.

Once more, the instant he stepped inside, an elf popped up between two bales of hay.

"Hi, Santa, what's up?"

"Oh, hello there, Marvin. I just wanted to drop by and check on the reindeer."

Marvin smiled proudly. "They're all set for tomorrow night, Santa. I've fed them and brushed them and made sure they have enough water. They'll be fed tomorrow afternoon, that way they won't be too full to fly." He chuckled at that, finding it amusing.

"Good, good, excellent. I want to see them."

"Of course, right this way." Marvin led Santa deeper into the stable until he stopped at a wide barn door. Opening it, he gestured for Santa to go first. As he did, he entered a large room the size of a three car garage. Here, the reindeer were basically lounging around, a few sitting while others stood. When they saw Santa, they all stood up and came to him. Santa reached into his pocket and pulled out a handful of oats, which he fed each of them in kind. He counted them, making sure they were all there.

"Ah, Dasher, Dancer, Prancer, Vixen, Comet, Cupid, Donner and..." He paused. "Where's Blitzen?" Santa asked.

"Huh? I don't know, he should be here," Marvin said as he counted the reindeer.

Then, from behind a small wall of hay, Blitzen appeared. He trotted over to the rest of the group and Santa patted his head. "Ah, there you are, old friend, I was worried there for a second."

Blitzen snorted like a horse and ducked his head. Santa smiled widely, letting out a loud bellow of laughter. "Ho-ho-ho! Well done, Marvin, they look fit and ready for their long journey ahead. I don't know what I'd do without them, you know."

"Take a plane?" Marvin inquired.

Santa laughed again and patted the short elf on the head, much like the reindeer. "Very funny, I highly doubt that would work as well as my reindeer do. Well, I'll be going now, I will see you boys tomorrow," he said to the reindeer as he left the stable.

All was well, or as well as it could be given his lack of communication with the outside world. At least whatever was happening hadn't affected his village.

Now that it was getting so close to departure, he had to admit he had a bad feeling deep down inside. Of course, it was possible something silly had happened. But for the entire world to go dark and cease communications, well, that couldn't bode well.

Either way, he would find out tomorrow night when he went on his yearly trek to deliver presents to good little boys and girls. Until then, he would have to wait and do what he did every year, which was to eat. He had lost some weight over the summer and had been doing his best to bulk up. After all, no one liked a skinny Santa.

Hoping Martha had baked those chocolate chip cookies she had promised earlier that morning, he headed back home to check.

"Now you be safe, dear," Martha told Santa as he finished checking his sleigh. The bright red sled was sitting outside the stable, the reindeers harnessed and ready to go. More than ten elves were all rushing about; making sure Santa was as ready to go as he possibly could. There was only one large sack in the back of the sleigh, as that was all that was needed.

Using Christmas magic, the one toy sack had an infinite bottom. All Santa had to do was reach inside it and pluck out the toy he needed. After all, how else could he deliver all those toys all over the world in only one trip?

"That's a funny thing to say, Martha," Santa replied as he stepped up into the sleigh. "What makes you say that?"

"Oh, I don't know, it's just...well, we still don't know why there's a blackout across the world, and for all we know there could have been some calamity or natural disaster."

"That's silly, Martha, you're being overdramatic. If it was something like that, then we would have felt the effects here in the village, too."

"Not if it was something viral. Maybe one of those Middle Eastern countries let loose a biological agent or some awful thing."

He chuckled, his ho-ho-ho, barely a whisper. "Martha, I swear, you've been watching too many horror movies. I'm sure there is a perfectly rational explanation to whatever has happened. Now, my love, it's time for me to leave. Boys and girls everywhere are waiting for me."

She stepped close to him and kissed his cheek. "I know that, and that's why you're Santa Claus. Just promise me you'll come back in the morning, no matter what."

He sighed and with a nod, decided to humor his wife. "I promise, I'll be back, no matter what." He picked up the reins and gave them a gentle tug.

Blitzen was in the lead and when Santa gently nudged him, he snorted and began to move, causing the other reindeer to do the same. Santa circled around the stable until he was in an open clearing used for take-offs and landings, and with another tug on the reins, he let Blitzen know it was time to go.

All the reindeer began to jog, then run, and soon they were galloping across the snow-covered ice. And then, when Blitzen jumped, the others followed suit and the sleigh lifted into the air, floating on a cloud of Christmas magic.

Santa banked around the roof of the stable and with a, "Ho-ho-ho! Merry Christmas!" he flew over the village and into the clouds, soon lost from sight, the tinkling of sleigh bells wrapped around the reindeer's necks also fading.

Martha hugged herself as she stared up into the night sky, her mouth set in a slim line. Rufio walked over to her and tugged on her apron. Looking down, she saw the elf frowning.

"You look like I feel, Mrs. Claus," he said. "Care to share why you look so worried."

She nodded slightly. "Oh, Rufio, I don't know why I feel this way. I should be happy. After all, it's Christmas Eve. But for some reason, I have this feeling of dread that I just can't shake."

"Yes, I feel it, too. It has to do with us losing communication with the outside world. Whatever the reason, it can't be good."

"I agree," she said. "I just hope he comes back to us safe and sound."

Rufio plastered a wide smile on his face, only half of it forced. "Hey, of course he will, after all, he's Santa Claus."

After crossing the ocean, Santa came in for landing in a small town in Maine.

He noticed that the town was dark, which seemed odd to him. As he flew over the town square, he saw the Christmas tree was dark, where it was normally lit up, a beacon he would normally use to find the town.

This was his first stop. From here he would continue across America and then head out to other countries.

There was a small park near the first house he planned to visit and he landed in the white fluff of the light snowfall. In the wan light of the moon, the snow glistened like glass, reflecting the light as if a thousand stars had fallen to earth.

Climbing off the sleigh, he patted each reindeer in turn, the animals sniffing and growling playfully. Each reindeer was covered in a thin sheen of perspiration from the long flight from the North Pole and their breath blew out on great clouds as they exhaled.

No sooner did Santa turn and walk away, then the reindeer began to root under the light snow, searching for tender grass. Santa looked all around him, making sure it was clear. A spell of invisibility covered the reindeer, but only from sight. If a passerby stumbled into the sleigh or the animals, they would be in for quite a surprise. Thus was the reason why he landed in the park and from there would make his rounds in a large section of the town. Then he would fly to the other side and do the same there. He rarely landed on rooftops such as the stories told as there was no room. Much like an airplane, he needed room to take off and land.

With his magic sack of toys over his shoulder, he began walking to the dark house fifty feet away.

As he exited the park to cross the road, he did see one lone figure in the shadows at the end of the street. He stopped to see what the figure would do but as he watched, the figure turned and shambled away, as if he or she was drunk. What was odd was the figure didn't seem to be wearing a coat, but looked as if he or she was wearing only pajamas. Shrugging his shoulders, deciding someone was out for a late night walk and must like the cold weather, Santa crossed the street to the house.

He scurried up the side of the home like a squirrel, using his Christmas magic to make himself lighter than air. Once on the roof, he made himself thinner and down the chimney he went.

Like a ghost, he shimmied down and came out into the living room, solidifying back into himself. He smiled as he shook his arms, the feeling always leaving his entire body tingling, much like when a person's leg falls asleep to then come back to circulation with pins and needles, only minus the pain.

The room was dark as well, the lights on the tree dead. He saw presents under the tree but they looked like they had been opened already. Or perhaps an animal had gotten into them. Ribbons and wrapping paper was scattered across the floor and he had to be careful not to step in it, or the crunch would awaken the residents.

Santa reached into a pocket and pulled out his magic notebook. Whatever house he was at, the notebook would show the names, ages and what the children wanted.

He saw there were three children in this particular home. Little Maggie, who was five, little Timmy, who was eight, and Baby Suzy, who was only a few months old. He read that Maggie wanted a dolly that sang songs and Timmy wanted a new video game system—the Z BOX.

He also read that both children had been good, or had been up until a month ago. Since communications had gone down, he wasn't able to update his notebook.

Santa reached into his magic toy sack and pulled out each present, placing them under the defunct tree.

He was about to leave when he heard the sound of small footsteps coming toward him. Turning around, he saw two small figures come running out of a side hallway and charge into the room. Before he could do anything, the two children were upon him, each lunging for him.

Little Timmy jumped high and latched onto Santa's right sleeve, his teeth trying to bite him. Only Santa's heavy red suit protected him from a wound. Little Maggie stayed on the floor and jumped for Santa's right boot. Her small teeth began gnawing on Santa's black boot like it was prime rib, while her tiny arms wrapped around his ankle.

"What in the name of Christmas?" Santa yelled at the two wild children who seemed to be trying to eat him, of all things. Though he would never hurt a child, he acted on instinct, too startled to think about what he was doing. Before either child could do him any damage, he plucked each one off him and tossed them to the couch a few feet away. The small bodies bounced off the cushions and rolled onto the floor. In a split second, both were on their feet again, each crouched low and growling. Timmy had material in his mouth and Santa realized it was a piece of his red suit.

Pulling a flashlight from his pocket, Santa turned it on and aimed the beam at the two tikes. He let out a gasp when he saw their faces.

Instead of two sweet visages of innocent youth, he saw two little monsters. Their eyes were sunken into their heads and their lips were pulled back on their faces, as if the skin had dried and pulled taut. Their teeth flashed in the beam of the light and their growling increased.

Santa saw both children's pajamas were covered in what looked like dried blood, and their eyes were a milky white, for all purposes void of emotion.

With a snarl and a moan, they came for him again, and he kicked out and sent them both rolling across the floor.

Not knowing what to do, fearful for the two children's well being, he broke his rule about being seen and ran deeper into the house, in search of the parent's bedroom. He found it easily enough, and with his flashlight bobbing up and down, he entered the room.

As the beam of light landed on the bed, he let out another gasp at the sight greeting him.

The mother and father were there in their bed, but they weren't *all there* exactly.

As Santa's eyes took in the scene before him, he saw that Mom was missing her arms and Dad only had one leg. All three of his other limbs were long gone and where they had been detached looked raw and torn, as if small teeth had worried away at the meat.

Both parents had large holes in their heads, as if something had been borrowing in their skulls, searching for the tender brains within. The bed was soaked in blood, and the once white sheets were nothing but a dark brown now. Flies buzzed about and the smell knocked Santa nearly on his butt, the charnel house odor potent beyond belief.

As he stumbled away from the murder scene, and back into the hallway, he looked back down the hallway to see the two children coming for him. Looking to his left, he saw another room and he dashed into it. He realized it was the baby's room. There was a crib in the corner and he stumbled over to it. But when he pointed the beam into the crib, all he saw were raw baby parts. A tiny arm, a piece of leg, a half a foot, and something that might have been an ear was all that lay in the crib. The sheets of the crib was also stained a dark brown, thanks to the blood drying weeks ago.

He turned when the door was forced in and the two children dashed into the room, both attacking Santa again. He used the flashlight and hit Timmy over the head, dazing the boy. When Maggie came for his leg, he kicked her away, then pushed Timmy with his free hand. Both little monsters fell into the corner. Acting fast, Santa pocketed the flashlight, and in the gloom of the room, he spun, picked up the crib and flipped it over, then used it like a cage to trap the two children. Baby parts spilled out to fall onto the floor as the two little monsters became trapped. They reached through the wooden bars of the crib, trying to reach him, but the bars were close together and they could only get their hands part way through.

Needing to catch his breath and try to make some sense to what was happening, Santa sat on the crib, thus trapping the two tikes.

Timmy and Maggie hissed and snarled as they fought like wild animals to get free.

Santa didn't get more than a few seconds respite before a shrill scream rent the night, followed by another and another after that.

Though the screams sounded almost human, he knew immediately it was his reindeer.

Jumping up, he dashed out of the bedroom and into the living room. No sooner did he leave the two children, then they pushed the crib off them and ran after Santa.

But Santa was already gone, up the chimney and onto the roof.

As he climbed down the side of the house, he stopped and cast a glance over his shoulder.

In the dark house, at a window facing the street, were the two children, clawing at the glass. One managed to smash a pane but neither could climb out, as the single pane was too small. They snarled and hissed as Santa ran across the street and back to the park.

Upon entering the park, Santa stopped short, his mouth hanging open at the sight before him.

Where his eight reindeer had been waiting for him, there was now nothing but bloody carnage from end to end. As for his reindeer, they were all dead, torn apart by what seemed to be *people*. There had to be more than fifty people huddled around his dead reindeer, each tearing at the carcasses, chewing on the meat. Some had their heads so far inside the stomachs of the reindeer that they couldn't be seen, while others had organs hanging from mouths as they chewed and swallowed, chewed and swallowed. Many of the people had stomachs so bloated with raw meat they looked ready to burst, and Santa took a step back in horror.

"Donner, Cupid, Comet, oh God no!" he yelled, too shocked to realize that calling attention to himself probably wasn't a very good idea.

As he yelled out, every person feeding on the carcasses stopped eating and poked their heads up, much like a wild animal would do upon spotting prey.

All eyes went to Santa Claus, who with his bright red suit, stood out like a white spot on a black piece of paper.

"Uh-oh," Santa said softly as he stared at the crowd of zombies with blood covering their faces and soaking into their clothes. In the moonlight, Santa could see their eyes, and he saw the same dead look that had been in the two children's.

Crunching snow caused him to spin around, and when he did, he found another dozen or more zombies surrounding him. As he watched them come for him, he put all the pieces together and realized the reason there had been no contact with the outside world from his village was that there had been a zombie apocalypse.

Santa found he had nowhere to go, all avenues of escape cut off. His mind raced with ideas of what he should do.

He knew about zombies from when he delivered toys to Haiti, and he knew to remove the head or destroy the brain would take them down for good. But he had no weapons, only the toys in his magic sack.

A zombie lunged for him, the first in the group, and Santa jumped out of the way, the body falling to the snow. Santa kicked the ghoul in the face, sending bloody teeth to splatter the snow like red hail. He spun when another zombie came for him and he used his belly, butting the ghoul in the chest as it tried to wrap its arms around him. Like a trampoline, the ghoul snapped back and fell into others.

Desperate for a weapon, Santa reached into his magic sack and pulled out the first thing that came to mind.

One half of a pair of women's ice skates.

The skate was black with white trim, and the blade was honed to perfection. It was suppose to be for a girl named Cindy, who lived in the next town. She wanted to be a figure skater.

Spinning the skate so that the blade pointed out, Santa used it when the next zombie came for him. This zombie was female with a red Christmas sweater on with a green Xmas tree on the front. As she lunged for Santa, he raised the skate and brought it down on her head. The skate slid into her skull like butter and he sawed it back and forth, cutting deep into the scalp and the brain within, nearly slicing her head in two. The woman dropped to the snow, all her Christmas cheer leaking out of her to soak into the snow.

Santa spun and used the skate on another ghoul, but when he whacked it in the head, the skate become stuck! Letting it go, he pushed the body away and reached into the magic sack for something else.

He came up with a handful of music CDs. Cracking the cases, he used them like mini throwing stars, adding a little Christmas magic to see them find their targets. The silver circles flew threw the air to become embedded in faces and chests. But this did nothing to stop the undead crowd and Santa went back in the sack for something else.

He came up with a hockey stick and he swung it like a madman. The blade connected with heads, and those that had muscle and tissue missing from their necks, found the hockey stick was more than a match for their weakened throats. Heads went flying and blood sprayed into the night air as Santa went to town on the undead horde.

Head after head went flying into the night until the hockey stick cracked and the tip broke off. Using it like a spear one last time, Santa jammed it into the chest of an attacking ghoul. It didn't stop the dead man but it did allow Santa a moment to reach into his magic sack and pull out another toy.

It was a toy train, the age level under three. It was made of soft plastic and had wheels that made noise when you squeezed them. Santa stared at it, wondering what he could do with it. Then he saw the pull string on the front. It was made so a child could pull it around the house, hearing the sounds it made as he did it.

Grabbing the pull string, Santa used it on the closest zombie. He wrapped it around the ghoul's neck like a garrote, then pulled it taut. String sank into dead flesh and as he used his bulk, he pushed on the zombie's back with his knee, causing the head to snap backwards and the back to arc. As the string severed the spine from the brain, the body collapsed to the snow.

More zombies surrounded him, and seen from above, he looked like one red dot surrounded by a sea of bodies.

His magic sack was pulled from his shoulder and he tried to get it back but was too slow.

As the ghouls came for him, he reached into his pockets and pulled out candy canes. Using them like small daggers, he jammed them into the eyes of the zombies. Sometimes the candy canes would go so deep that the brains would be punctured and the body would fall to the ground, but most of the time only blindness was the result.

From between the legs of the attacking horde, two smaller monsters crawled.

Little Timmy and Maggie had managed to wiggle through the broken window of their home and they were still hungry for Santa's flesh.

While Santa fought off the ghouls from on high, the two ghouls attacked from below, and Santa let out a cry as they wrapped their small arms around his legs. As he reached down to pull them off, his left sleeve rode up on his arm, exposing the pink skin of his wrist.

A geriatric zombie with a balding pate and a Christmas shirt that said, *KISS ME, I'M OLD, MERRY CHRISTMAS*, saw the opening in Santa's armor and took advantage of it. Yellow teeth sank into Santa's wrist, but not very deep and Santa barely felt the bite. When he spun to throw the kids away, the old man was knocked away also. Santa kept on fighting, oblivious to his wound.

He pushed through the undead crowd to try and break free, but there were too many! His eyes went to the zombie standing before him, one that was holding his magic toy sack!

Before the zombie knew what was happening, Santa reached out and pulled the sack back to him. Thinking of a toy he needed, he reached in and pulled out a high-powered BB gun.

It was fully loaded, and as fast as he could pump it, he shot each ghoul in the face, aiming for the eyes. It took more than one BB to put a zombie down, but when enough BBs penetrated into the brain through the eye sockets, down they went.

He exhausted his ammunition and then reached into the sack for more toys.

This time he was creative and he pulled out a large handful of firecrackers, M80's being a few of the more powerful ones.

As the zombies came for him, trying to bite, he lit the fuses and jammed the fireworks into their gaping maws.

There were muffled pops each time the firecrackers went off and a few heads exploded like a watermelon hit with a sledgehammer as the powerful firecrackers ignited.

But though he fought the good fight, Santa knew he was losing fast. Surrounded on all sides, he knew he couldn't keep up the battle indefinitely.

He came to a section of the park that the snow was crushed flat and he reached into his magic sack and pulled out two big handfuls of glass marbles. Tossing them onto the ground, the zombies began to slip and slide as they stepped on them, some falling so hard they cracked their heads open on the ice, staining it red.

Santa tried to see over the undead crowd to find a way to escape, but there was none.

He was about to give up hope and accept his reality, when a shadow flew over him, causing him to look up.

It was Blitzen!

Santa quickly realized he was mistaken when he had seen his reindeer killed and being eaten. With so much blood and animal parts strewn about, trying to count all the carcasses had been impossible and it was now clear that Blitzen had escaped, flying out of harm's reach.

And now he had come back for Santa.

Acting fast, Santa reached into his toy sack and pulled out two cans of silly string—yellow and pink. He sprayed these into the faces of the zombies, causing the ghouls to sputter and spit out the foul tasting foam.

Some were blinded momentarily and Santa used this as his chance to break free of the horde. Running as fast as his chubby legs would allow, he reached a small clearing in the center of the park.

Overhead, Blitzen floated down, and before the first zombie could reach them, Santa jumped onto the reindeer's back, Blitzen taking to the air once more.

As they flew high into the night sky, Santa looked below. Now, the dark town came into focus and he fully understood what it meant. As he looked on the horizon, where there should have been the lights of other towns, there was nothing but pitch darkness.

Breathing hard, Santa repositioned himself on Blitzen and said, "Let's go home, boy, there's no reason for us to stay here any longer."

With a snuff, the reindeer turned north, flew into the clouds and continued toward home.

Hours later, Santa and Blitzen arrived back at the North Pole.

Everyone gathered around, not understanding why Santa had returned so soon and why he was riding only one lone reindeer and was minus his sleigh.

Martha walked up to him and Santa kissed her on the cheek.

"It's as you feared," he told her. "It looks like there was a zombie uprising and that's the reason why the world has gone silent." He quickly filled them in on his night and what had happened to the other reindeer.

"Oh my lord, no," she said. "Those poor reindeer. Are you all right?"

He nodded, patting her arm. "Yes, yes, I'm fine. As I said, I ran into a town full of them but I managed to fend them off. But I have to be honest. If Blitzen hadn't arrived when he did, well..." he trailed off and she knew exactly what he was trying to say. She hugged him and muffled her sobs of happiness that he had returned to her.

Rufio pulled on Santa's jacket. "Santa, what are we going to do now?"

Santa shrugged. "There's nothing we can do, Rufio. The world as we know it is gone. There's no use for toys in a land of the walking dead. I guess we're out of business."

Other elves standing around them began to talk and murmur amongst themselves.

Santa raised his hands in the air to calm them. "Now, now, it's not so bad. At least we're safe here at the North Pole from whatever caused this terrible thing. We'll be fine and someday, when this is all over, we can go back to what we know and love. There's sure to be survivors."

More murmurs began and Santa quelled it once more. "That's enough for now. Tomorrow afternoon, there will be a village meeting in the main toy workshop. That's where we'll discuss what to do next. Now everyone, go back to your homes, I know for me it's been a long night and I need to rest."

Everyone began to shuffle away and Rufio pulled on Santa's jacket yet again. "Are you sure you're all right, Santa? Is there anything I can get for you? Do you need the village doctor?"

"No, Rufio, I'm fine, really, I'm just tired. I just need to sleep." Santa patted the elf on the head with a wan smile. Santa and Martha walked to their home, Martha asking question after question.

When they finally arrived home, Santa took off his blood-covered, torn red suit and went right to bed. He was so tired, which he didn't fully understand. He was immortal after all and normal ailments didn't affect him.

Martha made him a cup of hot cocoa and after he drank it he quickly he fell asleep.

He slept so heavily, some would say he slept like the dead.

As he tossed and turned, mumbling to himself about zombies and his slaughtered reindeer, the small bite on his wrist pulsed slightly as thin blue lines of infection crawled up his arm.

The next day would indeed be a memorable one for the North Pole, for in the morning, Santa would be a brand new man.

Or is that *dead* man?

GIFT EXCHANGE

RICK MOORE

Frank slid out of bed slowly, careful not to wake his wife, Melissa. The occasions were rare when she was able to have a lie-in, and just because his own internal body clock woke him at 5 a.m. without fail every morning, he saw no reason why anyone else should be woken as a result of it.

With this in mind, Frank slowly pulled closed the bedroom door, then stealthily made his way through the house toward the kitchen. His children, a boy aged fifteen named Andrew, and a girl Sandra, who was a year older, probably wouldn't emerge from their slumber for hours, well, not without repeatedly striking a gong next to their heads, so it was really only Melissa he needed to show any consideration to.

In the living room, Frank turned on the TV, hitting the mute button, knowing there was a five second interim between the transference from black screen to an actual picture. The night before, Melissa and he had watched *It's A Wonderful Life*, while the kids were in their rooms with the doors closed, doing whatever teenagers did when they retreated to their inner sanctums.

Probably playing video games or talking to their friends on line, Frank thought. *Or watching those dumb horror movies both of them were so enamored by of late.*

Frank knew it was only a phase, one they'd grow out of, but it sure bothered him to think of all that terrible stuff they sat watching day after day.

What had Sandra said the other day? Yes, that was it. She'd said the original *A Texas Chainsaw Massacre* was a classic. A classic!

On the TV, he saw *Miracle on 34th Street* was playing. Now that was a classic. And it had been on only a few minutes at most. He hit a sequence of buttons on the remote and the captions appeared at the bottom of the screen. In the movie, Mr. Gailey and little Suzie were watching the parade, commenting on a costumed character with an enormous head that had gotten turned around the wrong way.

`MR. GAILEY`: Looks like they're having a little trouble with the baseball player.

`SUZIE`: He was a clown last year. They just changed the head and painted him different.

Frank smiled, already being drawn into the movie, knowing every scene from seeing it so many times before, but still wanting to enjoy the experience all over again. He hurried to the tree and turned on the lights, then dashed to the kitchen to make coffee. As soon as the pot began to perk, he poured some Pumpkin Spice creamer into a mug, then returned to the living room to watch the movie.

The second he sat down on the couch, the commercials came on. The image of small children happily building a snowman was persuasive enough to hold his interest, but when Mom appeared carrying a silver platter laden with Holiday Burgers—turkey burgers that all the fast food joints were pushing this year—and the tykes abandoned their task in favor of tucking in to the grub, Frank shook his head disgusted, deciding instead to take a few moments to appreciate his Christmas tree.

Even though it was fake—Melissa detested real trees because of the needles they shed—he thought no Christmas tree could look more perfect. With the blinds still closed, it looked real to him. The effect of the twinkling lights shining off the ornaments was magical. Frank smiled, looking at the presents piled beneath it.

His smile suddenly faltered.

Now what the hell was that?

There beneath the tree sat a box-shaped package wrapped in brown paper and tied with string. The paper was wet, that much was obvious even from across the room. Whatever was inside must have spilled, because the bottom was even darker with wetness than the top, and whatever liquid the package contained was oozing through the paper, creating a stain on the carpet.

Was this one of the kids' idea of a joke? he wondered.

Frank was a temperate, placidly natured man, who rarely experienced anger, but he felt it now. The carpet was going to be ruined! And they'd only had it a year and a half. They hadn't even finished paying for it yet.

Frank jumped up from the couch and took long strides across the room. He squatted in front of the tree, then got down on his knees for a better look at the package. Written on the top in black marker, were the words, '*To Frank.*'

Melissa would never do such a thing, which meant one of his children had to be responsible.

Frank's heart was hammering so hard it felt like it would break through his chest. At his temples his pulse pounded; never in his life had he been more furious.

He reached out and touched two fingers to the oozing wet stuff at the base of the package. The stuff had a gluey, tarry quality and when he looked at his fingers, they dripped blobs of deep red gunk.

He was ready to raise hell, to go storming into Andrew and Sandra's bedrooms and demand an explanation. But when his hand reached for the string to lift the offending article, he found himself tugging the bow loose instead. The impulse to see what was inside could not be controlled. It was as though some other force had taken command, compelling him to open the package.

He yanked the string free and cast it aside. His fingers tore at the thick brown paper, which came away in sodden clumps. He stared in horror when he saw the box.

It was comprised of what appeared to be an intricate network of sinew and muscle. The box trembled slightly. Dark red fluids oozed and bubbled from the lid and sides, dripping like molasses and pooling on the carpet.

The sound Frank heard was unmistakable. It was the soft expulsion of air and the shallow intake of breath. The box was breathing—it was *alive.*

Frank's revulsion quickly morphed into panic. He wanted to run screaming, to get as far away from this aberration as possible, but when he tried to turn away, his limbs refused to move.

Shopping for gifts at the mall a few days earlier, Melissa and he had encountered a puppeteer's presentation of Tchaikovsky's *The Nutcracker.* Now he felt as though he'd been physically transformed into one of the wooden soldiers, with some unseen puppet master working his strings.

Despite his attempt to resist the impulse, his right hand reached out and touched the lid of the living box, caressing the interwoven threads of muscle.

"Help!" Frank tried to scream, but the only sound his throat produced was a soft clicking.

His hand took hold of the lid and flipped it open.

Again he was denied the need to scream. As he looked into the box and saw what it contained, his mouth twisted into a crooked 'O' shape. The quiet gasp that escaped him—or escaped whatever controlled him—contained only a fraction of his terror.

The head in the box was alive and it looked up at him with wide unblinking eyes.

"Hello, Frank," the head said. "Merry Christmas, my friend."

Aside from being decapitated at the neck, the head showed no other signs of abnormality. It was the head of a man, roughly the same age as Frank. The head's hair was cut in a short conservative style, much like Frank's own, and the face was clean shaven.

"Now where are my manners?" the head said. "The name's Frank. Well, Frank too. What I mean is, Frank Two."

"What..." Frank managed to whisper. "Are you?"

"Are you fucking deaf or something?" the head asked. "I just told you. Christ on a Christmas tree. Not too sharp are you, Frankie boy? I'm Frank Two. Got it? No? Well, tough shit. Explanations bore me and you wouldn't get it even if I tried. Can we just get on with it? You have no idea how long I've been waiting inside this fucking box. I hope you've got something to drink in the house. Fucking parched I am. None of that weak frothy stuff either. A man's drink, that's what I'm saying. I don't suppose you've got any weed laying around here somewhere? Or a bit of Charlie? What I wouldn't give for a couple of lines. Well, it is Christmas after all. If you can't indulge at Christmas, when can you?"

"What..." Frank said through vocal cords that felt as though some invisible hand constricted them. "Is...this?"

The lights from the Christmas tree shone in the eyes of the head in the box, making them *appear* to glow red. Wait, not appear to glow, Frank realized. They really *were* glowing. Then they started flashing, green, blue, red, yellow and white. As the eyes continued to flash their festive spectrum of colors, the head opened its mouth and a scratchy gramophone recording flowed out, as a full choir sang.

Ding dong merrily on high,
In hell the bells are ringing,
Ding dong! verily the fires
Are writhing with demons singing.
Glor-or-or-or-or, Or-or-or-or-or, Or-or-or-or-or-or, Gloria.
Lucifer in Excelsis!
(cracks and pops, and a stuck needle)
Lucifer in Excelsis-Excelsis-Excelsis-Excelsis.

The head's mouth abruptly clamped shut, the tinny sounding carol continuing, muffled now that the thing's lips were closed. The head swallowed, an exaggerated gulping sound emitting from the area of its throat, and the music was gone.

"I could answer your question, Frank," the head said. "I could. But I won't. You'll find out my friend. In the fullness of time, you'll understand everything. Right now though, there's the little matter of us completing our gift exchange. My gift to you was the surprise of a lifetime. You know the beauty of a gift like that, Frank? The beauty, is that it's the gift that keeps on giving. Don't believe me? Look over your shoulder. Go on. Take a peek at what's standing behind you."

Frank heard the soft patter of feet on the carpet. He felt the force that had taken complete control of his body loosen its hold. When he tried to turn his head, it moved without resistance. Looking over his shoulder, he saw all his family standing behind him.

His boy Andrew only had on a pair of boxers. His hair stuck up in clumps. His daughter Sandra was wearing the oversized shirt she always slept in. Melissa, his wife, stood there naked, which was how she preferred to sleep. All three wore the biggest grins Frank had ever seen, their mouths stretched wider than he would have thought possible.

Looking at them, he knew the thing in the box had to be controlling them, too, manipulating their flesh to produce the frozen rictus expressions they wore.

Though their eyes were open, they were rolled back in their heads, so that only whiteness showed.

In unison, Frank's family called, "It's Christmas! Merry Christmas one and all!"

Smiling and speaking English never went hand in hand—grinning less so. What actually came out was, "It's Clistnas! Nelly Clistnas ong ang orr!"

Their mouths suddenly relaxed, regaining their normal shapes, but their eyes remained rolled back. As one, the three of them burst into song. "Good tidings we bring, to you and your head, we wish you a Merry Christmas and a Happy New Year."

"Aww," the head cooed appreciatively, sounding genuinely touched. "Isn't that special, Frank? Doesn't it just warm the cockles of your heart?"

Frank looked back at the head in the box, or rather his head swiveled with no real direction. From the corner of the head's right eye, trickled a blood-red tear.

"Sorry, Frank," the head said. "I always was a sucker for a bit of mawkish sentimentality." Somehow the head in the box shook from side to side as though to clear away what it was feeling. The tear became translucent, then disappeared. Composed, the head smiled up at him. "Okay, family!" it called. "On with the festivities. Melissa, the table cloth, please. Andrew, be a good lad and plug in the carving knife. Sandra, if you'd be so kind as to be my escort."

Frank's wife and son went off to the kitchen. Sandra moved past her father and picked up the head in the box. Frank's limbs jerked, and he awkwardly stood. Again, he tried to resist, to will his body to do as it was told. Again, his efforts made no difference. In herky-jerky fashion, he lurched then lumbered, lurched then lumbered, until at last he stood facing the kitchen table.

Melissa had spread her best table cloth over it, the luxurious red and gold one they used every Christmas at dinnertime. She was sitting in her usual place, to the left of the table head. Directly across from her sat Andrew, also in his usual place, the carving knife plugged into an outlet and set before him. Sandra moved past Frank to the place where every father traditionally sat. She set the box down, then reached in with both hands and gently removed the head. Blood dripped from the neck and ran through her fingers, pattering the table cloth. Sandra set the head at the head of the table, then moved away, taking her usual place beside her brother. Her eyes, like her sibling and mother, were still rolled back, the white they showed glistening off the light coming through the kitchen window.

"Why the long faces?" the head asked. "It's a celebration! Smile family. Smile!"

At the head's command, as though invisible fingers were hooked into either side, the mouths of all three stretched wide, and were pulled upward, exposing their upper teeth.

"Let us pray," the head solemnly intoned.

Frank's wife and his offspring clapped their hands together as though in supplication, elbows jutting.

The head exaggeratedly cleared its throat. "For what I am about to receive, may my Lord make me truly thankful. Amen."

"Amen," those gathered at the table repeated.

Frank's hips twisted and turned. His body was flung across the table—landing back first with a heavy thud—his neck snapping back and his head connecting hard enough with the cloth-covered wood to make spots dance before his eyes. He tried to push himself up but to no avail. He felt as though his arms and legs were tied by unseen ropes and four hundred pounds of pressure weighed down on his chest.

"If nobody minds," the head said. "I think I'm going to open my Christmas present early. Andrew, would you mind doing the honors?"

Frank's son stood up. He picked up the carving knife and used his thumb to push down on the power button. The knife's serrated teeth buzzed to life, the sound of its motor and rotating blades breaking the silence.

Frank, reduced to a terrified mind trapped inside a body no longer his to control, could only lie there, watching as his grinning white-eyed son leaned in with the knife. He felt the blades chew through the skin of his neck. Felt the cold, alien sensation of steel sawing into his Adam's apple, splitting it in two, and the searing pain that followed. Andrew continued to work the knife, cutting deeper. Frank's vocal cords snapped. Blood sprayed out, coating his son's fingers, splashing both his wife and daughter. They only sat there, grinning insanely as his blood dripped from their faces and pooled on the tablecloth around his head.

A sanguine bubble formed on Frank's lips, his final breath pushing it from his mouth. The bubble burst, flecking his cheeks with the last of his life force. A hot jet of blood squirted from his neck and hit him in the left eye, blinding him on one side. Moments later, his vision dimmed in the right side also, as he dropped into darkness and died.

*　*　*

Frank's eyes snapped open as he woke from the worst nightmare he'd ever had in his life.

Thank God, he thought. *It was all a dream. That'll teach me not to eat mince pies before going to bed.*

He blinked a few times, realized it must still be night, and waited for his eyes to become accustomed to the darkness. He tried to sit up in bed and couldn't move. A moment before light flooded his world, it dawned on him that he wasn't breathing.

It took a few seconds for his eyes to become accustomed to the sudden intrusion of light, and a few more for the indistinct shapes to form and take on meaning.

In front of his face was pulsating muscle and sinew. Moving his eyes to the left, he saw the same, and the same again to the right. Directly above, three inches away from the top of his head, on either side and in front, were three straight edges. He didn't need to see the fourth edge, beyond his field of vision, to know that he was inside a box. Or more specifically, that he was now the severed head inside the box. He knew this because of the world that existed beyond the confines of his new home.

His family were out there, seated at the kitchen table; nothing about them had changed. They were still in their white-eyed trance-like state, lips peeled so far back their gums were exposed, cheek muscles pulled taut, straining to hold their grins in place.

Some time must have passed because each now wore a party hat. Melissa, naked except for the crepe paper crown, was in the process of unwrapping one of the gifts he'd bought her.

When the packaging was removed, she opened the small box and took out the earrings, holding them to her ears. "Frank, they're beautiful. Thank you."

It sounded like, "*Vang. Ve're vuvival. Vang u.*"

"Don't mention it, sweetheart," said a voice from behind.

Then Frank saw who had spoken. He leaned in, the head that was in the box—the head that was now attached to Frank's body—leaned in close to the box and smiled down at Frank. There was a thick line of scar tissue at the neck, raw and pink.

"Nice choice, Frank," Frank Two said. "She's going to look lovely in them. I think I'll have her wear them tonight while I'm fucking her."

Frank Two withdrew and went around the table. He leaned over Melissa's shoulder so she could plant a thank you kiss on his cheek. The thing that had stolen his body reached out and squeezed Melissa's breasts, then held each in his palms, weighing them. "Nice titties for a woman her age. As for me though..." Frank Two walked around to the table's other side, and rested his chin on Sandra's shoulder. He reached around with both hands for a grope. "I like 'em young and firm. I think the left one might be a little larger than the right. But then again, as Francis Bacon put it, 'There is no excellent beauty, that hath not some strangeness in the proportion.' Right, Frankie boy?"

Tears welled in Frank's eyes and ran down his face. When he tried to speak, he felt a vibrating sensation where his vocal cords had been severed, and understood that he'd become one with the box, fused to the living-flesh out of which it was constructed. "Please..." Frank begged, the word a hoarse whisper. "Please don't do this."

"Already a done deal, Frank," Frank Two said. He stopped fondling one of Sandra's breasts, then used the free hand to rub at the scar line across his neck. "Now you see it..." When the hand came away, the scar was gone. "Now you don't. Your family won't even know anything has changed. Not even when I let them come almost completely back from where I sent them. Nobody will know. They never do. I'll be the same Frank to them I always was. This isn't something new, Frank. The old head switcheroo, it's as old as...well, as old as Christmas."

Frank's sobs turned to soft laughter, laced with the first fall of madness. "You become me and I become you. Is that it?"

"Well..." Frank Two said. "Not exactly. You'll find out soon enough."

From the front door came the sound of somebody knocking.

"Looks like very soon."

Frank Two picked up the box containing Frank's head, carried it to the door under one arm, and opened it.

"What about its lid?" inquired a voice like a thousand whispers echoing for all eternity.

"I suppose you've seen enough nasty stuff for one day, Frankie boy," Frank Two said, then held out the box and addressed the owner of the voice. "I'll run and get it."

When Frank's head looked up and saw the living nightmare that had come to collect him, he was thankful his replacement still retained some notion of the Christmas spirit.

CHRISTMAS EVE AT PARK THEATER

ELIZABETH MARSHALL

The proscenium glittered with tinsel and icicles. The carved wall ornament was hung with wreaths. Red bows and mistletoe dangled from every ceiling coffer and chandelier. Waiting outside Park Theater, the crowd chattered and laughed with the anticipation that always colors Christmas Eve. This year's production was rumored to be more fantastic than ever before. It was to have its usual features—elf dancers, red and green, Santa and his sleigh— but with a twist at the end. Everyone was excited. That is everyone except Stage Director Thomas Monroe. Closing night was moments away and the star ballerina hadn't been seen in hours.

"Josephine will have to take her place!" Thomas declared. "Sandra, help Josephine get into costume. Thirty minutes till curtain!"

Josephine obediently followed Sandra backstage.

"I can't do this," Josephine whispered, shaking her head.

"You'll be fine. You've practiced it a thousand times," Sandra soothed.

"I just wasn't planning on this. I'm not ready," Josephine continued as she slipped the flimsy white dress over her head.

"Just breathe," Sandra said, pulling the skirt down from where it had collected at Josephine's waist. "This is your chance to be the star. I would kill to play Snow Queen for a night."

Josephine nodded shyly. The truth was, there was nothing Josephine liked less than to be the center of attention. And she knew Marlise—wherever she was—would be furious with her for stealing the spotlight.

The orchestra was playing a whimsical rendition of 'We Wish You a Merry Christmas' as the doors opened and the crowd poured into the lobby. Joshua Brennan, a small boy of eight, gazed around in wonder. Not an inch of space had been left unadorned. The already decorative walls had been splattered with ornaments, wreaths and garlands in the richest reds and golds. The central chandelier dripped with holiday decorations. Tinsel and mistletoe hung from every dangling crystal. The curved staircase and bar area overflowed with the sounds of pleasant conversation and laughter. Everyone wore a smile.

Despite the jubilation surrounding him, Joshua felt a sort of unease. The chatter and clinking glasses seemed to meld into a dissonant noise that almost hurt his ears. The mouths and teeth forming such cheerful words seemed for a moment to gnash at him menacingly. Joshua looked around in a quick panic, searching for a way out of the crowd. He spotted the main lobby doors, the curved staircases leading to the mezzanine, the restrooms. He breathed in and out. He looked down and closed his eyes. His tension began to fade.

"Joshie, are you okay? You look scared," his mother asked, bending forward. She placed her blood-red lips on his cheeks in a comforting gesture. "Are you worried about Santa coming? I wouldn't worry. I have it on good authority that Santa's coming tonight!"

For some reason, this gave Joshua little comfort. As sweet as she was, Joshua's mother had always underestimated him. Joshua, of course, knew that sometimes his anxieties—as his mother called them—came in anticipation of not so good things.

The chaos settled as everyone took their seats, and the audience filled with hushed murmurs about the show. Some thought the surprise ending would involve aerialists; others thought it would incorporate pyrotechnics. There were rumors of a snow machine. No one was certain what was coming. The orchestra was playing 'Jingle Bells' as the crowd waited.

Before the final chord resolved, Bernard Bartlett, Master of Ceremonies, leapt onto the stage. "Ladies and gentlemen!" he began, "Welcome to Christmas Eve at the Park Theater! Tonight, you will watch the unique and beautiful tale of a large white-haired man and his eight tiny reindeeeeeeeerrr!" His voice boomed, echoing through the auditorium to the upper reaches of the balcony. A flautist in the orchestra trilled a high, sharp note. The audience applauded wildly.

Joshua clapped softly with the crowd, denying the discomfort once again stirring in his belly. He couldn't quite place his fear. Christmas Eve was usually such a careless time.

Bernard continued, his words quickening, "You, of course, know the story of Santa Claus and the challenge he faces every year, delivering presents to every good little boy and girl in the WORLD!" Pausing several seconds, Bernard then concluded, "But you likely have not heard about the trouble he ran into on a Christmas Eve very much like this one, when he encountered an evil Snow Queen and her band of violent thieving elves!" The flautist trilled again, this time a higher, sharper note. The audience once again cheered with the passion of an angry mob.

But the Snow Queen is usually a good character, Joshua thought. He was confused.

"TONIGHT, ladieeeeeess and gentlemeeennnn, the conclusion of this story is one the likes of which you've never considered. It will, my friends, not be told quite this way ever again. Be prepared for a spectacle beyond your wildest dreams! A spectacular performance! A fantastic show! Excitement! Surprise! Ladies and gentlemen, I give you... Santa Clauuusssss and the Snow Queeeeeeenn!"

The crowd roared.

The curtain went up in a violent jerk, revealing a collection of glittering silver trees. A lone dancer clothed in a flowing white gown gracefully twirled her way through the forest, pausing to leap and pose in beautiful curving positions at each clearing. Josephine didn't actually look at the audience until she reached the apron of the stage, turning a series of slow pirouettes in front of a full-length mirror. Cotton snow fell gently around her as she transitioned into a stunning arabesque. The audience applauded. The loveliness of Josephine's movements was astounding. As her legs relaxed, Josephine realized she had never, until that moment, been so fully herself. She felt reborn, as if leaping into the world for the first time. The audience cheered its overwhelming, thunderous approval as she struck her final pose, holding it a few moments longer than the music required.

Backstage, Thomas moved in the shadows, covering Blitzen with a sheet. Before her mysterious disappearance, Marlise had dropped Blitzen off at the theater to be dressed in his reindeer costume, mentioning to Thomas that the dog hadn't been right since getting in a minor scuffle with another very aggressive dog that morning. Blitzen had walked away with only a small bite. The vet thought he'd recover, but then Thomas found him dead. Concerned that the dog's sudden and strange demise would upset the cast mid-show, he hid Blitzen's body in a dark, backstage corner. He didn't want Marlise finding out about her dog after everyone else.

Following her solo, Josephine rushed backstage, climbing a ladder to the catwalk extending across the fly tower. She shuffled into a waiting sleigh positioned just behind the top of the curtain. The audience couldn't see the shining red vessel, which was set on an automatic timer that would initiate its flight downward at the conclusion of the next scene.

Josephine watched from above as the elves pranced toward the front of the stage, skipping into formation.

The lead elf, Christine, was a petite, young woman. She leapt through the other dancers, her pointed toes lifting high in the air, effortlessly propelling into a series of grand jetés and fouetté turns. Her balance was near perfect until her third leap, when her eyes started to itch. She began to blink erratically as she spun, using every inch of strength in her muscled legs to maintain her balance. A chill cut sharply through her body.

Christine looked nervously over the audience as she danced, feeling her control slip. She focused briefly on a man and woman sitting in the third row. Something about their expressions caught her attention. Their eyes, bright and eager only moments before, had begun to narrow. Christine wondered if one of the dogs had come loose behind her or if one of the holiday wreaths had fallen. She completed two revolutions, spotting the couple again on her third twirl. The couple's faces had shifted, their worry clearly about more than disrupted decorations.

Blitzen had emerged from his resting place. He looked skeletal—dead, even. He was missing large patches of fur. Snarling and pawing at the stage floor, he was in a rage. He jerked his neck in quick, hectic movements as he looked around. His teeth gnashed and his red eyes bulged. Chunks of clotted blood dripped from the massive hole by his jaw. He moved very quickly toward Christine.

Before she had a chance to react, Blitzen pounced, his teeth sinking into the meat of her calf, ripping the flesh of the bottom half of her leg entirely off in one vicious jerk of his head. He spat out the meat, letting a deep, wet growl escape through his spasms. He began devouring Christine's lovely calf, stripping the skin and muscle as if he'd been served a fried chicken leg. Christine had built up such momentum in her series of turns that the stump where her leg used to be propelled her around in one final revolution. Spurting from her wound, a stream of blood sprayed the audience as she spun, catching the couple in the third row in the eyes and mouth. Some of the blood struck Joshua's mother. Joshua screamed. His mother clawed at her face, frantically wiping the red goo from her eyes. Christine finally toppled over, shrieking as an ever-widening circle of gore flooded the stage around her.

While the crowd ran frantically for the doors, one man flew to the stage to help Christine. Leaning over the young dancer, he used his shirt to tie a clumsy tourniquet at her thigh. It was too late. Christine was already dead. Moving with great urgency, the man tried again and again to resuscitate her.

Christine's heart had stopped for minutes when she began to stir. She opened her eyes again, looking up at the man who was hectically moving his open mouth over hers blowing air into her lifeless lungs. She was glad to have a snack ready and waiting.

Attempting to save face, Bernard Bartlett once again got on the microphone.

"Its all part of the show, folks!" Bernard declared from one of the high, false balconies flanking the proscenium, throwing his shaky voice to the back of the auditorium.

But it was too late. Santa Claus came up slowly behind him and ripped out his throat. Chomping wildly at Bernard's delicious raw flesh, Old Saint Nick filled his big belly. He was ravenous.

Joshua and his parents ran for the lobby. As they exited their row, Joshua took one last look at the anarchy on stage. Christine was twitching and eating, red flesh spewing from her mouth and pouring down her chin. The man who had rushed to help her was mostly dead, although his feet kicked slightly as Christine plucked an ear from his head as if pulling a thick grape from a vine. She snacked and chomped slowly, savoring the taste. Santa shambled onto the stage and began grabbing and devouring several of the slower elves that had stayed to help poor Christine.

The orchestra's cheery, staccato version of 'Here Comes Santa Claus' ended as quickly as it began. A pile of hungry, frenzied reindeer pounced on the conductor, ripping and clawing at his eyes and mouth. The conductor stabbed Comet through the eye with his baton before succumbing to the dogs. Comet struggled briefly and fell to the ground, dead for the second time that evening.

Joshua's parents pulled at his arms, leading him out of the auditorium. Thousands of other people ran with them, jamming together in the exit rows and hallways until they reached the lobby, which was so packed with fleeing pageant-goers that no one could move. Joshua could see only legs and midsections of those who had corralled him in. He began breathing in and out very quickly, the panic rising in him as he realized he was trapped. The crowd reached the lobby to find that the main doors were, of course, locked.

Joshua looked up in a panic at his mother. She was rubbing her face where Christine's blood had stained her skin, forming an odd, crusted death mask around her eyes. She had grown very pale, her eyes red.

"I don't... feel so..." His mother's voice trailed off as her body jerked and fell to the ground in a violent spasm.

Joshua's father fell to the ground beside her, feeling her mouth and cheeks with his face to see what was wrong.

"She has a fever," he announced desperately as her body went limp in his arms. "We have to get her out of here. Find another way out!" Joshua's father commanded desperately as he hoisted his wife's dead weight over the low height walls of the concession stand. "We'll wait here! Be careful, son!"

Joshua instinctively ran for the large, curved lobby stairs. Despite the droves of people pushing their way down from the mezzanine and balcony, Joshua was small for his age and able to slip through the crowd with relative ease. He clamored and climbed his way upward.

There must be another way out. There must be another door, he thought.

He reached the mezzanine lobby, where the crowd had thinned. A few people were still fleeing their seats, each running toward the stairs wearing the terrified expression of a person who knows he is last to escape.

One of the wild, bloody elves Joshua could swear he had seen crushed by Santa on stage only minutes before was squatting on the bar, feasting on the arm of an unfortunate man who now ran dramatically for the stairs, screaming at an unbearable pitch as blood surged from his wound, sprinkling those around him with each squirt.

Joshua ran by the bar, the elf too consumed in her affairs to notice the small delicious boy. Taking the stairs two and three at a time, Joshua threw his body upward, climbing as high as he could in the ancient theater. Perhaps there would be a door to the roof or another place where he and his parents could hide. Or perhaps there would be another elf waiting for him at the very top.

The stairs ended at a hallway. Draped in tinsel and ornaments, the gaily appointed space was flooded with light and filled with the cheerful sounds of holiday music. As he ran toward the waiting, open door that would lead him to the upper reaches of the balcony seating, young Joshua completed what would have, under normal circumstances, looked like a scene from a greeting card—a small boy galloping through a decorated space in his red and green holiday sweater. Circumstances were, however, not normal.

The balcony seating area was very dark, the lights having been dimmed for the show. Emerging from the hallway, he moved slowly, cautiously. The area had been entirely abandoned, the ghosts of five hundred empty seats outlined against the bright stage lighting below. It wasn't until that moment, when he briefly felt safe in the quiet balcony area, that Joshua allowed his brain to process the horror he had beheld. The silence of the balcony contrasted sharply with the screams and yells that filled the rest of the theater, making the terror more present—more real—than before.

Even if he found a way out, he would have to go back down there, with the bloody elves and reindeer, with the hungry Santa and whatever else waited. He blocked from his mind the real source of his mounting anxiety. There was now a great distance between him and his parents...and his mother was very ill.

Josephine had been watching the events taking place on stage in quiet horror, too scared to consider leaving the safety of her hiding place. She didn't notice the sleigh was moving until the bells began to sound. She grappled quickly for the ladder, but was too late. The ladder was already out of reach.

Designed to depart diagonally from its position behind the curtain to center stage, the sleigh was supported on a thin wire cable. It was planned that, concurrent with the sleigh flight, a series of silver bells would chime a bold cheerful song that would be piped throughout not only the auditorium, but also the lobby and restrooms. The brilliant carol, marking the dramatic entrance of the Snow Queen, reverberated throughout the theater on schedule.

Josephine watched in horror as the blood-stained things that had become of Santa's little helpers looked up. Wide, dripping grins spread across each of their small faces as Josephine began her unwilling descent. The elves flailed as they shambled toward the sleigh, their arms out, ready to receive the Snow Queen. Those who could no longer walk crawled and slid through the river of blood that now soaked the stage floor.

Apart from the scene surrounding her, Josephine was the image of an angel. Her sparkling, snowy costume reflected beads of tiny white lights on the ceiling and walls. Her hair, with shades of gold and amber, tumbled over her shoulders, framing perfectly the soft features of her face. Her ordinarily healthy, flushed cheeks were, however, at the moment an unnatural shade of white.

Dead. They were dead, she thought, struggling to believe.

Only minutes before, the elves had been happily whirling their way through the silver forest, and now gnawed wildly at everything in their path. Shuffling, writhing and clawing in their slow, jumbled dance, the elves hissed, spit and laughed as she moved inexorably toward them, the bells hollering and taunting, announcing her arrival. Josephine's eyes followed the cable, looking everywhere for something she could grab to lift her out of the path of the waiting mouths below.

She knew she had only ten seconds before the sleigh would complete its flight, maybe nine. The only thing within reach was the icicle garland that dangled in low scallops from the proscenium. She grappled desperately for the tinsel-covered wire, grabbing hold as tightly as she could, in the hope that she might use it to lift her from the sleigh. She didn't know if she would be able to hold on for long, but seeing no other option, grabbed at it with all her strength.

Secured with only small tacks, the icicle garland came off easily in her hands. She screamed in dismay, her eyes widening. The bells continued their intolerable jingle. She couldn't think. Only five seconds—if she was lucky—from the termination of her ride, mid-air above the stage; there was nowhere to go.

There were at least twenty of them waiting for her. The flimsy plastic icicles affixed to the garland would be poor weapons. She wasn't sure she was even capable of using them if it came down to it. She couldn't imagine the feeling; piercing that oozing, red flesh with a dull plastic spear. She nearly vomited at the thought.

Looking down with terror at the gathering crowd that pawed and leered at the falling sleigh, waiting for her arrival with their bloodied mouths open crazily, she knew she wouldn't have even the smallest chance of fighting them off. They moved slowly, but there were too many of them. Looking up, Josephine noted that the sleigh's flight had been quick, traveling over twenty feet already. As the sleigh passed through a circular spotlight, she remembered briefly the triumph of her earlier performance. There had been nothing more terrifying to her than taking center stage—until now.

She knew the only chance she had was the cable.

In the final moment before the sleigh landed and was descended upon by the flesh-hungry monsters, she leapt upward, grabbing the thin cable supporting the sleigh, her legs swinging wildly as she transferred her weight. She knew the thin cable would slice her skin if she put all her weight on it and it did. She grabbed as tightly as she could, slashing her perfect white palms deeper every moment. Small droplets of blood rained onto the stage, taunting the hungry sharks below as they swiped at her dangling feet. Luckily, the elves were petite and couldn't quite reach her toes. Santa was, however, very tall.

Upon hearing the bells, Joshua had rushed to the balcony edge, watching Josephine's slow descent in horror. Relieved, he saw her avoid Santa's lumbering, six foot frame as she leapt from the cable to the stage. She had just enough time to escape up the steep stairs into the fly tower. Santa didn't seem to have the coordination to follow. Josephine crept as high upward as she could go, climbing out onto the catwalk, where she waited.

Joshua had been distracted by Josephine's plight. His attention shifted when, amidst the shrieks and screams ringing through the theater, he heard a low growl not very far away. It wasn't loud, but before turning to look, he instinctively knew it was directed at him.

Blitzen stood at the topmost level of the seating, growling—louder now—at Joshua, who was perched twenty or thirty rows below, leaning against the balcony edge. Blitzen pawed the seat in front of him, his matted, crusted fur sticking out at odd angles, framing his terrifying hollow stare.

He began to charge.

Rushing forward, Blitzen galloped over fifteen rows of seats in a matter of seconds before leaping, his teeth bared, ready to sink into the boy's flesh. Joshua threw his body to the floor, narrowly missing Blitzen, who flew over the balcony edge, roaring.

Blitzen's howls were cut abruptly short.

Joshua peered over into the seating area, finding the dog impaled on a large glass icicle ornament that must have fallen from the decorations adorning the balcony edge.

As he leaned over, watching Blitzen in his final moments, he looked around the auditorium. His eye caught a sliver of strange light bleeding through a crack in an auditorium door. He realized the door was slightly ajar. Joshua moved quickly, making his way down the stairs to the mezzanine balcony overlooking the lobby.

Some people had managed to force themselves through the crowd blocking the main doors, to escape into the night. Others still ran about the lobby frantically.

There was blood everywhere. Joshua found the concession stand where he had left his parents. A bit of hope filled him when he spotted his mother standing with her back to him. She turned instinctively, looking up at Joshua, a bloody grin stretched across her dead face. His father was motionless in pool of blood at her feet. Horrified, Joshua ran back up to the balcony.

The fly tower was oddly quiet. Crouching on the catwalk, Josephine remained still, knowing even the smallest movement would cause the rickety walkway to creak and groan. Her heart pounded so fiercely she was certain its thumping would rattle the flimsy metal planks supporting her weight. She somehow maintained the silence for several minutes. It seemed the undead had lost interest in her. Then, she heard something.

The rhythmic thudding at first seemed far away. As it grew louder, she realized the thuds were slow steps. The sound wasn't getting louder—it was getting closer. One rung at a time, some-one...some *thing* was coming for her.

Thump! Thump!

The sound of flesh slapping metal, moving upward in deter-mined, clumsy steps. It wouldn't be long now. Allowing the catwalk to squeak loudly, Josephine stood, backing away from the mysteri-ous climber toward the end of the catwalk. The stairs were entirely shrouded in darkness.

She didn't instantly recognize Marlise, who shambled discon-nectedly toward her from the opposite end of the catwalk. Once a vision of grace, Marlise's lethargic, heavy movements nearly threw her off balance.

She continued toward Josephine, trailing a streak of clumpy dark liquid along the handrail as she steadied herself. She man-aged a grisly smile as she came fully into the light, looking right at Josephine. She growled a hollow, guttural noise at the crouching, terrified dancer. Despite her slow steps, Marlise was making progress and Josephine was running out of time. Josephine screamed.

In an unexpected grand finale, Marlise picked up some speed, wobbling at Josephine with her arms out, and awkwardly extended before her. Marlise intended to grab Josephine at the throat.

With no weapons and Marlise blocking the only means of es-cape, Josephine did the only thing she could. She removed her dress in one quick movement, throwing the white fabric in Marlise's face as she charged. The low catwalk railings, tipped easily and Marlise's already off-balanced lumbering form toppled over the catwalk, collapsing several Christmas trees as she fell onto the stage below.

Josephine leaned over the catwalk railing in her undergar-ments, watching Marlise's body twitch and thrash. As she looked up, she saw a young boy gesturing wildly from the balcony. He was waving at her and moving too quickly to be one of *them*. He was pointing downward. Josephine followed his line of site to a side door that was slightly ajar.

As he motioned to Josephine from the balcony edge, Joshua began to feel uneasy with his back to the seats. A low rumbling was churning in the hallway above.

Concerned with getting Josephine's attention, he hadn't noticed the group of ten or twenty of those disgusting undead things making their way toward him, shuffling and crawling, ambling in their dripping, carnivorous way. They had smelled his flesh.

Without thinking, Joshua clumsily threw his weight over the balcony edge, grabbing at the hanging beads and garlands, hoping something he held onto would be strong enough to break his fall.

Just as the thin string of garland pulled off the balcony, the undead pageant-goers leaned over the edge, unwittingly pressing their weight against the top of the garland, providing just enough tension for Joshua to dangle and drop to the auditorium floor.

Seeing Joshua's leap of faith, Josephine knew it was time. She ran for the dark catwalk edge where Marlise had climbed up only minutes before.

Slipping down the rungs of the ladder as fast as she could manage, she descended to the stage floor and sprinted toward the door.

The majority of the undead were rambling about the theater too slowly to react. Only Santa Claus stood in the way. A few steps ahead of Josephine, Joshua had avoided the bearded old man, flinging the door open and running into the night. Santa now turned his attention to Josephine.

The only thing Josephine had going for her was speed. If Santa reached the door before she did, she knew she was finished.

She would never be able to get the door open with Santa's weight pressing it closed. She had only seconds. Santa clawed at her, wobbling toward her with outstretched arms as she passed, his fingernails slicing the skin of her arm as she ran by him, flinging the door open and running into the night.

Josephine spotted Joshua emerging from the shadows where he had waited. There was nothing worse than to be alone on Christmas Eve. The two ran without talking, moving down the center of the street, avoiding the slow-moving bloody things that were emerging from homes and buildings throughout the neighborhood.

The two paused to look back upon the twinkling lights of the city, only when they were far enough away that they could no longer hear the screams.

Josephine suggested they rest briefly. She was feeling a little dizzy and her arm had started to itch where she had been scratched.

IT JUST DOESN'T TASTE LIKE CHRISTMAS

DANE T. HATCHELL

Little Freddy Purple's most favorite time of the year was Christmas. The house became a cozy place adorned with the spirit of the season. The electric candles in the window, the Christmas tree in the living room, and the purple colored lights strung with precision out front. The house became a shiny shrine; a modern way to celebrate the winter solstice. A time of love, he and his whole family would share together.

When he would look out of the window, at all the snow and lifeless trees, it would be the fireplace that would bring him hope. It was secure, a refuge during the frozen emptiness of winter. The sizzling flames would make the wood crackle; ejecting blue, orange, and yellow sparks in the firebox. Freddy would sit and watch it for hours.

The fresh cut Christmas tree stood proudly in the living room. It was uniquely lit by strands of purple light bulbs, with purple ornaments hanging from the branches. The purple theme matched their purple-colored mailbox in front of the house. Freddy's father, Dan Purple, took every opportunity to emphasize the family name.

The scent of pine from the Christmas tree put that special magic in the air. That and the pine scented air spray his mom, Beth, would use after Thanksgiving. Sometimes he would pick a few needles from the tree and break them in half and smell them, just for that extra *burst* of aromatic fragrance. One time he made the mistake of spraying the pine scented air freshener in his nose. All he remembered was that it burned and made him gag. He would never do that again.

When Freddy was three, his dad had videotaped the Christmas family gathering. Freddy was dressed in red flannel pajamas with jolly Santa Claus faces printed from top to bottom. He was having such a happy time. Scurrying around the room from one family member to another, and begging for a bite from whatever item of food was on their paper plates.

Uncle Barry was calmly sipping on his eggnog, when Freddy ran up to him and pointed at the cup. Barry turned and saw the red light on the camera, and lifted his glass to Dan in a mock toast.

Freddy pointed to the cup, and said, "I want that."

Barry shrugged his shoulders and carefully placed the cup to Freddy's mouth and tilted enough for him to get a taste.

Freddy took a sip and backed away, looking bewildered as he smacked his lips.

"What's the matter, you didn't like it? You don't like eggnog?" Dan asked.

Barry laughed, but to his surprise, Freddy came back for more. So he gave him another sip, and then another, until the cup was empty.

"Say, little man, you like eggnog, don't you?" Dan asked, to which Freddy nodded in approval. "What's eggnog taste like, Freddy? What's eggnog taste like?"

Freddy hesitated a moment and said as best he could, "It taste like *Cwistmas!*"

The entire room erupted in laughter. And from then on, the family joke around Christmas time about what things tasted like would be, "It tastes like Christmas!"

All that happened four years ago, Freddy was seven now. It was Christmas Eve, his mother's family was over, and waiting for the arrival of Santa Claus.

This Christmas was going to be very special. Freddy and three of his cousins were going to be awake this time when Santa arrived. Freddy had been extra good this year, and Santa was coming at 5 p.m. as his reward.

The doorbell rang while Freddy was watching the fire, wondering what Santa would bring. He heard his mom say, "Come on in," and then she yelled, "Freddy, Brian's here!"

Brian was Freddy's next door neighbor, and his best friend. Both were the same age and had been constant companions at home and at school.

Brian came running into the living room all excited. He would be seeing Santa, too, with Freddy and the rest.

"Hey, Brian, who's that present for?" Freddy asked, pointing to a green, foil-wrapped small rectangular box.

"It's your Christmas present. Here, open it." Brian shoved it towards Freddy, eager for him to see his present.

Freddy's eyes were wide open in anticipation. He scratched around on the paper until he found a seam and peeled the paper off. He opened the box and pulled out a rectangular metal tag. It was edged in green and brown camouflage plastic, with a thin metal chain attached. Freddy let the box drop to the floor, and carefully examined the tag.

"It's a name tag. It's got your name and address on it. Look, I've got one, too!" Brian reached into the neck of his red sweater and pulled his dog tag out, letting it dangle on his chest. "Now when we play army, we can be just like real soldiers."

Freddy quickly put his around his neck, picked up the tag, and looked at it again. "This is great! Thanks, Brian." Then Freddy frowned. "I got you a present, too, but Mom said to give it to you tomorrow, so you'll have a present to open on Christmas Day."

"That's okay. Santa's gonna be here soon, and I'll have lots of stuff to play with," Brian said, jumping up and down. Freddy jumped, too, and clapped his hands in excitement.

It would be the last time the two would share a happy moment together.

A light snow had kicked up, adding another layer to the crusty six inches already covering the ground. That, and the fact that the sun was going down, made it harder for Freddy and Brian to see as they sat by the front window.

Freddy craned his head around. "Mom, what time is it?"

"Five forty-five," she said, arms folded, giving her husband cross-eyes and a frown.

A 1999 Honda Civic was slowly coming up the street. It came almost to a stop in front of Freddy's house, then picked up speed and went down the road. Freddy's eye's followed it; he thought he saw a man wearing a white beard driving.

Could this be Santa?

He had asked his mom if Santa would be coming in his sleigh, but she said no. Rudolph and the other reindeer had to rest for the big night ahead. When he asked how Santa would get to their house, she said she didn't know, and to ask him when he arrived.

The car pulled to the side of the road at the intersection a block away. Freddy could barely make out a figure wearing red clothing getting out of the car, and opening the hatchback.

"Brian, look over there. Is that Santa Claus?" Freddy asked, pointing.

"I don't know, but he's wearing red and he's pulling a big sack out of his car."

The hefty figure walked down the road towards Freddy's house. With each step, it became clearer it was Santa, and he was on his way with a bag of toys for good girls and boys!

"It's Santa! He's coming!" Freddy yelled happily, running to tell his mom and dad, Brian following at his heels.

"Thank God," Beth said, over shrieks of excitement from her nieces and nephew. Dan powered up the video camera that was hanging from its strap around his neck. Beth picked up the digital camera; this was a Christmas she wanted to capture, and remember forever.

Most of the family gathered behind the front door, in anticipation of St. Nick. Beth and Dan were to the right of the door, so when it opened, they could get shots of the kids' faces when they saw Santa.

The entire family was there, including Freddy's Grandpa and Grandma, Ralph and Susan, his mother's sister and her husband, Amy and James, their two daughters, Tracy and Karla, his mother's brother, and his older sons, Barry and Kyle. Finishing the group was Brian's mother, Grace. Brian's dad was a policeman and on patrol, and fortunately, his shift would be ending soon.

A knock on the door and the joyous sounds of bells jingling from the other side, brought ear to ear grins to the young children.

Beth stooped down, making sure she wasn't blocking the video camera's view. She turned the door knob and pulled the door open.

"Ho, Ho, Ho!" Santa bellowed, adjusting the sack slung over his shoulder, as he stomped his feet dry of slush on the welcome mat. "Santa's here with Christmas cheer for all!" He stepped inside to the flash of the cameras and the squeals of delight from the children.

Beth got a *whiff* of Christmas 'cheer' and B.O. as Santa stepped past her and into the house. His suit looked like it might have been cleaned as recently as two years ago. His beard was turning urine yellow from its original gray. The broken veins on his nose and cheek plastered across his ruddy face looked like a road map.

Despite the appearance of the hobo Santa, it was the bandage wrapped around his left hand that was her biggest concern. It was starting to show early signs that the wound it was concealing wasn't healing and becoming infected.

Beth herded everyone into the living room. The Lazy Boy chair was set up for Santa to receive each of the children one by one.

Dan leaned into Santa's ear before entering the living room. "You're late. What happened?"

Santa whispered, "Me and the elves were having a little nip after our shift was up behind the department store, when this bum comes our way with a bunch of cops chasing after him. I tried to slow the bum down so the cops could get him, in case there was a reward. But that good for nothing sucker bit my hand before the cops got him and hauled him off. I had to stop at the drug store and patch myself up before coming here."

The unpleasant odor of garlic, baloney, and the sweetness of an unidentifiable rye whiskey assaulted Dan's nostrils. He took a deep breath to purge his respiratory system and showed Santa to the Lazy Boy.

Santa shifted the sack off his back, carried it in front of him using both hands, and placed it next to his chair. Dan had noticed his weak legs, attributing his shaky walk to his near three hundred pounds of weight and the whiskey. But when Santa sat down, his eyes were bloodshot and looked tired, beads of perspiration forming on his brow. He put the back of his hand to his mouth and expelled a low, long burp. "Excuse me. Now, who wants to be the first on Santa's lap?"

Karla was the youngest at four. Amy, her mother, lifted her and placed her on Santa's lap. Karla made an embarrassed grin and her eyes followed her mom. She was contemplating crying out and bolting for freedom from the strange looking man.

"Now, little Karla, Santa's over here," he said to her, trying to get her attention. Karla continued to crane her head towards her mother. Santa decided the only way to get her attention was with a bribe. While balancing her on his left thigh, he leaned over to the right and reached in his sack for one of her presents. As he strained to find one with her name on it, more gas from his stomach escaped to freedom, announcing itself this time from his trousers.

The kids laughed, while the adults cringed and looked at each other. How were they going to handle this situation without ruining it for the kids?

Santa sat up straight, giving up on the present. His eyes started to flutter, and his head slowly shifted back and forth as he pushed Karla off his lap. He leaned forward with his head drooping between his legs, and he threw up a stream of green and yellow bile.

Like a mother hawk, Amy dashed to Santa's side and snatched Karla to safety. Freddy and Brian looked at each other in disbelief. Kyle started gagging, and Tracy ran to be with her mother and Karla.

Santa fell forward into the pool of vomit. The adults surrounded him, waiting for someone to make the first move to go to his aid.

Dan had all of it on film, and decided it was well past time to turn the video camera off. *Ho, fucking ho*, he thought.

James was the first to bend to a knee and roll Santa out of the bile and on to his side. He knew better than to lay him on his back, as he could drown in his own vomit. He reached down with his right hand and pulled Santa's left eyelid open. The pupil was dilated, not a good sign.

Then, before he could make a report to the others, he felt an incredible pressure latch down on his little finger. He let out a yell and jerked his hand away from Santa, staring at a bloody nub where is little finger used to be.

James sprang from the floor, holding his right wrist with the hand extended, biting his lower lip in an attempt to muffle the series of curses pouring from his mouth. Susan ran to Ralph's side and clung to his waist, jostling his second rum and punch drink. Amy grabbed a dish towel laid out by the sink and ran to James' side, wrapping the towel loosely around his bleeding hand.

"We've got to get you to the hospital!" Amy yelled to James. "That looks bad!"

James shook his head. "I thought that fat bastard was dead! Look what he did to me."

Barry came up to them. "Maybe it was an involuntary twitch, he's lying still now."

"I'm calling the police," Beth said, receiver in hand and dialing 9-1-1.

Santa twitched again and this time it was his whole body. Then slowly, in an ethereal sort of way, Santa rose to his feet. The stump of James' little finger protruded from the right corner of his mouth, and blood trickled down his beard. Santa started to chew.

"What the? He's eating my finger! Hey, stop it! They might be able to reattach it!" James hollered, taking a step toward Santa, and then hesitating before taking the next.

Screams and cries of protest clashed together as the hulking Santa stood and chewed the finger down like a French fry. His eyes were void of emotion, void of life itself.

Barry wasn't known for any physical prowess. "What should we do?"

"The line's still busy at the police station," Beth said.

Dan pulled Beth by the arm. "Women and children get down the hall and close and lock the door. We'll figure something out. You too, Gramps, keep an eye on them."

In other words, Dan wanted Grandpa to stay out of the men's way.

Amy gathered her two kids and shoved them toward the hall. Grace and Beth were right behind Freddy and Brian. Barry brought up the rear with Kyle, and told him to 'listen to Grandpa' before he closed the hall door behind him. He heard the click of the lock from the other side. Barry's bowels quivered as he walked down the hall to face the man-eating Santa.

Santa was still by the Lazy Boy, the fireplace to his left, and the Christmas tree to his right. A love seat was positioned to his forward right, and a couch sat eight feet directly in front of him.

Dan and James had moved behind the couch, facing Santa, uncertain of their next move. Barry joined them, standing behind them, keeping an additional layer of safety between him and Santa.

Santa raised his arms and took a stiff walk forward. The three men watched, uncertain what to do next. Santa continued walking like an un-oiled robot. When he reached the front of the couch, he stopped. The three men took one step back out of reach.

Santa leaned over as much as he could, but he couldn't get his hands on the three men. He then turned and walked around the couch. The three men matched each step he took in the opposite direction until Santa was now at the back of the couch and they were at the front.

"How long are we going to play ring around the rosy?" Dan asked James.

"I don't know, but my hand is throbbing. I need to see a doctor," James replied.

"I hope someone is still trying to contact the police. If we take matters into our own hand, we might get sued," Dan said.

"Maybe we can take him down and tie him up until the police get here. This is your house and we're in fear of our life. Screw the courts, we've got women and children to protect here," James said.

Dan waited until the circular walk brought him back around to the fireplace, and he removed a cast iron poker from the tool station. He gathered up his nerve, then sped around the couch, hoping to catch Santa off guard. He did, and slammed the 'S' shaped end of the poker into the side of Santa's knee.

Santa turned in Dan's direction and made a grab for him. Dan managed to keep his distance, maintaining equal distance by hurrying back around the couch.

"I hit him with all I had. My hands sting and my elbow hurts. This guy took it like he felt nothing," Dan said, wringing his hands.

"Guys, I don't feel so good," James said, looking white as a sheet.

"Okay, get back there with the rest of the family. Get some water from the bathroom. Try to lie down and keep your hand elevated. And keep trying 9-1-1..." Before Dan could finish his words, James passed out on the floor, with Santa only five steps from him.

Instinctively, Dan and Barry kept their distance, but were ready to make some kind of move if James was attacked. He wasn't, which surprised them as they continued to walk around the couch, away from Santa, and were now forced to step over James.

"On the next go round, let's grab James and drag him to the hallway," Barry suggested. "We can all get behind the door. I don't think this fat-ass is fast enough to catch us, and I don't think he can open a locked door in his condition." It was the first contribution Barry had made. And right now, it sounded like the best plan of action to Dan.

As those words left Barry's lips, Dan stepped over James, and when Barry was about to step over him for the final round, James' hand went up and grabbed him by the leg.

Barry hit the floor and tried crawling away but James held tightly. Tight enough that Barry actually started pulling James across the floor with him.

Dan came to an abrupt stop and tried to shake James' grip from Barry's leg. Santa was on him before he knew it. He fell to his back and the blubbery mass in a red suit fell on top of him. Dan put his arms up, pushing against Santa's chest, keeping the gnashing teeth at bay. The nasty vomit-soaked beard tickled Dan's chin, the smell making him gag.

Barry was still held by James, unable to break the grip. James was on his stomach now, and was crawling toward Barry who kicked with his free leg. First at the hand that held him, then at James' face when it got too close. Barry could hear Dan making low sounds of distress, which turned into coughing.

James was relentless. The room was charged with pheromones of fear secreting from Dan and Barry. James had a faraway look in his eyes as he clawed and snapped his teeth at Barry. Santa's gaping mouth was inching ever so slowly towards Dan's neck. The strain of the attack was about to get the best of Dan.

Suddenly, the kitchen door crashed opened.

"Everybody! Pack up, we've got to…" A man standing six foot four, dressed in mossy oak winter camouflage stepped into the empty kitchen. He looked towards the living room and saw Dan struggling underneath Santa. "What the…"

"Get him off me, John! Get him off me!" Dan used up the last of his remaining energy to call to his brother for help.

John moved forward, reared his foot back like he was going to kick a ball, and sent his steel-toed boot smashing into Santa's side. Ribs snapped like cracking wood in the fireplace. The sheer force of the kick sent the flesh-crazed zombie off of Dan, and rolling on to the floor.

John stood with his fists raised in a defensive position, then saw Barry struggling with James on the floor. The couch had hidden them from view from the kitchen.

John looked at Barry and yelled, "What the hell is going on here?"

"Stop him, John! Don't let him bite me! Don't let him bite you!" Barry screamed.

John grabbed James by his feet and pulled him away from Barry, who also slid backward, still unable to free himself from James' grip.

"James, what's gotten into you? Knock this crap off," John snapped, holding James' feet off the ground by his side like they were playing *wheelbarrow*.

Dan was on his feet, his strength returning to him. Santa was on his feet too, with death in his eyes and hunger in his mouth.

"John!" Dan shouted.

John turned his head and saw the zombie Santa lumbering forward. He dropped one of James' legs, reached in his jacket, and pulled out a small pistol. He pointed the gun at Santa. A small red dot from its laser danced on the zombie's chest. "Stop, I'll shoot if you don't stop!"

Zombie Santa didn't stop and John fired twice. One bullet found its target, and one went to the left as James kicked John with his free leg. The bullet didn't slow the fat zombie's approach.

Dan stood motionless, unsure what move to make next. John had a gun, and James was still fighting to get at Barry.

"Crap," John uttered under his breath, and dropped James' other leg. He turned and faced zombie Santa, gripping the gun with both hands, and placing the laser mark on Santa's forehead. The *crack* from the barrel sounded and the bullet penetrated Santa's skull. A hole from the back of his head erupted blood and something that looked like partially digested hamburger meat.

Zombie Santa collapsed at John's feet.

"Guys, a little help here!" Barry yelled.

John put both his knees in James' back. He leaned forward and grabbed James by the wrist of the hand holding Barry. Using both of his hands with great effort, he managed to break the grip from Barry's leg, and twisted the arm behind James' back. Dan rushed to John's aid and grabbed the other arm, twisting it around until both hands were touching. James was squirming like a worm on hot cement.

"Barry, get over here and get a tie-wrap from my pocket," John called out. Barry crawled over and pulled out a wad of plastic tie-wraps, and hurriedly threaded one around both of James' wrists.

John quickly pulled a tie-wrap from the pile on the floor and tied up James' legs by wrapping his ankles.

Before the three men had a chance to catch their breath, the sound of glass breaking came from the back of the house.

When the first gun shots rang out, Grandpa told everyone to lie on the floor. They had already moved from the hall to the master bedroom. Brian had been looking out the window, when he heard the gun shot. He turned around, placing his back to the frame. Freddy was on the floor, looking at his mother, waiting for her to tell him that everything was going to be okay.

Something hit the window that Brian was standing by. Everyone's head turned in time to see a pair of arms come crashing through the glass and pulling Brian to the world outside. Blood was dripping from the remaining shards of glass of the broken window.

Freddy's heart sunk, a wave of fear and nausea sweeping over him. Brian's mother screamed and dashed toward the window. She stuck her head out of the window frantically, calling Brian's name. Then she was pulled out head first by unseen hands.

Everyone was off the floor and up and running out of the bedroom and down the hall, deciding to take their chances on the unknown rather than the known. Grandpa led the group with Beth pulling Freddy by the hand, bringing up the rear.

The hall door opened and everyone spilled out into the living room. John, Barry, and Dan were soon standing between the writhing James and the other horrified members of the family.

It was Amy that first recognized that it was James tied up and struggling on the floor. "James! What the hell did you do to my James?" Amy ran forward but John and Dan wouldn't let her by them. They each held her by an arm, as she watched the father of her children twist like a wild beast on the floor.

"My God, what's wrong with him?" Amy asked softly.

"I'm not sure," John said. "But on my way back from the deer camp it started looking more like Halloween than Christmas outside. People were wandering around looking like zombies out on a hunt. Some looked like they had been dead for years. I tried to get some news on the radio, but most of the stations were nothing but static. I did get some info on the CB radio..." John hesitated and looked at the children. Then he looked at the adults. "The zombies were attacking people. That's what the guy on the CB called them. He called them *zombies*. He said they were...eating people alive."

"We don't have time to talk about this!" Beth interrupted. "They broke our bedroom window and took Brian and Grace."

"Oh God, no," Dan said, feeling even worse than before.

"That settles it, grab your jackets and let's go. We don't have much time. This town is crawling with zombies!" John's military training took over. The enemy was attacking, it was time to move. "Five people can ride with me, the other five go in Dan's Cherokee. Let's go people! Move! Move!"

"What about James? We just can't leave him here," Amy said to Dan.

Beth came to her sister's side. "Amy, we can't take him with us. Not like this. We can come back for him later."

"No, no I can't leave him. Take the girls and come back for us later," Amy said.

John grabbed Amy from behind and slung her over his shoulder like a wounded soldier on the battlefield. Amy screamed her protest, which only made her children more upset.

The family followed John out of the door and into the garage. He put Amy into the back of the Jeep Cherokee and Beth directed Amy's two daughters to sit next to her.

"Freddy, I need to be with Aunt Amy," his mother said. "Go with your Uncle John and the others. There's not enough room for you in here. Listen to what Uncle John says. Don't worry, everything's going to be fine."

Freddy nodded his head and followed behind John as the garage door rose up. He felt better now; his mom had told him that everything was going to be all right.

The door came up and the cold wind blew in, the street light dimmed by the falling snow. Freddy was behind John, and he heard John's handgun fire twice in rapid succession. It startled him but he pushed forward, right at the heels of his uncle.

"Get in the truck, now!" John hollered. The gun popped off three more times as the others ran and got inside the truck.

John went to the rear bed of his truck and unzipped his shotgun from its case. There were two zombies coming up the driveway and he didn't want them to get in the way. A quick aim at one, pull trigger, *BAM*, one down. Another quick aim, pull trigger, *BAM*, two down.

Buckshot rules! he thought.

John hurriedly got into his Ford King Ranch, handing the butt of the shotgun to Barry, who was sitting on the passenger side. The gun stock rested on Barry's lap and across Freddy's. John needed it handy. Kyle, Grandpa, and Grandma were huddled together in the back seat. They were shivering more from fear than the cold.

John started the engine and pulled out onto the street. He waited for Dan to back out and get on the road behind him before setting out for safety. It was back to the deer camp for him and his family.

The deer camp was more than just a place to sleep to a survivalist, of which John was. The camp was his intended refuge for a variety of catastrophes. It sat high on a hill, making it safe from flooding. It was in a remote location to avoid contact with people during flu or other infectious disease pandemics. The camp's close perimeter was cleared of trees and brush to avoid the flames of a wildfire. There was enough food stored for five years and a supply of potassium iodine in case of nuclear fallout. And last, but not least, enough guns and ammo buried on the property to take on a small army.

John opened a can of Skoal retrieved from the side pocket on his door, and shoved in a big dip. The saliva in his mouth mixed with the pungent ground tobacco in his lip and delivered a much needed nicotine fix.

He rolled his window down halfway and spit.

A country-boy can survive, he thought.

* * *

"It just doesn't taste like Christmas," Freddy said, dropping his turkey leg on his plate and chewing slowly.

211

"Alfred Purple! How ungrateful!" Beth yelled at him from across the table, which caused Dan to jump in his chair, nearly spilling his grape juice.

"Son, how can you be so selfish?" Dan asked. "Uncle John spent hours hunting that turkey so we could have a special Christmas Eve. You could be eating venison again or an MRE. Your mother slaved to make us the best meal she could, considering our situation," Dan said, feeling like it was his duty to come to his wife's side.

John reached over and snatched the turkey leg from Freddy's plate and started eating it. "Taste just fine to me."

Freddy's lip began to quiver. He put both of his elbows on the table and rested his chin under his hands.

Beth felt a little guilty for her outburst. Sometimes the burden of the last two years would pile up, then come crashing in an inadvertent out-lash.

Her mother didn't hold up well and had died before the spring of the first year. Dad didn't live a full month afterward. It was hard on Freddy, seeing his grandparents die that way. Death came to them because of the end of hope. At least they weren't eaten by the living dead, like her sister Amy was.

Amy had snuck out before dawn after the first night they spent in the cabin, presumably, to go back after James. She left in the Jeep and it was a couple of hours before anyone woke and noticed her gone. John followed her after arming the rest of the family to the teeth before he left.

He found the Jeep with a flat tire forty miles away. Amy was gone. But the windows on the Jeep were broken and there was blood on the seat and in the snow by the vehicle. There were also remnants of a bloody and shredded shirt. John didn't recognize it, but couldn't remember what she was wearing anyway. He didn't stay to look for her. The story the scene painted had an obvious ending.

Beth looked around the table, thinking of last year's Christmas Eve. Karla and Tracy had sat to her right, Barry and Kyle to her left. Those chairs were empty now.

Last year's winter was harsh. The lake had frozen over by Christmas day. Barry and Freddy had been ice fishing, with Kyle and Amy's two daughters ice skating nearby. The ice gave way under the three playing children. When Barry rushed to their aid, the ice collapsed under Barry's weight, and he fell into the frigid waters. Barry had called out for Freddy to go get help.

Freddy ran faster than he had ever run in his life. But it was a full ten minutes before John, Beth, and Dan arrived to help. By that time the kids were no longer on the surface. Barry was so stiff and cold he could barely move his arms. Dan tied a rope to his waist and crawled out to Barry's side, grabbed on to his right arm, and John, Beth, and Freddy struggled with all their might and pulled on the rope to bring Barry to safety.

Barry was unconscious for twelve hours. When he awoke, he was despondent. He sat with a blanket wrapped around him and cried, ignoring any comfort his family offered.

"I'm going outside to the bathroom," were the last words that Barry said. He shot himself in the head just a ways from the cabin, by the graves of his parents.

Beth took a bite of beans and chewed without tasting them. She looked around the cabin she had decorated for Christmas, for Freddy. Pine cones were tied together, interlaced with mistletoe, and hung to make a wreath on a bare wall of the cabin. She had whittled little crude figures from wood in shapes resembling Santa, his elves, and even his reindeer. A six foot pine tree stood in the corner with an aluminum foil star on top. Other shiny pieces of food packaging had been twisted or shredded to form colored ornaments.

She tried to swallow. Her tears welled in her eyes and the lump in her throat made her spit the beans back out onto her plate. It just didn't taste like Christmas.

* * *

It was Christmas morning, the sun shown faint orange rays through the trees, casting shadows on the snow-covered ground.

There were no presents under the tree that morning. No new bike, no new electronic toys, nor any wrong-sized clothing to return to the store the next day. The day brought the hardships that every day brought since the dead began to walk.

Freddy was helping his uncle John with gathering kindling for the day. He was dragging a plastic garbage bag and filling it with pine cones and small dried twigs and branches, shaking off as much snow as he could before placing them in the bag.

He had wandered from the watchful eye of his uncle and was busy working on a broken fir branch with his hatchet. Fir made excellent kindling, and this branch had been dead for some time and was nice and dry.

Freddy heard the metallic sound of a chain rattling nearby. His Uncle John had animal traps set throughout the woods. The areas they were located were marked with orange flagging tied to the tree branches above them. He followed the sound twenty feet deep in the woods, and froze when he saw what was held captive by his uncle's trap.

It was a young living dead boy. He was straining to walk in one direction but his foot was held tightly in the clamp of the trap. Freddy hadn't seen any of the living dead since that Christmas Eve two years ago. There had been a few stray ones come on the deer camp property, but he only knew that because he had overheard John tell his parents about them. The camp was in a very remote location. He hadn't even seen another living person in those two years.

The zombie child changed directions, and the chain rattled behind him until it became taut again. Then he stopped, tilted his head in the air, and turned toward Freddy. The zombie boy walked twice as fast as before until he was jerked back by the chain. His arms were outstretched, clawing at the air.

Freddy could feel the zombie's wanting desire to eat him alive and cold fear washed down his spine. He wanted to call out to John but couldn't find his voice.

The sun caught the face of a metal object hanging from the zombie's neck, causing Freddy to focus past his fear. He gave it a double take; it was unmistakably a plastic dog tag.

Freddy thought about the dog tag. He also thought about the red sweater the zombie child was wearing. It looked just like the one that Brian had worn that night he was snatched from the house. In fact, except for the clothes being tattered and dirty, it was wearing the exact clothes Brian had worn.

This couldn't be Brian, could it? he thought.

That thought scared him more than the zombie did now. He turned to run and find his uncle John, and ran right into John, who was standing a few steps behind Freddy, pistol drawn, and aiming at the zombie child.

Freddy pressed his face into John's stomach, and his head jerked when John pulled the trigger. He wanted to cry, thinking how things used to be with his best friend Brian.

"There, there, Freddy. He won't bother anyone anymore," John said softly.

Freddy walked over and looked at the emaciated form of his friend. The face was ashen-white with dark circles around the eyes. Parts of his arm and shoulder were missing chunks of meat and frayed like ragged cloth. This looked nothing like the Brian he knew and loved.

Brian was on his back, a hole on the left side of his forehead, and the dog tag lying below his chin.

A spent cartridge from John's gun was hung up in the injector port and he was busy working to extract it.

Freddy stooped down and eyed the dog tag. The camouflaged brown and green plastic on the edges were chipped in places, but Brian's name and address were still readable.

Freddy wanted the name tag. He wanted to put it on his chain, so that the two of them could be together again. He slowly reached his hand down, and as soon as he grabbed it, Brian's entire body shook uncontrollably for a few seconds. Freddy leaped backwards and rolled on the ground, away from Brian.

"Freddy, what is it?" John asked. He had finally pried the spent casing out of the injector port and cycled the slide to load another bullet.

"He moved!" Freddy yelled, clutching the name tag secretly in his hand.

"Moved huh?" John walked over to the zombie child and fired two more rounds into the small head. "There, that'll keep him down for good. Let's get you back to the cabin. Your dad and I need to make a quick perimeter sweep to see if any more are around."

Freddy walked behind John back to the cabin. He opened his hand and examined the dog tag again; it brought so many memories of his friend flooding back. He noticed something sticky and red was on the plastic guard, and then noticed a small scrape on his index finger, and a trickle of blood. One of Brian's teeth had scraped his finger when he retrieved the dog tag.

"Look at the poor boy, he's traumatized," Beth said, stroking Freddy's hair as he lay in bed, shivering under the covers. "And he looks sick."

"He must have gotten a cold," John said. Oh well, this is something he needs to get used to. Even a cold can be serious now. We've been lucky for a long time," John said, pushing the last shell into his bandolier.

"John and I won't be gone long," Dan said. "We're going to take a look around and make sure there aren't any more of them wandering around. Keep the doors locked and don't forget the shotgun is loaded and ready to shoot. Just take it off safety before you pull the trigger," he instructed, squeezing Beth on the shoulder before he and John left the cabin.

Beth closed her eyes and held back her tears. It seemed lately that she was always on the verge of crying. It wasn't that she wasn't thankful for what they had. It was just that this horrible situation didn't have a conclusion to look forward to. Just surviving day after day, living in a constant state of uneasiness, with the fear of the world that Freddy would inherit.

She left Freddy sleeping in his bed and gathered her sewing kit and a pair of pants she was working on to modify for Freddy. The boy was going through a growing spurt and she had a limited supply of clothing to work with. John had left the cabin a few times over the last two years for additional supplies and to check out the order of things. His last trip out he was unable to find any diesel for his truck and barely had enough fuel to make it back. He did bring back a load of clothing on that trip he found at a good-will store. There were no other supplies to be found. And as far as the order of things, it was as chaotic as it had ever been. The dead walked, the living hid.

Beth put on her reading glasses and threaded a needle after pulling a chair close to a window for better light. She heard Freddy stirring in the background. This made her smile; he was going to be all right. He just had some growing up to do. She knew it was going to be hard on him. Growing up was hard for a young boy in any situation, and she was going to make sure she gave Freddy every advantage she could to help direct him to be a good man.

Beth felt Freddy's arms wrap around her from behind and give her a strong hug. Her smile broadened across her face and her heart melted, feeling the love through the embrace of her only child.

Freddy pressed his cold dead lips on his mother's neck, and tore off a large chunk of meat with his teeth. Her screams of anguish fell on a soul dead of recognition, dead of compassion. He only felt hunger now.

It was Christmas day, his first day as a member of the living dead. From now on, he would be feeding upon the flesh of the living. This is what Christmas would taste like as long as his animated body would roam the Earth.

Every day would taste like Christmas.

ABOUT THE WRITERS

Rebecca Besser is a wife and mother who lives in Ohio. She's a graduate of the Institute of Children's Literature, a member of Write-On Writers and the Ohio Poetry Association (OPA). Her writing has appeared in the Coshocton Tribune, Irish Story Playhouse, Spaceports & Spidersilk, joyful!, Soft Whispers, Illuminata, Common Threads, Golden Visions Magazine, Stories That Lift, and The Undead That Saved Christmas charity anthology. As well as multiple anthologies by Living Dead Press and Wicked East Press, and one anthology by Pill Hill Press.

For more information visit her website: www.rebeccabesser.com

Brandon Cracraft lives in the historic district of Tucson with his partner and a black cat in a house that predates Arizona's statehood. He has published articles on various subjects including role playing games, health food, and the occult.

Jeremiah Coe lives in Portage, Michigan. His novel The Dead of Space Book One: Brave New World is available now. He also has two more novels soon to be released. The Dead of Space Book Two: Journey's End and Here Comes Santa. He has also authored several short stories and has created and written a vampire web series that can be watched for free.

Go to www.transitionstheseries.com.

Contact him at facebook.com/jeremiah.coe or you can email him at jeremiah_coe@yahoo.com.

Anthony Giangregorio is the author and editor of more than 45 novels and anthologies, almost all of them about zombies.

His work has appeared in Dead Science by Coscomentertainment, Dead Worlds: Undead Stories Volumes 1-7, and Wolves of War by Library of the Living Dead Press. He also has stories in End of Days: An Apocalyptic Anthology Vol. 1-4, the Book of the Dead series Vol. 1-5 by LDP, Zombie Zoology by Severed Press, and two anthologies with Pill Hill Press.

He is also the creator of the popular action/zombie series titled Deadwater and his action/ horror novel Dead Rage is being optioned for a movie.

Check out his website at www.undeadpress.com.

Dane T. Hatchell grew up in Baton Rouge Louisiana and has lived there all his life. In his youth he was a fan of old school horror movies, and a collector of magazines such as Creepy and Eerie. Now in his early fifty's, he is devoting his free time to writing to satisfy a lifelong passion. You can contact Dane at Enadious@gmail.com.

Elizabeth Marshall lives in West Hollywood, CA and works in historic preservation. She regularly researches and writes building histories, although prefers narratives where the historic structures are descended upon by the undead.

Kevin Millikin currently lives in Portland, Oregon. His previous stories have appeared in the books Dead Worlds 6, Halloween tales Of Terror and Emails Of The Dead. He's currently working on his first novel as well as a comic book series and can be reached via facebook.com/kevin.millkin

Rick Moore's stories have appeared in over thirty anthologies. These include 'The Undead: Flesh Feast', 'History is Dead' and 'Cthulhu Unbound' (Permuted Press), the Stoker Award nominated 'Horror Library 3' (Cutting Block Press), 'Dark Animus', 'The Beast Within' (Graveside Tales), 'Embark to Madness' (Coscom), 'Bound for Evil' (Dead Letter Press), and in numerous anthologies from Living Dead Press, including Book of the Dead Volume 1. This October be sure to check out his story 'The Church of Dead Music' (starring a before he was famous Elvis Presley) in the Halloween themed anthology 'Harvest Hill' (Graveside Tales). Recently Rick joined Dark Moon Digest as an associate editor. To earn his daily crust the author works as a Mental Health Specialist for the Arizona State Hospital. Originally from England, he now lives in Phoenix. Go to http://www.myspace.com/zombieinfection to contact the author.

Marc Shemmans is from Birmingham, England. He has had several short stories and novellas published in numerous anthologies and magazines. He is also a screenplay writer who writes original scripts based on the dark nature of life and the apocalypse which he knows is destined to happen at any moment. He has also written screenplays which are based on novels by Graham Masteron, Tim Lebbon and Guy N Smith.

Jody Page is a reformed bohemian with a wife, two kids, and a mortgage. He lives with his family in Calgary, Alberta, Canada. Working as a freelance writer he has had over fifty pieces published in local publications and on the internet. These range from feature pieces, reviews, and fiction. He cannot fix anything unless it requires black humor or sarcasm, and much prefers Halloween to Christmas, which is why he is currently working on a line of greeting cards for those who hate greeting cards - totallyrecarded.com.

R. S. Pyne is a freelance writer and science journalist now based in rural West Wales after two years as a Research Technician at Cardiff University. Previous fiction has appeared in: Albedo One, Delivered, Neo-opsis, Tainted - Anthology of Terror and the Supernatural, Star Stepping Anthology, Pen Cambria, Crimson Highway, Midnight Horror, The Orphan Leaf Review, Peccary, Apollo's Lyre, Hungur, Silver Blade, Flash Shot and others.

D.B. Reddick is a former newspaper reporter and editor who has worked in the insurance industry for the past 20 years. His previous short stories have appeared in Blue River Press, Pill Hill Press, Red Coyote Press and Whortleberry Press. He and his wife, Rebecca, live in Camby, Indiana. Check out his blog at: http://dbreddick.blogspot.com.

Marc Shemmans is from Birmingham, England. He has had several short stories and novellas published in numerous anthologies and magazines. He is also a screenplay writer who writes original scripts based on the dark nature of life and the apocalypse which he knows is destined to happen at any moment. He has also written screenplays which are based on novels by Graham Masteron, Tim Lebbon and Guy N Smith.

E.F. Schraeder studied literature and philosophy in graduate school, and currently publishes in several genres including creative nonfiction and poetry. Previous publications appear or are forthcoming online and in print at New Verse News, Haz Mat Review, and elsewhere. Creative work has appeared or is forthcoming in the anthologies: Gone with the Dirt, Damned if You Don't, Kicked Out, Caviar ,Coupons, and College, and others.

Charles Versfelt lives in New Jersey with his wife Doreen, daughter Kayla, stepdaughter Melissa, and Hazel, his beagle. He is a member of the New Jersey Writer's Society, Franklin chapter, and also has organized a writing group through a Yahoo Groups called NJWrite which meets in Bridgewater, NJ. He has two stories previously published in Dark Dreams, Tales of Terror, and is currently working on his first novel, the Jefferson Bible Code, a thriller.

UNITED STATES OF ARMAGEDDON
by Jeffrey Thomas Crooms
THE END OF A COUNTRY!

America's enemies plot a sadistic plan to destroy the population and armed forces so they can swoop in and rule the country.

Terrorists called the Horsemen smuggle in a deadly biological weapon straight to the heart of the United States and release it.

The result is a land covered with corpses, bloated bodies strewn from sea to sea.

A few desperate survivors battle through the blighted landscape on a last ditch mission to save the country from total domination.

But the biological weapon has a side effect, one no one would have ever foreseen, one too unimaginable to even contemplate.

Welcome to the future. Welcome to the Unite States of *Armageddon*

BOOK OF THE DEAD
A ZOMBIE ANTHOLOGY VOL 1
ISBN 978-1-935458-25-8
Edited by Anthony Giangregorio

This is the most faithful, truest zombie anthology ever written, and we invite you along for the ride. Every single story in this book is filled with slack-jawed, eyes glazed, slow moving, shambling zombies set in a world where the dead have risen and only want to eat the flesh of the living. In these pages, the rules are sacrosanct. There is no deviation from what a zombie should be or how they came about. The Dead Walk.

There is no reason, though rumors and suppositions fill the radio and television stations. But the only thing that is fact is that the walking dead are here and they will not go away. So prepare yourself for the ultimate homage to the master of zombie legend. And remember... Aim for the head!

REVOLUTION OF THE DEAD
by Anthony Giangregorio
THE DEAD SHALL RISE AGAIN!

Five years ago, a deadly plague wiped out 97% of the world's population, America suffering tragically. Bodies were everywhere, far too many to bury or burn. But then, through a miracle of medical science, a way is found to reanimate the dead.

With the manpower of the United States depleted, and the remaining survivors not wanting to give up their internet and fast food restaurants, the undead are conscripted as slave labor.

Now they cut the grass, pick up the trash, and walk the dogs of the surviving humans.

But whether alive or dead, no race wants to be controlled, and sooner or later the dead will fight back, wanting the freedom they enjoyed in life.

The revolution has begun!

And when it's over, the dead will rule the land, and the remaining humans will become the slaves...or worse.

KINGDOM OF THE DEAD
by Anthony Giangregorio
THE DEAD HAVE RISEN!

In the dead city of Pittsburgh, two small enclaves struggle to survive, eking out an existence of hand to mouth.

But instead of working together, both groups battle for the last remaining fuel and supplies of a city filled with the living dead.

Six months after the initial outbreak, a lone helicopter arrives bearing two more survivors and a newborn baby. One enclave welcomes them, while the other schemes to steal their helicopter and escape the decaying city.

With no police, fire, or social services existing, the two will battle for dominance in the steel city of the walking dead. But when the dust settles, the question is: will the remaining humans be the winners, or the losers?

When the dead walk, the line between Heaven and Hell is so twisted and bent there is no line at all.

RISE OF THE DEAD
by Anthony Giangregorio
DEATH IS ONLY THE BEGINNING!

In less than forty-eight hours, more than half the globe was infected.

In another forty-eight, the rest would be enveloped.

The reason?

A science experiment gone horribly wrong which enabled the dead to walk, their flesh rotting on their bones even as they seek human prey.

Jeremy was an ordinary nineteen year old slacker. He partied too much and had done poorly in high school. After a night of drinking and drugs, he awoke to find the world a very different place from the one he'd left the night before.

The dead were walking and feeding on the living, and as Jeremy stepped out into a world gone mad, the dead spotting him alone and unarmed in the middle of the street,
he had to wonder if he would live long enough to see his twentieth birthday.

THE CHRONICLES OF JACK PRIMUS
BOOK ONE
by Michael D. Griffiths

Beneath the world of normalcy we all live in lies another world, one where supernatural beings exist.

These creatures of the night hunt us; want to feed on our very souls, though only a few know of their existence.

One such man is Jack Primus, who accidentally pierces the veil between this world and the next. With no other choice if he wants to live, he finds himself on the run, hunted by beings called the Xemmoni, an ancient race that sees humans as nothing but cattle. They want his soul, to feed on his very essence, and they will kill all who stand in their way. But if they thought Jack would just lie down and accept his fate, they were sorely mistaken.   He didn't ask for this battle, but he knew he would fight them with everything at his disposal, for to lose is a fate worse than death.

He would win this war, and he would take down anyone who got in his way.

THE WAR AGAINST THEM: A ZOMBIE NOVEL
by Jose Alfredo Vazquez

Mankind wasn't prepared for the onslaught.

An ancient organism is reanimating the dead bodies of its victims, creating worldwide chaos and panic as the disease spreads to every corner of the globe. As governments struggle to contain the disease, courageous individuals across the planet learn what it truly means to make choices as they struggle to survive.

Geopolitics meet technology in a race to save mankind from the worst threat it has ever faced. Doctors, military and soldiers from all walks of life battle to find a cure. For the dead walk, and if not stopped, they will wipe out all life on Earth. Humanity is fighting a war they cannot win, for who can overcome Death itself? Man versus the walking dead with the winner ruling the planet. Welcome to *The War Against Them*.

DEADTOWN: A DEADWATER STORY
B OOK 8
by Anthony Giangregorio

The world is a very different place now. The dead walk the land and humans hide in small towns with walls of stone and debris for protection, constantly keeping the living dead at bay.

Social law is gone and right and wrong is defined by the size of your gun.

UNWELCOME VISITORS

Henry Watson and his band of warrior survivalists become guests in a fortified town in Michigan. But when the kidnapping of one of the companions goes bad and men die, the group finds themselves on the wrong side of the law, and a town out for blood.

Trapped in a hotel, surrounded on all sides, it will be up to Henry to save the day with a gamble that may not only take his life, but that of his friends as well.

In a dead world, when justice is not enough, there is always vengeance.

END OF DAYS: AN APOCALYPTIC ANTHOLOGY
VOLUMES 1-4
Edited by Anthony Giangregorio

Our world is a fragile place.

Meteors, famine, floods, nuclear war, solar flares, and hundreds of other calamities can plunge our small blue planet into turmoil in an instant.

What would you do if tomorrow the sun went super nova or the world was swallowed by water, submerging the world into the cold darkness of the ocean? This anthology explores some of those scenarios and plunges you into total annihilation.

But remember, it's only a book, and tomorrow will come as it always does.

Or will it?